STEALING

STEALING:

A Novel in Dreams

Shelly Brivic

Frayed Edge Press
Philadelphia, PA
2018

Copyright 2018

Published in 2018 by Frayed Edge Press

https://frayededgepress.com

Cover image by Jeremy Brivic.

Excerpt from "A Sequence of Poems for H.D.'s Birthday, September 10, 1959," *Roots and Branches*, by Robert Duncan © 2018 The Jess Collins Trust, reproduced with permission.

Publishers Cataloging-in-Publication Data

Names: Brivic, Sheldon.
Title: Stealing : a novel in dreams / Shelly Brivic.
Description: Philadelphia, PA : Frayed Edge Press, 2018. | Summary: Explores the relationships between the four members of a dysfunctional Jewish family, spanning from the early 1950s through the mid-1970s.
Identifiers: LCCN 2018945420 | ISBN 9781642510034 (pbk.) | ISBN 978-1-64251-008-9 (ebook)
Subjects: LCSH: Brothers--Fiction. | Families--Fiction. | Jews -- United States --Fiction. | Man-woman relationships--Fiction. | Bronx (New York, N.Y.)--Fiction. | BISAC: FICTION / Jewish. | FICTION / Family Life / Marriage & Divorce. | FICTION / Family Life / Siblings.
Classification: LCC PS3602.R5 S7 2018| DDC 813 B7--dc23
LC record available at https://lccn.loc.gov/2018945420

For Joe and Joanne

*I'm stealing, stealing, pretty mama don't you tell on me
I'm stealing back to my same old used to be.*

—American traditional song

Contents

A Note to the Reader — xiii

1 The Parents 1954 — 1

2 The Room 1954 — 19

3 Crossing Dreams 1954 — 33

4 The Pool of the Past 1950 — 41

5 The Cliff 1955 — 55

6 The Roof 1956 — 67

7 The West Side 1958 — 83

8 Falling, Apart 1959 1962 — 97

9 The Best Yet 1959 — 111

10 The Picnic in the Desert 1960 — 117

11 To the Shithouse 1960 1961 — 123

12 Save the County 1961 1966 — 145

13 The Nipple 1964 1966 — 157

14 Pressing Lidless Eyes 1966-67	167
15 Happiness 1967	173
16 Fishing in the Air 1967 1969	183
17 The Relay 1967-68	223
18 Stealing Back 1976	231
Glossary	259
About the Author	263

A Note to the Reader

This novel contains a number of words and phrases in Yiddish (or more broadly, German). These are indicated by *italics* within the text. For readers unfamiliar with these terms, a glossary is provided, starting on page 259.

1

THE PARENTS

1954

Judith thought or said, "How can you hear me, Shirley, when you're gone? I don't even know myself whether I'm talking or thinking. Which would you hear more truly? A blessed spirit, a beloved dream, can hear a silent thought better than a loud word. What are my thoughts in Yiddish but words heard by the dead?

"Such a saintly woman, you're filled with regret to keep hearing again and again that you're right. I should never have married Yoyel. The only ones who can hear what I say out loud are the boys, the fruits of my mismarriage, and it's better they don't hear, just a grand thank you that they don't understand. Yet they must hear, because the other room is the same room, the thoughts are a voice."

Ira was aware that the kitchen and the dining room were not two rooms, but rather one long room, divided in the middle by cabinets attached to the wall on either side, forming an eighteen-inch passage between the two spaces pretending to be rooms: "A place where we are in both. Marc and I share this divided space with our so-called parents. I'm hardly a child at sixteen, yet Marc may never stop being one though he's almost twelve.

"Mom, with her white hair, courtesy of Dad, is muttering to herself, mostly in Jewish. She doesn't know we can hear her, or maybe she wants us to, but we understand by the sliding of her sound. And beneath it the faint whispering hiss of carrots being skinned. Though she's at the sink in the kitchen and I'm at the table in the dining room, I can see the peeler slicing with its two blades facing each other. One blade slits the skin and the other, drawn across the surface in reverse, allows you to press it in without going too deep. Which blade is happier? I can see dirty orange shavings fall in curled strips on the newspaper in the sink. And I can hear what she's thinking. It's the opposite of what I'm reading about, freedom."

Ira was reading a history book about how Rousseau wanted people to be free and his younger brother Marc was splitting peapods with his thumbnail and pushing the peas into a pot. Ira thought, "He wanted us to be free as nature, but are animals free? How about plants? Can you be free without knowing it? Maybe that's the best way."

Marc thought, "Does it hurt the pod to have a thumb pushed into it, or does the plant enjoy being opened up, feeling my finger sliding on its smooth, shining inside?" But the boys worked fitfully, absorbed in what their mother was somehow saying, a bitter syrup in which they were suspended.

"Shirley, the worst thing about Yoyel is that he tries so hard to be good, to be right. He's sure he is, but it comes out backwards. The more he tries, the worse the situation gets. His trying comes out twisted around his fury that everything is wrong. He claims he wants kindness, but he can't bear it. His only way to reach out to anyone is to curse them. I'm pickled through and through with his resentment, but you're my witness that I started out wanting to help people.

"Remember in school I had a great wish to be a teacher, to use my mind to raise people up? I always liked to read, but I didn't get far." She opened her hands. "I had to quit high school before the second year was done to help in the house. Yoyel boasts about finishing high school, but he has no more refinement than a demented dog.

"Before Yoyel there was Erwin, who had some culture—Dostoevsky he liked—but he didn't have much drive. I wanted him to say something, but he seemed afraid, looking at the floor." Wistfulness was the natural expression of her gray eyes and thin lips. "Maybe it was my fault I didn't get him and didn't finish high school. If I was determined I could have gotten somewhere.

"And then I got to be too old. Our father, may he rest in peace, never made much money after we got to America. You say he didn't make any before." She lifted her fingertips as if touching a wall. "It was Dave who supported us all, his father, brother, and two sisters. I had a feeling I was a burden to you, even when I worked—with such money as I could make in those days trimming hats. So I wanted to get married in the worst way, *takeh*, and I got what I wanted. *Shoin fertig*."

The carrots were done and Judith put them next to the meat on the sink. Her thoughts began to shift more towards the boys as she moved toward the dining room.

"When Joel came along, he wasn't bad looking, then— *azoy* thin—and he had a regular job. With the Depression, a clothing salesman was a good job, even cheap clothes. The answer to a maiden's prayer. But I never really cared for him, or if I did, it didn't last long. Would you call that a style he has? It's a style you get from a pushcart with one wheel missing." As her vehemence carried her from the kitchen to the dinette, her complaint passed into speaking what the boys were already sensing and she increased the proportion of her English.

"Since I've known the man, he's never treated me the way a husband should treat a wife. I never had a decent life. Trash, garbage he lives in, the lowest filth. Whenever he got me anything, it was always cheap junk. Seconds, thirds, one side bigger than the other, coming apart in your hands. You see how he brings me home window trimmings from the store. That's some stuff, I'm telling you. When we got engaged, what did he get me? A pair of rubbers that you wear when it rains. That's my trousseau. Did he expect I should put them on in the house? And whenever I'm with him in public, I'm just ashamed of the way he behaves. He would embarrass a bear."

"I remember being on a bus with him," Marc thought. "He kept picking his nose and talking about how crazy his wife was. Everyone could hear his yelping from the driver to the back row, and he kept tilting his head to the side to get a good hook on the snot with his fingernail, and rubbing it off under the seat. Ira hasn't gone anywhere with him in years. Of course, she tends to sound like him when she attacks him, bound to pick up some of his ways after being with him so long."

Ira thought, "She enjoys it, her unsuccess story. Her life is perfect married to an abomination. If he was any less awful, what would she do with nothing to *kvetch* about? She wouldn't exist, my dear mother."

Judith kept going: "I remember I used to sit on the stoop of our old building in Newark talking to the women. At night, he came home from work and walked right by me without even saying hello. He said, 'Who wants to yap with your *yenta* friends?' I was so humiliated, sitting there and watching him go by with his hard face. I felt like a tramp. I wanted the ground to swallow me up."

It occurred to the boys that they wouldn't want to talk to the women on the stoop either, that if you said hello, it would lead to a ritual that seemed to go on and on, grinding at one's patience and requiring phony talk. Still, they were moved by the saga of her suffering, even though Ira thought, "The old hogwash." Through her grief they knew the sensitivity of their souls the way you feel the life of your throat and chest in yearning when you swallow without food. But Ira couldn't swallow, he gagged.

"It's only for the sake of the children that I stay with him at all. Day after day, it's the same party. Whatever I do is wrong. If I put salt on, it's too salty. If I don't put salt on, it's too bland. If I put it on top, it goes on the bottom; if I put it down, it should go up. If he knocks something over in the ice box, it's because of my booby-trap. You remember the time he threw my clothes in the hall?"

Marc didn't remember this, but Ira was the one she was talking to, and he knew everything she was saying inside and out.

"Who can live with that?" she asked, echoing her husband's style. "Whenever he's home, he walks around the apartment singing. His singing sounds, you should excuse me, like the wrong end. And when he isn't singing, he's having a tantrum, raving like a *vilde chaia*. Everything is my fault, including old age and the weather."

"What I hate most," said Ira, "is when he sings to himself going to the toilet: 'Yiddle diddle diedle dum.' You're right about it being hard to tell the difference. You can hear him in the next apartment and the one after that, both ends of him." Ira imagined his father on a toilet in a spotlight on a stage, with the audience booing.

"I suppose," said Marc, "he sings because he feels unhappy, to take his mind off what's eating him. What gets me is that he'll never admit he's wrong about anything." Yet once, late at night, when the boys were lying in bed, the door opened and the old man's voice had said, "Maybe I was too harsh about those dishes." Marc had said, "Thanks," and though he hadn't actually seen Joel, the yellow light of the doorway seemed to have grown brighter. But that might have been a dream.

"I want you to know your father's not a bad man. He works hard. He tries to be honest. He means well on his terms. He doesn't exactly refuse to sacrifice for the children, though he tries to cut corners. He never went with *bumicas* or drank, like a *goy*. But he's nervous." Judith had gone into the kitchen and was koshering a big slab of meat with coarse salt for future use, the white crystals scattered over the raw magenta. The boys had heard that when the Nazis would whip a Jew, they would rub salt on the wounds. Judith considered, "He's always been that way, touchy, high-strung. That man could pick a fight with a butterfly."

The boys chuckled, but were impatient with the defense of their father. "We're nervous too," said Ira, "but we don't go around ranting and raving at people all the time. It's disgusting, and it's disgusting the way you're always making excuses for him."

"Something gets hold of him," she replied, "and he can't stop himself. He can't back down once he starts up; that's not the way men behaved in the world he grew up in. Sometimes I almost sympathize with him, I mean, when he's not around. When he's around, he gets to me right away. And when your father gets to me, he doesn't stop. He just keeps digging and digging until a person doesn't care anymore what his excuse is. He's just unbearable. He makes me want to give up altogether."

"Don't give up," said Ira fervently. "Free yourself. Get your own place."

"Don't talk nonsense," she said. "Where would I go? How could I support myself and two boys as a milliner? Where would your education come from?"

Ira thought, "Where is she now? How many times do I have to confirm that it's hopeless? The rhyme of the ancient milliner."

Marc had seen such exchanges before, and was getting ready for Ira to say that if Joel was what she wanted, then Joel was what she deserved. But then the sound of a key clicking in a keyhole came to them from the other end of the long foyer with ersatz rococo trimming that led away from the dining room.

Ira glanced at the clock and said, "Here he comes now, folks," referencing a cartoon by Herblock. A crowd was gathered and a brass band was playing. Flags and banners adorned a rostrum on which an animated man with a microphone said, "Here he comes now, folks!" In the foreground at the bottom, a darkly dripping manhole cover was pushed up and Senator Richard M. Nixon emerged from a sewer.

Joel came in with a stride that was both important and questioning, as if he were experimenting with being a god. He was a stocky man with dark hair, piercing eyes, and a thin moustache. He was below average height, and his wife and both of his sons, Ira at sixteen and Marc at eleven, were now taller than he was. "Good evening," he said, giving three syllables to "evening." "Clothes are going out of style. The Jewish people will now go naked to save money, and hop around to keep warm. How's by you?"

Their father would walk around in his underwear in the house, and Marc remembered the time he had told him that people could see him through the windows. He had replied that if they wanted to look, that was their business.

"We're fine," said Judith in a sardonic voice, "as fine as silk." She had withdrawn to the kitchen and was focusing her attention on the sink.

"That's extra swell," said Joel. "I can see something is wrong around here. What is it? Did one of these guys break something?"

Marc, who was closest to his father, said "Nothing broke. It's been a quiet day."

Joel said, "Nothing broke? Now that's really something. Hallelujah. Praise the Lord and pass the ammunition. A *lebedike velt*. Next stop, things will start to put themselves together. Now this calls for a celebration."

Judith was at the stove and didn't bother to turn around. "He's complaining that nothing is broken. You can see he's a critic." The corners of the boys' mouths curled.

"I'm not complaining. I'm trying to be nice. Do you know what that means? Look it up in the dictionary, *n-i-c-e*."

Judith said, "You see? An educated man *takeh*."

"Try not to envy my education so *much*," said Joel. "Boy, it takes a hell of an effort around here. It's a big job. I come home from another long, rotten day at the store, a bunch of lousy J. B.'s trying to take the shirt off my back, and as soon as I get in the door, I see the three of you crouching there. The first thing I say when I look at you is '*Vayizmir!* Look at them. They're in cahoots. They're trying to do me dirty.' Then I say, 'No, they're my family. I should try to believe in them. Even if it's not true, I should try my darndest to believe in them. What else am I working for?' Other people enjoy their families. You should see what they do. Why shouldn't I have the right to a family that gives me anything but gall? Just a little bit of *nachus*. They can't be so cruel that they would cut me out like a dog. So I try like the dickens to be nice--and what good does it do me?"

"It cramps his style," said Judith.

"Now that's uproarious. Look at my own sons sitting there smirking at me. I can't escape for one minute the painful fact that I've come home to a nest of vipers."

Marc tried to lighten things up: "Vindow vipers."

"You know what I mean," Joel said. "Enemies, backstabbers."

"And whose fault is that?" Judith asked.

"Now you're asking the right question," Joel said, "because it's obvious to anyone who it is. It's as plain as the nose on your face, and that's saying something. The person responsible is the person who's spreading the poison—who's taking two young boys and teaching them to hate their father."

"Fine, but you still didn't answer my question: Who is **that?**"

"Admitting that you're stupid is one of your more attractive qualities," Joel said. "You should do that more often. It's not only honest, but it takes a little time off from poisoning my sons. What do you expect to accomplish if you succeed in bringing the boys up to be bitches?" He turned to them. "Don't you ever get enough of that evil Polack poison? You suck up to her when she's playing cuckoo and she goes over those lies like *davening.*

But what does it do for you? That's what I can't understand." His voice squealed with perplexed astonishment.

Ira sat at the table scowling, taut with tension. He was obviously tempted to say something, but for years he had avoided saying anything to his father. Joel was taking advantage of this prohibition. Both boys wanted to leave, but felt that if they stayed, their father would be under some restraint.

Joel flipped on the radio. "I wanted to live a normal life. We could go places and enjoy things like regular people instead of all this recrimination." The radio came on, playing a string orchestra version of "Begin the Beguine."

Ira slammed his book shut, though he hadn't really been reading. The sound of the radio was a conditioned signal to the boys that reading would now be interrupted. Ira gripped the edge of the table with white hands.

"Look at my oldest son. He's on his way to being a gangster, and once he's a gangster, he'll be on his way to hell. I wanted to do right by you, but it's a waste of time to talk sense to you because you just want to be rotten. It's that Polack poison she's always oozing at you. What boy can live right if he doesn't talk to his father? I sacrificed myself for you. A bicycle you got, a typewriter."

"The typewriter was from Uncle Dave," said Marc, "and Ira paid for part of the bicycle."

"Part of the bicycle. One wheel. Let him ride part of the bicycle," Joel hammered at the obvious. "He couldn't have gotten half of it without me. The only thing he ever got for himself with all his working is that damned fishing reel that he can't even use because he has no rod. Who gives him food and clothes?"

Ira suddenly exploded: "All I ever got from you was sickness. You keep trying to blame Mom because you know that it's your fault that the family is fucked up." His father tried flinging his voice in, but Ira kept repeating, "Your fault, your fault" loudly.

"That's it!" Joel said, like a movie director with a megaphone. "Perfect! That's exactly the way a gangster talks. Great language. Great ideas. You're on your way to the shithouse, mister."

"Your fault. Your fault," reiterated Ira.

"Don't go to *schul*, don't do anything right. Just talk like that. You're going to show the other crooks and wrongies how to do it! You'll be in the papers. You want to behave like a gangster...."

They stared into each other's eyes as they howled, as if they were actually hearing each other, each hearing in the other the truth of himself. "I'll *treat* you like a gangster!" Joel gave Ira a jarring slap on the side of the head, partly to stop him from repeating "Your fault," and partly because he didn't want to go on with his own invective. He said to himself, "It's a father's job." He couldn't imagine he was wrong unless he chose to be, and that was the heart of his insanity.

Ira's face went crimson and his rigid body shook. He leaped up, his brow twisted and the sides of his mouth contracted to a grimace, his blue eyes blinded. "You bastard," he croaked, "I'll break your neck!"

"No, you won't. I'd like to see you. I'm your father. You can't hurt me, buster, because you know the truth."

While Joel was speaking, Ira wrenched himself away and ran awkwardly down the foyer. He slipped on an area rug, stomping one of his feet to knock over with a jolt a candlestick on a blonde imitation Louis XIV table. He stumbled, recovered himself, and struggled out the door.

As he went out, Joel raised his voice in an effort to follow him into the hall, his rage pulled along in the wake of Ira's. "Where do you think you can go with that crazy sourness? You'll get further and further behind the eight ball. You'll live a bum's life." Though he yelled sharply, his rhetoric had fallen behind the situation, wailing as much in dismay as anger.

Marc stood up. Whenever he was sitting in a room where his father was snarling, he felt in danger of being smacked at any moment. Torn between the desire to leave and the impulse to protect his mother, he stood facing the doorway.

Joel turned to him. "You see? She glories in that. That's her pride and joy, her mama's boy. She's got him so filled with evil lies, he doesn't even know what he's doing. If she can get him to display some new level of crazy nonsense, that's a delight to her. It tickles her pink."

Marc struggled to get the courage to speak, as if he were trying to swallow, then said, "If he's angry, it's your fault. You hit him." Joel interrupted before he could finish the last sentence.

"Right. Now you're talking the way she wants you to talk, and thinking like she wants you to think. You're learning your lesson well so she can have a matched set of misfits. You're another one who wants to try your damnedest to be a wrongie."

Now Judith began to insert a series of sporadic comments in an undertone, even though Joel did not stop. "Wrongie," she said. "That's his idea of how to describe a person, his level of understanding. He's going to convince you that he's right. Notice how convincing he is."

Talking over her, Joel asserted, "I happen to be right from A to Z, and you know it, sister." At the same time, the radio was insisting, "You can solve those problems and put your life in order by taking advantage of Sincere Finance Company's new comprehensive plan. Just drop over to any of our friendly offices."

"They form a kind of trio," Marc thought, "with the old man dominating it. They go together better than the radio goes with them because they're Jewish." He had seen a TV ad for brotherhood that showed Benny Goodman, Lionel Hampton, and Gene Krupa—a Jew, a Negro, and a Christian who formed a famous trio. The jingle was, "If you want good harmony/Takes more than one/ Takes two or three." His father's shrill voice was like the wail of Goodman's clarinet, Mom's icy asides were like Hampton's vibraphone, and the deep announcer was the drum. Marc listened to snatches of it as it went by:

Let me tell you how her mind works. I'm an expert.
Why shouldn't you be impressed? Anyone can see he's
there's no need to suffer any longer! Because now

She wants you to think that if he's a gangster, it's my fault.
Trying to impress you with his intelligence. He must spend a
soothing relief from soreness and embarrassing itching can be

Can't you see she wants you to get addicted, like he is?
lot of time thinking about it. He sure spends a lot of energy.
yours today if you just try new improved Preparation H.

    Marc saw that the parents were getting involved in this volley to avoid thinking about Ira's terrible exit. Marc himself took consolation from the scene by concluding that Ira's outburst was so negative and incoherent that it would not break his arduous and exalted rule to not talk to the old man—and Ira would know that.

    His pondering was soon interrupted by Joel, directly supplicating him through a repeating line: "You should see other boys with their fathers. They have fun. They go to ball games, boat rides, parades, shows. They enjoy life. If you could just have the right attitude, things would be so much brighter." He was a salesman, and his speech reminded Marc of the last commercial; but was too insistent to sell anyone who wasn't already sold. A sales pitch should suggest something being sold other than a fantasy.

    "You should remember to take those vitamins," Joel continued in a confidential tone. "You'd be surprised how important that can be." He put his hand on Marc's ass. The touch was soft and affectionate, but Marc felt disgusted by it. "Stop it," he said, and stepped away.

    "So you want to be cold and bitter like your mother, heh?" Marc remembered seeing his mother move away from Joel's hand on her rear end. Joel said, "You won't listen to reason, another one who wants to end up behind the eight ball."

    The encounter jolted Marc into retrospection: "When I was about five, I was in bed with Dad and he asked me to go under the covers with him. In the darkness, he said, 'This is my sword.' I stayed away from him, but I wondered what was the mystery of his *schmekel.* Since that time, I've worried about whether I might be a homo, but I can't be because boys don't attract me."

"You should know," Judith said, "how much your sons love you and why they feel that way."

"I don't want to hear your bitchiness right now. Save it for Saturday. That's your double bitch day. I know what you're saying before you say it. You want to alienate my sons from me because you're sick and you have a sour face." He shrugged. "Now that doesn't even sound logical, but it's the kind of crazy logic you live by. I had to study it carefully over the years just to manage to survive."

"Your precious logic," Judith continued. "You should put your logic on the market. You'd get rich. Then you could buy a hundred radios and blast yourself from all sides." The radio was playing a mambo version of "Makin' Whoopee."

"I can understand why you'd be bitter with a face like yours. Who would want to look at that miserable grey puss with those dried out eyes, and a potato for a nose. Your sweetheart brother knows how bitter you are: that's why he keeps away from you except when he wants to take your money."

Judith thought, "This he says, Shirley, to cover up how Dave is embarrassed by him even though he helps Yoyel out financially. Especially he has to blot out how Dave got us this apartment."

"He says that," Marc thought, "because what she says is cleverer than what he says."

Joel said, "Your sons will grow up to realize what your swindler brother already knows: that you can't live because you can't be happy. You only want to be miserable. You're crazy like your whole family is crazy, bunch of evil Polacks."

As far as Marc knew, both of his parents were Polish Jews. The only difference was that his father's family had come to America a few years before Joel was born, while his mother had come with her family when she was about eight years old. Marc said, "Stop picking on her."

"Picking on her? I'm just telling a little bit of the truth, that's all. It's a free country. I've got a right to tell the truth every once in a while, in my own home, I think. Boy, she's got you so bamboozled that you need a little truth desperately. If the truth hurts you, that's because there's something wrong with you. You have to see the light."

"Go see if you can find your brother," Judith said. "I've got some lamb chops in the ice box and they'll be ready soon."

Marc hesitated, feeling that if he stayed, he might keep them talking to him rather than each other. But it didn't seem to be working that way, and besides he could be eavesdropping. "I'll go," he said to Joel, "if you'll keep cool."

"*Me* keep cool?" Joel exclaimed. "Of course I'll keep cool. I always keep cool. She's the one with the nasty mouth. We're a jazzy couple. I'm cool and she's crazy. Aggravation is her element. She thrives on it."

Marc started down the foyer, pausing to stand up the lustrous fallen candlestick.

"You see what you're doing to them?" Joel said with a dumbfounded voice and staring in amazement. "I wouldn't believe it if I didn't see it with my own eyes, but the truth is apparent."

Marc thought, "The truth is a parent."

"The truth is that you're taking healthy young boys and turning them into diseased criminals with your insidious lies. It really is horrible, *takeh,* a tragic nightmare. You know, it's your good luck and the boys' bad luck that you're married to an easygoing fella. Any reasonable person, thinking about what you're doing to those two boys, would wallop the hell out of you."

Marc was pulling his jacket from the closet at the other end of the foyer and stopped to hear what would happen. He was hoping for a lull so that he could open the door without worrying about meeting neighbors. But instead, they were building up. It did not occur to Marc that they might be doing it for him, perhaps without knowing it; that they wanted to get some good choruses in before he went, though they weren't even sure he could still hear them.

Judith had to shout to interrupt Joel, but her shout was not as loud as his declamation. In fact, she could outsound him by screaming, but as usual, she chose to play it tough. "You're welcome to try it, big shot, but you tried it before and you know what happened. This time you can be sure you'll never see me again."

"You *enjoy* talking like that," he said, "don't you?" She asserted, "Yes, I *do* enjoy it." But he was louder: "You, you get a *kick* out of tormenting me. You witch! She-devil! You're destroying the children worse than any disease in the book because you don't know what it means to be a mother. When in hell am I ever going to get anything nice out of you?"

"If I was smart and had some backbone," Judith said, "you'd get something nice from me in a hurry. Let me tell you what, my darling husband. If I put up with you this long, it must be because I'm made of iron, but even iron wears out. You take it and you take it and then there comes a point where you can't take it anymore. If I was strong, I would go jump off the roof and leave you to live with your music and your garbage and be happy. *Shoin gut.* You can find a woman who likes to be tortured every day."

"The roof," thought Marc. "There she goes with that one again. She doesn't realize I'm still here. Compared to Ira, I'm small potatoes. The fact that she's said that so many times proves she won't do it."

Despite Joel's bluster, his wife's statements disturbed him. But he continued: "Now that's very clever. That's a grand idea, what they call 'ginger peachy.' Did you think of that yourself or did you find it in one of those books you read that twist your mind? All you want to talk about is dying. It gives you a thrill. I guess something has to give you a thrill."

Marc slipped out the door. He wanted to get away, but just as he closed the door, the racket increased. And since no one was in the hall, he couldn't resist listening a little longer to what was quite audible even with the door closed. His father was whining in a caricature of his mother, "When are they going to let me in the box? I can't wait to get in the box."

"If that's what I want," she said, "It's a logical reaction to you. Living with you, I'd have to be crazy not to want it. The boys both know all about you, mister. That's why they're both running from you like the Kentucky Derby."

"You pulled the wool over their eyes," he said. "A kid can't stop himself from being buttered up good by his mother. But when they get to be men, they'll see the truth. They'll know what I had to put up with from you. They'll understand what an ordeal it's been for me to live with your frigidity."

"Sure, frigidity. A few minutes with you, Mr. Glogover, would make Mae West frigid. Her *tsitskes* would run into her underarms to hide."

"Your nasty jokes are just trying to cover up the fact that you know you're wrong. Or don't you even remember that you're supposed to be my wife? You think it's funny that you're poisoning the souls of the children. Even your jokes are unhealthy. Your whole attitude stinks to high heaven. Wait'll you see the results of your nastiness. God will judge you, sister."

"Oh, of course," she said. "God is very interested in your *mishegas*."

"If you think you can laugh at God, you'll just bring disaster on yourself. Smart alecks like you always find that they can't fool the Almighty. He knows what a father should be, what a wife should be."

Marc thought, "He's so sure that God wants what he wants, which is unbearable. God shouldn't let Dad use Him to bully people, to hold us in this miserable merry-go-round. But where has Ira gone? Hope he hasn't run away again. I'm going to have to do some arguing myself to get him home to eat supper." He dashed off down the maroon hall.

2

THE ROOM

1954

Just a regular guy with a touch of interference is what I am. A little patter that doesn't quite matter if I merely tune it out. Like a good scout. I should really think of building up my mind, floor by floor. The most profitable subject for contemplation is not a nasty old creep whom I can easily keep at a distance. It's a miss-dance to worry about what isn't there, the outsides of words. I pondered how to get the worm out of the soup, but there was no soup. Stay in your group. I'm just a trifle unclear about who I'm talking to.

I know exactly what my words mean when I talk to Marc, even when he's not there—he's never there. To live upbeat, I gotta believe that good thoughts have value when no one hears, but evil thoughts can't hurt without objects. That must be possible cause here I am. A *lebedike velt mit gelt*. And these solitary goodies are aimed at the one I can speak most honestly to, the closest of those who are not there. It may not be best to be limited to my kid brother, but it's only logical. I'm the step before him, so he knows how right I am to say that the old man has his clothes on backwards. Who else could I speak to?

We are where we belong, near the famous Bronx Park Zoo. Half a mile southwest of us as the crow flies, more by foot, but we get there when we can. It tends to smell from elephant shit, but it's a heap nicer than Bronx Park East, the exotic or Oriental zoo in which Marc and I and all of us Glogovers are on exhibit, comical to the general populace and aghast at the imprisonment to which we have subjected ourselves, longing for an escape that's impossible to a homeland we can't find. There are amusements for the animals, but they hardly relieve our sense of being caught since the object of amusement is ourselves. In Newark there was a tree in the park with a branch you could sit on above the people.

I go beyond who I'm talking to, the guy I can't reach. When I was twelve, I hung around the zoo for hours every day, since you could climb into it for free. Before the entrance to the zoo, Fordham Road passed over the Bronx River and there were stone railings on the bridge with curved pillars. I'd climb over the railings and go down a slope to the water. You were little then and only went with me a few times. At five years apart, we weren't usually the right age to do things together. There was a pool to the side of the zoo with a circular island where it was said there had once been monkeys, but we never got there and it looked deserted.

Through this side entrance it was easy to walk into the zoo and save the entrance fee of fifteen cents. I tried to make friends there, having none outside. My favorite was a spectacled bear, with white rings around his eyes. I'd put my hands through the bars to feed him peanuts. I called him "Glasses." He seemed to appreciate it, and was a whole lot easier to get along with than Joel. The zoo was filled with children and grown-ups cautiously letting themselves wonder. If I could have hid out there, both of us, we could live on the unfinished food people threw in waste baskets, whole halves of hot dogs.

The parents say they moved to the Bronx for the *kinder,* to give us a chance to go to the splendiferous City College. A better environment than Newark, everything for the *kinder*. But zoos are not much fun for the critters stuck in them, and Yiddish loses a lot in translation, even if the original is lost to begin with. *Kinder* is not kinder. Is it kinder to put us on display this way for people who see us as *schmutz*? Animals there are not judged the way people are here. It's supposed to be good for us, to make us better, the dream of the boys. But the dream of the promised land sent the parents bonkers, so we had to move from the plebeians to the classy folks, and we're always being caught with our fingers in our noses, or someplace worse. It was for them, for Joel and Judith fleeing the *tsuris* of the Depression and anti-Semitism, that the dream of the enchanted boys was born, a dream that got lost.

We're supposed to develop class, but class may always be on exhibit or it wouldn't be class, and zoo folks seldom enjoy being peered at. They'd rather hide in a corner of the cage that's their own. Mom has an idea of what class could be, but what it actually is is a permanent affliction 'cause of Joel, who's always saying we should turn out the lights or we'll end up in the poor house. So we end up in the dark. This doesn't help us to read, but he thinks reading is bad for our minds, not to mention our eyes.

Joel the star exhibit, the astonishing fat man who can make your hair stand on end and jump out of your head. He chases people from the zoo. Sometimes the chimps cause problems by throwing their frockey at people.

We keep getting tropical fish and the old man keeps turning down the thermostat. So the fish end up drooping their fins, humping their backs, turning silver, and limping along until they lie on the bottom, twisted and staring, waved by the water. Joel has saved them from the poorhouse. Why do I have to be talking to anyone? What I have to say is bad news. Only with junior I can enjoy being the one who knows, long as he doesn't know what I know. A sparkling treat, as good as happiness can be. With Gornstein, I can never catch up, I always want too much; but fooling Marc is heavenly, sliding down a slope of orange Jello.

Us ideal youths, who slept in the living room in Newark, now have a special room appointed for us. It's our own aquarium, with these aqua walls and shiny orange maple furniture, with rounded corners and dulled brass handles—innocent and cheerful as Debbie Reynolds. So we're even proud of it, and God knows we enjoy having our own corner of the cage, the stories I tell and the card games; but somehow this space draws us apart because it's really their space, not ours. We were closer in Newark, where we both slept on the sofa bed, breathing the same breath. The parents impose themselves on the room all the time, just as they control its furniture, with those doilies on top of the chest of drawers, like "don't touch" signs. Designed to keep us away from ourselves. You should know this, but you don't really see it because you're happy, an infection from which you may never recover, which I gave you by saving you.

The desk, the place we're supposed to think, is Joel's sewing machine. The top folds open to become a table for clothes and you pull the black Singer engine heavily from the hole in which it is buried and you lower a flap to hold it up with its silver spindles and wheel. Then when you lift the machine and release the flap, it sinks back into its coffin while you hold it to keep it from crashing. With the machine and the top lowered, it looks like a desk, but when you pull the drawers, they swivel open on a slant to hold needles, threads and razors for a machine that can only write by piercing, cutting, and binding.

Joel does lots of sewing with it on weekends, fixing clothes with holes and making pants longer for his tall sons. He has to play the radio loud while the machine is droning, and he sings along with both of them. It's hard to tell the yammering of his yiddle diddle from the hammering of the machine or the farting of the radio; it makes the area uninhabitable. What does their yammering say? "Cheap, I'm cheap, I'm cheap." The room and the whole place chirp it in their cheesy attempt to be fancy.

Sitting at the machine, I look out the window at the trees with the sun shining through them. The leaves stir and flutter in the breeze and the light on my arms slishes into itself wildly, scattering, shattering beams across my glowing skin. I look back for you.

We were always in trouble because our games had drastic consequences, worried about when the latest thing we had broken would be found, being yelled at or waiting to be yelled at, so the parents would loom over the room even when they weren't in it. The walls of the apartment express by a fervid coagulation of bright paint a striving for lavishness. They are mostly either a sort of maroon-mauve or aqua, stippled and with patterns stenciled on them in gold paint, but they're poorly made. They have bulges, air bubbles and flaws that break easily if hit by a rubber ball or an elbow. So they're spotted with plaster gaps that are grey and inclined to crumble. Even when they are painted over, they remain spots because the gold tracery can't be continued, and the tiny bumps of the stippling are interrupted by flat parts. What the gaudy walls are trying to cover can't be covered. They're only a frozen sea of distress.

One thing we know is that Spaldings are the supreme rubber balls because they bounce almost as high as the point you drop them from. You'd watch me drop two pink balls parallel to each other to see which one would rise higher; for handball, stickball, or catch. We couldn't help bouncing off the walls of the apartment with those balls, but when we bounced, something broke. We would see how high we could throw a ball against the grayish-yellow front of the building's six stories. Remember when I threw it over the top, and when we went to look for it on the roof, it was gone? Though the building was almost as deep as it was high, the ball must have bounced a number of times and gone over the back or side. It was never found. The ball that resigned from the earth.

Even though we lived on the ground floor, the neighbors complained about us running, yelling, and bouncing balls, so the fun we had in the house got more restricted as we got bigger and noisier. Growing up as a series of losses. Sometimes you and I had pillow fights, walloping each other with these massive slidy-soft cushions. A few times the pillows broke open and filled the air with floating swirls of tiny white feathers like Chinese egg-drop soup, the beauty of crime, of breaking things open. The softness of the feathers on fingers, like the inside of a mouth, suspended around us.

When Mom got angry, she threatened us with a leather belt, and at pillow fights she'd whip us across the legs with it, leaving feathers stuck to our skin. But it was the fat boy we hated and feared—hysterical and unpredictable. Mom's blows hurt more, but we could stand up to her lashes. We braced ourselves, there was a hot streak of pain or two, we winced, and it was over—or on the way toward stinging less. And she stopped hitting us, but his didn't really stop. They continue.

Joel's blows, mostly slaps to the head, come at the end of a spell of tension and fury that makes them devastating explosions. They speak with the thunder of a curse. The rasping snarl of his voice is the crack of his palm on the side of my brow, a curse that keeps growing. Every word of it strains to say something worse, every explosion gets more devastating and hateful as it reverberates. We feel her anger as cold indignation and his as hot, seething rancor. She punishes what she loves and he attacks what he hates. He only hit me less than once a week, and he rarely hit me after I got older and stopped talking to him; but it always seems as if he's about to when he's here, even when he's working. His real work is smashing my brain. Jabbing his needle into my fabric. Click click click. As if what reverberates is most real, what erases my thoughts. [Yet you'd insist things aren't so grim. If I write to see life, I must aim at some cheer, and this must be true if I'm thinking, and I must be thinking. Marc would say I should look upward.]

When the boys could feel the privacy of their room, it was a treat. Late one afternoon Ira, the better of the two at math, was doing his algebra on the sewing-machine desk. Marc was on his nearby bed reading *Plasticman* comics. Tall and thin, he identified with the hero who could stretch in any direction.

Marc looked up. "Hey," he said, "do you ever dream of flying?"

The question of what Ira dreamed about wiped the algebra out of his mind. He thought, "What would hold me up? A flock of birds with silver wings. I would fall and crush them." He exhaled and took on an air of patience: "A little."

"I've dreamed about it a lot," Marc said. "Especially lately. In these dreams, I can lift myself off the ground by concentrating, or sometimes I just find myself in the air without meaning to."

"You're in the air when you're awake, my bucko. *Schmendrick* the magician."

Marc went on: "Of course, sometimes it doesn't work, or it only takes me a few inches. I have a feeling that there's a right way to hold myself, to think, a part of my body to focus on, but I'm not sure what it is. Most often I think it's on the bottom of my brain. Sometimes I hit it and begin to rise. But when I try to remember exactly how it feels, I can't get it clear. Generally, I try to think about lifting and controlling myself while being calm at the same time, but I can't stay calm. I'm not sure whether to calculate where I am in the air or pay no attention to it. It works best when I'm not thinking about it, and then I find suddenly I've got it. The movement seems to be there and I catch it and fly with it. But then I realize it and start to fall."

Ira was thinking, "This boy's daft, but I'd better not let on. Only upset him further." Marc noticed that Ira's mouth was pushed up in the middle and his eyes were looking down in a sly way. This made Marc wonder what the use of contact he was trying to establish could be. Nevertheless, he was driven onward. "'Times I've gotten up twenty feet or more. I remember looking down at a street lamp and its yellow circle of light on the sidewalk. When a bully or something threatening appears in a dream, I usually try to fly. And even when I'm awake, I sometimes feel I've got this ability if I could only grasp it. I'm convinced there are times when I jumped up and came down more slowly than I should have."

Ira squinted his eyes. "If I had the misfortune to be you, young moon, I'd have a care with that stuff. Every so often one hears of a likely lad who comes to the conclusion that he's Superman and ends up making a personal pizza on the pavement. Of course, looking at the bright side, there's not much danger in your taking too many risks. Anywho . . . all of this balderdash definitely reminds me of a story about Looiyoo. It dashes so baldly. It's bald with such dash."

Marc dropped into a listening position, sitting with his chin on his palms. But he did it quietly, for if he looked too eager to hear the story, it might dissuade Ira from improvising. Ira found his younger brother's delight in the Looiyoo stories embarrassing. The style of Looiyoo, who wore a Napoleon hat, held his right hand under the left breast of his jacket, and farted a lot, was heavily influenced by *Loony Tunes* and *Pogo Possum*. Somehow, Ira enthralled Marc by presenting this regressive figure who always succeeded, with a good deal of *joi de vivre*, in not getting away with anything at all.

"In fact, this here rib-tickling rouser is nothing less than a colossal Looiyoo epic, the Looiyoo story to end all Looiyoo stories."

Ira sat down and looked out the window at the empty back yards of the private houses across the way. It was almost dark outside and he saw reflected in the window his own dark silhouette against the brightly lit aqua wall behind him. The outline of his reclining form was filled with the dark, lifting, swaying leaves of the outside trees. One of the leaves, above another, fell on and stroked it, then rose to its natural height, then was bent down by the wind to touch the one beneath again. "I'm too big to be telling kiddie stories," he thought, "and ashamed to enjoy it."

Left to stop and think, Marc noticed an impression that Ira was trying to avoid something by the rush of his talk. But Marc didn't like to think of this, so he hoped Ira would go on, and he lifted his chin a little in eagerness.

"From the time Looiyoo was a weenchly toddler, he had a prodigious desire to fly, to go smooching through the air, like a debonair affair."

Marc felt an urge to laugh, but he kept it quiet by holding back the convulsion with muscles under his eyes. Without looking, Ira was aware of the level of his non-laughter. "He tried running, jumping hard, and flapping his *fleegles*." Ira pumped his elbows energetically. "After a massive dose of serious calculation, he launched a plan to take off like a helicopter. He'd run around in a circle, faster and faster, trying to grab his own *tuchas*. But though he tried to be like Plasticman and almost thought he reached it a few times, it always was gone when he got there. Expressing its defiance, as asses tend to do. Did his fingertips brush it or was it only the wind? After a few hours, he thought he smelled success, but it turned out to be gas. Then he felt that he was lifting off, but it turned out he only fainted. But was he put out by this? Did he grovel in despair? He most certainly did not, that schmuck of all schmucks.

"Someone once asked Looiyoo what the word 'defeat' meant, and what did he answer?" Marc looked up at Ira, who pointed to Marc's head, then his arms, then his legs, saying with a dopey Looiyoo accent, "'This here's de head, there's de arms. There's de legs, and then there's de feet!' And what do these words of Looiyoo reveal?"

Marc replied, "That he didn't know the meaning of defeat!" and burst into a snort of laughter, as if he hadn't heard it before, or it was renewed by the context.

Ira said, "Prezactly! Believe it, beloved! The blasted idiot was actually too dumb to give up! Too fucking dumb! The lad just had to cause himself even more misery by continuing to try. It's like paying to buy a pie in your eye."

The leaves were agitated by the wind as if they were in pain. Ira thought, "Well at least I can make this yuck laugh. I hope he doesn't figure out how much time I spend thinking about this drivel."

Then Ira jumped up and said, "Did I say this was an epic or did I say this was an epic?" Marc thought, "He sounds like Dad, asking questions that answer themselves, even though Ira hasn't spoken to him in four years. Making fun of Dad, but he sounds like him." Ira lifted his arms, threw his shoulders back, and bellowed with the voice of the Coming Attractions for a movie: "SWEEPING ACROSS THE SCREEN!" Then he started ostentatiously, suddenly crouched, and did a laborious imitation of an old man pushing a broom. Marc chortled deliriously.

Ira went on: "Looiyoo would spend hours standing on a chair trying to pull himself up into the air by tugging at his hair. He'd lament to himself, 'If only I had the guts or the muscles to pull a little harder.' His most successful flight was achieved by putting a garden hose up his *tuchas* and turning it on ice cold and full blast. He did nine feet high and sixteen feet forward this way, but it was a bit rough. Left him without a foundation, with standing room only."

"Can anyone fly without a plane?'" asked Marc, though he had said he could.

"Not as I know of, junior, though maybe there's a way they haven't thought of yet" (he lowered his head to the right). "But I doubt it" (lowered to the left). "Anywoe, just as Looiyoo was getting exciting results, his project was nipped in the butt. As soon as he sat down, he realized that he couldn't keep trying in this half-assed fashion." Ira made a point of stirring uneasily in his seat. "He had to be systematic, had to get down to fundamentals and learn the principles involved if he was ever to get anywhere. In fucked fact, he had to go to school, as don't we all. To scummy drool.

"So Looiyoo went to school and he communed with all the higher intellectual types in an effort to understand things to their roots, to stand under things. But what he found when he looked school over really shook the lad up. He found scads of people who were great at all flavors of fancy mouthing. I mean they could hold forth indefinitely in the most splendiferous fashion, but if you asked them what it meant, they were stumped, in the dark, didn't have a clue. So Looiyoo decided he'd have to do it for himself; he'd have to write a book that would explain life completely. What our breath is saying, what our farts are saying, and the difference between them." Ira raised his eyebrows as his mother did to signify a most comprehensive conception.

"You want to be a writer, don't you?" Marc asked.

"You bet your bottom buttock I do, and I will be one, one way or the other, probably the other."

Marc thought, "These shticks with words. Even though he hates Dad, they're like Joel when he gets cute with his wise cracks."

"Well, anyway, Looiyoo started his book, and ideas began to spout out of him profusely, like baby guppies, and he was getting on copacetically. Ah but then, after a few days, he began to hear this rumbling sound and he felt something gnawing at his insides. He soon realized that he was hungry. So cavernously hungry that he had to look for a job immediately. He thought that if he had a pile of moolah, he could write all he wanted. So he looked for work and got a respectable position freezing Band-Aids. He would line these Band-Aids up on big trays and put them in a freezer, and he did quite well at it, too, winning ferocious admiration from the other Band-Aid icers and achieving superior success."

"What did they want frozen Band-Aids for?"

"Well, generally they use them for cold-cuts. You figured out the crucial question in less than two hours, suggesting you're more intelligent than I thought you were. On the other hand, so is dog doo." Marc withheld further questions.

"So our boy began to make good money, but then he became aware of something drawing him to the side, like he was doing a samba. There was an empty space beside him that felt hollow, so he soon realized that he was going to have to look for a girl. Well, he set about it with his peepers on high gear, and after a while he found one, and she was scrumptious. Her public parts were so good they were private, as a result of which it hurt severely to look at her. So he wined her and dined her and made a grand speech. And then he was just about to give her an extra-large kiss, when suddenly something grosped his guts: he had this raging desire to go to the bathroom. So he tearassed over to the toilet; but just as he was about to let fly, a monster appeared, popping right out of the potty." Ira stood up eagerly. "Now this monster was fat and disgusting. In fact, I hate to say it, but this here monster had a considerabobble resemblance to something we know." He extended his head sideways at Marc and wrinkled his eyebrows in perturbation.

Snirting through his nose, Marc burst into giggling. "You mean Dad."

"Except that actually the monster was three-and-a-half times as smart, a hundred and thirteen times as nice and twelve times as good looking as dear old dads. So Looiyoo fought the monster while holding it in." Ira enacted the gestures of someone with rigid legs swinging a sword and then thrusting home. "He killed the monster and then he said, 'Huzza' and took a shit—on the monster—and this gave him a stupendulous feeling of relief. He felt exactly as if he was flying high.

"Unfortunately, when he got back, the girl was gone. He was done left in the lurch. But did this bother him? No siree! Not that nitwit! He just did his old dance." Ira hinted at a few steps of a sort of ponderous polka in slow motion. "You'se heard of the turkey trot? The bunny hop? Well this is the weasel romp!"

The musical part of this was a familiar formula to Marc. In the old days it was accompanied by a song, the meager words of which centered on the refrain "Wes'll romp across the floor." For a few years, the song had become too embarrassing to actually sing, but it was still in their minds, and Ira's movements indicated its rhythm. Coming at the close of the story, the song tended to lead to a moral. In this case, "And Looiyoo, that putz, said 'I'm a lucky guy. 'Cause I got to do two things I really wanted to do.'"

Marc laughed and exclaimed, "But what he wanted to do was better at the beginning than in the end, wasn't it?"

"True enough, m'lad, and his reasons were also better at the start than later on. They went downhill from the highest to the lowest. And yet . . . ." Ira sat down again. "Well, he's had his moments of satisfaction to remind him of his old dreams, and the story's not over, is it? And maybe if you do something now to make up for something you once wanted to do, maybe you're doing the other thing too on some level. So maybe when he plopped on the old man, he was making the world a better place and bringing about enlightenment. It was his way of flying, or maybe making love. Hmmm. The important thing is that he was happy, whatever that means. Half a pee is better than not peeing at all."

Marc couldn't tell if Ira was serious or joking. He wondered how Looiyoo could be happy with his dreams put off, but he thought that later he would understand. He said, "Then you're always sort of doing two things at once?"

"Sure," said Ira, "Must be at least two. For example, there's the thing you're actually doing and the thing you really want to do. Now the thing you are actually doing is generally vile. In fact, it's enough to make a waffle vomit. This is especially true in your case, but more or less true for everyone. We spend ninety percent of our time on humdrum chores, or meanness, to teach other people lessons they'll never learn. And the worst part is we don't even know what we're doing because we're too busy thinking of what we want to do. So that at any given moment the average Joe is basically taking a crap, but he thinks he's doing something very useful, part of a noble effort to help humanity. Sometimes I get the feeling that what I say actually means something, a surefire sign of decline.

"The thing you really want to do is to go back to something that's gone, maybe even to go back to something that's gone that stands for something that's even goner." He looked Marc in the eye. "You'll never get back there. The situation is hopeless—so it's just as well that you're a pinhead."

Marc laughed, but he felt that he would never be as sharply perceptive, as courageous, as Ira. Ira was a stern realist, while he was a weak dreamer. Ira could face the fact that the old man was hopeless, while he kept trying to find some justification for him. Ira saw the upper leaf tap the lower one for half a second.

3

CROSSING DREAMS

1954

Marc usually left the television after the eleven o'clock news and went to bed before Ira. And when Marc was alone (no worry when Ira was there), he was careful to pull the cover over every inch of his extremities. If he left anything except his head sticking out, he was afraid something would seize it while he was asleep. His head would be conscious of any touch, even when he slept, but his limbs were less aware and could be snatched.

The snatcher stayed hidden, but the most common image it assumed was that of a vampire with green skin and red, glowing eyes. Sometimes in his thoughts the eyes were closed, and then the monster might part his cloak and reveal one large burning eye in the middle of his chest. Marc imagined this creature in shadowy corners, behind doors, and in closets. When he left the garbage bags downstairs on the table, he rushed back to the elevator, dreading to think of the dark, unknown rooms in the recesses of the basement. He could not bear the thought of looking in that luminous eye. If he saw what was inside it, a blank space that looked at you without being seen, it would penetrate, transform, fuse with him.

Marc was long and his parents were obsessed with saving money, so the blankets he slept in were usually not quite long enough. Sometimes he had to sleep diagonally, with his feet wrapped under a corner of the blanket, and most often he slept curled up on his side to avoid sticking out. Ira's bed was parallel to Marc's, on his right if he was on his back (which he rarely was), and less than three feet away.

When Ira came in to sleep, Marc was usually snoring, a peaceful sound that helped Ira to drift off.

One night in summer Ira dreamed that he was going to mail a letter to a girl he liked named Joanne on a fine sunny day. Outside the dream Joanne did not exist, but inside it she did.

He was striding on a neat grey road in a clean small town when he heard a faint bell ringing in the distance. The vibration drew his head slightly to the left in the dream and on the pillow. His closed eyes were concentrated, but no one could see them knitted and striving, pupils straying.

As Ira listened to the chiming, it divided and clarified itself into the singing of a bird, a whispering whistle of lifting tones.

On the same night, perhaps, Marc dreamed that he saw the sea beneath him and he was falling toward it spread-eagled with his head below his body. He was puzzled by the fact that the sea was both a field of wave ridges, a surface with its own visual existence, and also a window into buried depths and shadows. Then he was frightened but fascinated by the thought that the whole globe could be an eye, with a dark center and a green iris with a gleaming ring around it of grey flecked with darker streaks.

It was focused on him as a microscope focuses on a tiny creature, and a slogan he had heard on TV slipped through his mind: "Big Brother is watching you."

(Perhaps there was a bird singing outside their window that night, for Marc heard a bird too, a seagull in the distance. Its cawing seemed to open an enormous space over the sea, an ocean of empty sky, and the water seemed to sink further away. Yet these dreams may have taken place at different times. There is no way to know, for dreams cannot know what is outside them, just as the outside cannot know the actuality of dreams.)

Ira was in a buoyant mood because he thought that the letter expressed what he wanted to say and she would be touched by it, but the ringing birdsong began to intrude on his thoughts uncomfortably.

The notion started to occur to him that he detected a high pitched voice behind or beneath the shrill chirping. A core of meaning syncopated deep in the vibration of the song that he began to articulate as words, as if the music were a language if we could understand it, but we don't dare.

Ira realized that the words were "Keep your thoughts from darkness." And whose voice was that, distorted into the unnatural purity of a warble? It sounded like Marc's. It was sensible and concerned, but for him, it wasn't right. It might mean that he should stay cheerful, but it might also mean that darkness was waiting to draw his mind into itself.

Marc's own weight, hanging over him, was pressing him down toward the ocean, and he felt that the darkness at the center was a tunnel he could be sucked into. But he had power in his mind, he was free, and he was moving away from the darkness, away into the air.

Wondering why he was falling upward, as if it could be explained, Marc started to move and realized that he was not falling now, but braced numbly and leaning over the side of a gondola, a big basket made of thick wicker and attached to a balloon. Then he grew apprehensive about following his thoughts and obeyed a strong pressure to just watch what was happening.

(If he had followed his question about where the balloon came from, he might have realized he was dreaming and waked, and it might have occurred to him at the point of waking that the questions were asked by Ira.)

(Now their dreams seem to be leaning toward each other, almost touching. The outer edges of the biggest spaces on their horizons may be the same. But it is as impossible to know what they dreamed as it is to know what they might have dreamed if they were different people. Perhaps the dreams are the same dream in different languages—the language of life and the language of death. But which is which? Perhaps the language of death speaks of hoping to live and the language of life speaks of hoping to die.

So the two dreams can never understand each other, and there may be no contact between them at all, though they may be the same. There is no space for what speaks between the dying brother and the living one. There are no words for the conversation by which they live and die in each other. It is outside of any point of view. And when the two boys wake, the dreams may be completely forgotten, never to have existed. This cannot be spoken.)

Ira told himself that it was pessimistic nonsense to think that the trill of a bird concealed a warning. He controlled his mind logically and listened to it again and heard nothing but warbling. "That's better," he said. "My mind is okay."

Then he got to the mailbox, an ordinary looking, squat steel mailbox, painted and repainted, dark green and bolted to the pavement. It seemed to be making a sincere effort to look solid and trustworthy.

Ira opened its slot and looked in to see if other letters might be visible. But he couldn't see anything inside,

Marc found himself in an old-fashioned hot-air balloon, shaped like a big electric bulb and colored orange. One of those very old bulbs with a point on the top, and the basket that held him was at the end that went into the socket. But how could he see the point? Looking around, he saw that there were many other balloons in various bright colors filling the sky, and each had a gondola with someone in it. Some had long gondolas like boats, with groups of people in them. It seemed to be some ridiculous holiday in the sky. He and the others tried to call perhaps because the sunlight was so bright. The inside seemed to be awfully dark, as if the box were filled with black velvet. Then he remembered what the bird might have said, and he became anxious as he lifted the letter to the slot. "I can't let myself be sidetracked by imaginary voices," Ira thought quickly. "If I don't mail this letter here, I'll probably find some bad omen at the next mailbox. I may never mail it. Either I can live in the real world or I can't, and what kind of life would it be if I can't communicate?

So he dropped the letter in the mailbox, and as he dropped it, he pushed his hand forward and opened it a little—maybe a bit more than was necessary, as if to wave goodbye, or to wave hello. As he did so, he felt a chill in the loose, tender skin between his thumb and his forefinger; and the chill shot up his arm to his spine and reverberated through his body. He
to each other, but they could only hear faint, indistinct echoes. They were too far apart, and the air was too filled with movement.

The sky was swarming with people in gondolas. When they approached each other, the balloons gently rebounded from their bubbles like soft rubber balls, separating themselves, and there was a faint sense of frustration, of gaping space. Yet the fact that they couldn't get together didn't seem serious. People smiled and waved and shared a sense of buoyancy

Marc thought he saw Ira in one of the gondolas in the distance, and he seemed to be enjoying himself like the rest. The sun lit everything brightly, but the balloons provided shade. Below, patches of foam wandered over the ocean. Marc felt pleasant, but he had a vague sense that there was something serious somewhere that he should be attending to.

was shaken out of himself by the tremor, and he heard a whisper: "Life is given, life is taken." Then he realized that it was his own voice that was whispering, but coming from someone else.

(If we cannot know each other's dreams, nevertheless we need to believe we know those dreams insofar as we believe in love or in art or in ourselves or in others. Certainly we are most awake, most alive, when we hunger for the dreams of others. Such hunger is inclined to attack those others, which is a way to discover their dreams, to feed on them.)

The letter hit the bottom of the mailbox with a tiny tap, and Ira found himself inside the box, looking out through the slot into his own eyes. They were gleaming with pleasure, and staring at him with a hard, knowing look that stung him to the quick. He realized this meant that the spirit or demon that was waiting for him in the mailbox had taken over his body, that whatever he had to say would always be lost in transmittal, could only be spoken by another alien to him.

The slot clanked shut and Ira, in the dark, felt riveted to the pavement. He wanted to cry out, but as soon as he tried, he felt throughout himself that he was made of steel, too cold to make his life known.

If he could only make the metal hot enough, he could cry, but how could he warm it up? It was rigid, like frozen fire. The only language he had access to

The balloons were moving together, swaying among each other like a school of fish, moving upward. As they ascended closer to the clouds, Marc saw that on the side away from the earth, these clouds were piled in many clearly-defined layers that looked like cities. There were terraces. parapets, towers, bridges, and lifting trees of bright vapor, dazzling in the unblocked sunlight. They were so huge and elaborate that they must be organized. There must be cloud people living their floating lives in those soft, radiant spaces. Their refulgent lines were not straight or symmetrical, but that somehow made them more intelligent.

The clouds were so beautiful, so stately, that Marc was clutched by a desire to jump for them. But he was passing them now, and too far away. He couldn't figure out any way was not in the range humans could detect.

So he had sent his letter to himself, and everything in it had turned out to be false. Perhaps if someone came and put a letter in him, perhaps if it were a true letter, he could gain a new life. But what kind of life would it be? A life whose features were unknown to him.

to control his balloon, and he began to wonder how high he could go. Wouldn't it be impossible to breathe at a certain height? Perhaps as he drifted over the clouds, he could jump onto them. Certainly they would be soft, softer than down, as soft as air.

And why did it have to be taken from someone else, based on cruelty? Worst of all, he felt that as time went on, locked in this scraping darkness, he would turn bitter and mean, and he would long furiously to possess someone as he had been possessed.

(What if Ira were lifted to the sky because he needed it so much that his lifting filled him? And Marc could complete his yearning and pass through the cloud to reach the earth? No one knows which one dreamed what, not even themselves. Wasn't it Ira who called out and couldn't be heard in the other balloons? And Marc who confidently sent the letter? Each speaks for the other, declaring by his living what the other wants to hear.

Meanwhile, outside, a grey bird may have fallen asleep and entered the world of dream. More than once, in the park, the bird had come close to people lying on the grass or on a bench, sleeping peacefully. Now, in her dream, the bird was human (as humans dream of flying) and so she could lie down and sleep on her side. She felt herself relaxing, firmly supported, resting peacefully. She dreamed that she was really asleep. But her dream could never be recorded at all, so maybe that dream was the deepest one, the dream that could sleep forever, that could never be reduced.)

4

THE POOL OF THE PAST

1950

"The sun makes me feel so light," Marc thought. "The word *light* means two things, a light color and a light weight. But the light you see also comes in two kinds. One falls on things and gets lost in their colors, folds, and shadows. The other is bright and spreads and rises to the sun. Does the bright one lift you up? A bubble is a rolling brightness that shines in rising. That's how I feel. With my feet in the water, I'm like a bubble in a bubble pipe, resting on liquid. The sunlight all around presses my head, and the squeeze of brightness on my sides makes me feel like the moment when the gleaming walls of the bubble begin to narrow, to give in at the bottom, bending and— what is it—wobbling?"

Marc thought, "I don't know that *wobbling*. Ira could help. There's more in this life than I can hold. Think of the bubble. It sways (is it sways?) to the side as if it thought of lifting from its ring, a wave of "should-I-go-this-way?" that can't last. Either the bubble will take off,

Ira would have said "quivering" or even "inhaling." His swing swung back and up and he felt his breath come into him, felt the strain of strength through his arms holding the chains apart to lift his body.

"A great swing," he thought. "The seat's solid and it's rounded so it won't cut into its bottom waving wildly, or it'll pop. It almost breaks as it trembles onto the air, almost dying of its uplift. But the light goes on, hushing itself, filling me with feeling I don't understand, as if I was disappearing, like a bubble about to leave its pipe, getting bigger, changing shape, filling itself completely with nothing. What does a bubble know about the life it sees shining? It only looks like it's asking a question, a question mark.

"What holds the bubble together? When I asked Dad what makes bubbles, He said the air outside pushes against the air inside. 'It's called air pressure.' The way Dad stops when he says a new word I don't know, like it's my fault. Ira says that even when Dad is nice, he's a pain in the ass. Ira's right, there's no use talking to him. Yet Dad can be funny with those Jewish curses, and when he read to me I got smart. And not to talk to your father, the way Ira does . . . it gives me a chilly feeling, like subway tracks going out of sight that your legs. The thick chains are stable but swingable. This hotel is the best place we've ever been. Up, up, and away! It's Stupidman! I should be able to go sailing over the top, the bar the chain pulls at, to look at that thick pipe painted dark green on the top, scratched silver-grey on the bottom, like a fish."

Ira watched the white pebbled ground accelerating toward him as he exhaled, then it whipped down behind him as he lashed forward to feel his hips in front, above him, thrusting at the sky. The most beautiful moment was the beginning of the top of the forward swing, when he felt himself coming to be suspended in air before he was dragged down backwards. As this moment arrived, he would slowly inhale and lift himself a little from the seat, pressing the backs of his legs against its curved front and grasping the hardness of the chains so that his body said, "Here I am," while swinging the clouds across the vacant blue.

Now Ira left his past behind, as if the weight of his

echo a train whistle against walls you can't see.

"I like the color of the tiles I'm sitting on, blue green. They're smooth and even, like that picture of the Holy Land stretched out under the sunbeams that I saw in that . . . *Coronet* magazine. The water in this pool is heavy to push against, but it's empty and brighter than air. Is it rising in the center, heaving up? It breathes in, then breathes out, like Gail's chest."

Eleven feet from Marc, on the concrete beside the pool, Gail was kneeling, fixing up her teddy bear and murmuring to it. She was six, a year younger than Marc, and though he hardly knew her, he thought she might have been watching him when he did not see. The black water of her straight hair fell over the soft curve of her shoulders. He felt her breathing, light and delicate, her chest making its tiny silent movements as regularly as if nothing moved but air. When he tried to look at her face, though, his eyes stuck to the tiles.

"Why can't I move my eyes up? I can't do things like regular consciousness would not catch up. The sky opened, expanded as he lifted toward it, and he had a glimpse of a new self that could be detached from his old one. And then, as his flesh caught up with his bones and nerves to swell the racing stillness in which he was held, there was a quick hint that maybe he would not come down. But he was no child, and when he became aware of this hope and the downward drag of the swing, there was a touch of shame: "Whoa there. Get a grip on yourself, my boy," as if speaking to his brother.

As he began to fall, the slumped figure of Marc sitting at the edge of the pool swung across his vision. He hesitated in his pumping to watch Marc, and the chains holding the swing slacked off, their links slipping into each other. Then, when he hit the bottom of his curve, his swing jerked the chains taut, snapping his body into a jarring clash. He got a kick out of being shaken up this way. The jolt gave him a sensation of having two points of view at once, something he people. Why should she talk to me if I can't talk to her? She's in another place. Now I can look up and see her when she's apart from me. Listen. The dabbing of water against the side of the pool, calm as her breathing, as quiet as the sound of a mouth opening. Here and there are squeaks that scratch it from the swing at the other end of the hotel's field. My brother is swinging. I can feel the power he's feeling." He sensed Ira's plunge and lift, his strong body moving ahead of every motion of his pumping, grabbing energy and striving to plant himself in the air. "I feel safe with him around."

At first the water had been cold, but now Marc found it mild. Its warmth gently sucked his feet and shins down, bathed him smoothly from in front, from above, while its coolness wafted upward to lift his ankles and calves. The brightness of the sun fused everything into clarity as if he were in a sparkling fish tank. He knew too well to think of it, that the shining quality of things was bright with their distance from the couldn't express without hearing something else.

Ira's perceptions came together as he continued swinging: "That bubblehead is in a daze as usual. The little *nebbish* will always be lost in a dream. Sitting by that pool mooning and he doesn't have the foggiest notion of what he's thinking about. You have to remind Marc to breathe. If there's one thing I know, it's him. I wrote the book, pull the strings, except for the interference of his weirdness. What does he have of his own? A certain wandering nervousness that hesitates to be me, a fear of getting lost in me."

Ira leaned his head back as he fell rearward, and as he felt himself plunging away from a whirling sky, he remembered plunging, hands lifted pointing forward, into a dull green swelling of water. As he swung upward and backward with its motion, he felt the weight of the bay lift him. He saw the heavy, grey-green suspension of underwater, like a transparent pudding, swaying almost too slowly for the movement to be seen. His arms and legs dimly lit malignity of his home, with its haunted shadows; and he could see in Ira's powerful swinging the same liberation. Ira could face how bad things were and knew how to separate himself from the parents.

"Only a few feet away," Marc thought, "Gail is sitting there, as if she was with me. She doesn't seem bothered by me at all, but then maybe she isn't aware of me. As she talks to her teddy, the holes on her nose open up. I've never seen that part act so alive before, as if it was a tiny bird about to take off. Her white suit drifts across her smooth tan skin. What could I say to her? Other boys know what to say. If I told her she was pretty, she'd think I was fresh. I'd make a fool of myself. We're only kids. It's better not to think about it.

"Look how peaceful the world can be. The tiles are lined up in a neat row at the edge of the pool, a roadway hanging over the water's glow, leading from me to the distance, the future." They were so polished that drops and tiny puddles of water were sharply outlined on their aqua surfaces, little maps

pumped the swing, and they remembered drawing together to pump him forward under the water. There was nothing to hold him, so he held himself, and the stain that enwrapped him was washed away.

When he came to the surface, he was already beyond most of the kids on the beach. As his breathing calmed, he saw little crests of pale foam rising on points of glassy, murky green water. He took a deep breath and launched into a crawl, swinging his arms and waving his feet in a steady rotation. He coasted on the swing and remembered, moving his arms and legs easily, more resting than active in Passaic Bay.

After he had gone around eighty feet, Ira stopped to breathe, lunging up out of the water and flipping on his back like a seal, so that he could float for a while. Everyone was far behind him now, and with a loose, regular motion he paddled his arms and scissored his legs to stroke himself further out. The buoyancy of the water drifted along his sides in cool currents and its somnolent of unknown countries against mirrors the color of the sea.

"There are more tiles at home in the bathroom. It's big for a bathroom. That's because the apartment used to belong to a doctor. But the tiles in the bathroom are small, hard, and discolored white, with eight sides. And the bathroom has something shadowy in the comer at night that frightens me. One night I saw it move out from the comer and slide to the middle of the floor, a thin figure wrapped in dull blankets, holding itself over the tiles. There is nothing like that on this vacation. Everything is light and clear, a new world."

But here the tiles were not quite flat. They lifted from the edge of the pool in a slow curve that seemed to shift as his eyes moved along the side, changing their angle as they got further away. He felt as if they were slowly moving, or as if he saw them from two places at once. It must have been the sun's fault, melting the air into waves. It was unsettling, like giving his mind to someone else, or carrying someone inside himself.

swell arched his back, opening his belly to the sky. The shore was a faraway margin of beige, only a suggestion of what it was.

"We could almost see the ocean from the top of that steep hill I bicycled down outside Newark, where the doors tilted off the streets. Well, it was a haze in the distance, and I shouldn't have told Marc it might be the ocean, but I wasn't sure myself that it might not be water. I guess the sea's always in the distance. Perhaps it's because I can't touch anything that I can't believe I'm here, even though I'm deep inside it."

A little chill whispered on his spine and he felt the big, cold space growing deeper beneath him that felt alive. He was leaving something he hated to name to go toward something he could never know.

"Where could I be going that gives me the feeling of going someplace?" Ira's memory of the sea thought, "Where is the farthest I could go? Up ahead I guess there's Jersey City and maybe the Atlantic. So what I'm going toward must be the ocean of not going back." He

"But then if I'm thinking," Marc thought, "I must be talking to someone. Who is it that hears what I think? He's like whatever is watching me from the mirror when I'm careful not to let the mirror see me, when I keep off the edge of the sight of it, or turn the mirror away in the bathroom. I can't see anything in the mirror but the room and myself, yet I feel someone behind it. Sometimes when I catch a glimpse of the mirror in the dark, I can almost see his shape or the gleam from his eye brushing through the shadows, but I try not to look at that. Ira would say it's childish.

"I depend on Ira more than on Dad. As long as I could figure, I've liked and trusted him more. Ira's with me all the time, so I don't have to think about him. I see things the way he sees them as far as I can. Looking at him on the swing, I can see him holding himself in the air with his hands clutching the chains, feet slicing the breeze—and I can feel the ground coming toward me. He sees it better than me because he's older, but I can almost see it his way because heard the water sizzling nearby and clucking to itself further off, and was glad to hear himself surrounded by peaceful voices, cold and lonely as they were.

"To be headed in that direction, even to think I could be, casts a rosy glow on everything, even these swaying ripples of green shadow, this deepness beyond sight, beyond dream." The push of his sweeping limbs circled him, but his eyes were closed and his mind was in the water.

"What do I have to go back for? There's nothing to say. I can't talk to either one of them anymore. In my mind I start talking and I lose control. I say, 'Dad, listen.'" He turned over and swam to expend energy to make up for what seized him. That building feeling shook him even now on the sunlit swing.

"Listen, Dad, you should never talk to her like that, never. Human beings don't talk like that to their wives. Animals wouldn't talk like that. Any five-year-old knows that only a slimy creep would tell his wife she's ugly." How shrill my voice gets. "You understand?

he's my brother. If I try to see like him, I can see more. So if I try to see more, it must be his sight. What I see is meant for him, like a story he tells, a story of the strivings of the helpless Looiyoo."

Held by this shifting context, Marc stared at the water, its fleeing points of light that glared mysteriously below the surface. Suddenly he started. "Huh." Gail had risen and was walking away. "I must have been half asleep, and she woke me when she got up and slapped her foot on the tiles. I can see her glowing body walking away and her movements are saying something I will remember. Oh well, no use bothering myself about it. I never really expected to talk to her. I was hypnotized by the mysterious water. How is it moving? Ira would understand, he'd know what to say to Gail.

Marc had no words to describe the pool. Waves and bumps on the surface of the water did not follow their own directions. They were moved up, down, and sideways by other movements under the

It's completely crazy. If you say that again, I'll strangle you. I'll rip your goddamned throat out. Tear it open... Wait!" His swing had jerked out of line and was twisting around. He had to concentrate on straightening it out or plunge off it. "Damn. I had trouble swimming, too." He willed to keep going, as he had in the sea, focusing his pumping on recovering a smooth swing. "I can't even say it to myself. He's always pressing on me. I coughed and choked in the water, had to turn on my back to rest, trembling."

On his back in the water, Ira's memory thought, "Nothing I say to him will do a drop of good. He sees me shaking and knows I'm short-circuited and that makes him pounce on me, call me a mental case or a gangster. Every time I get worked up about that situation, it seems more impossible, more degrading. What I have to do is be absolutely sure there isn't the slightest possibility of communicating one atom of information to either one of them, of any kind in any way."

Then Ira heard a voice say, "Hold on there, big fella. These water. Movements Marc saw as a flinging network of bright unstraight lines and light blue shadows lacing and crossing the body of the pool. Every gulp of water was pushed and pulled so that he could not tell where it would go invisibly. There was a core of light in the middle of the pool that changed shape quickly—a guitar, a pair of melting windows, a ship. He could decide what it looked like because he was in tune with it, swimming in its music.

"Of course, I can't swim, but I remember the feeling I had in the bathtub, steamy and quiet. I put my head underwater and opened my eyes—Ira said I could—and felt clean and light and free, as if I had escaped to a dream inside the water." He watched part of the pool's surface lift itself, bulging, and then sigh and fade and soothe itself into a glassy dip. "Ira said when Mom's eyes are sad, they go into themselves."

The water licked the sides of his knees. He reached his foot into it, easing the joints of his toes, ankle, and knee, and felt it slowly inch up and gently kiss a ravings are making you jerk so much you can't float peacefully." A realistic voice sounding like the least realistic creature on earth, Marc. The bay made a creaking sound like a swing. The voice went on, "Do you have to be so rigid?"

"If I'm only reasonable about this," Ira replied, "I'll soon go back to arguing with him when I see him picking on her. Done this too many times. Got to stop for my own survival. The more I argue with him, the more I become like him. This business of trying to prove people wrong is his specialty—Joel's word. But what should I do? Pretend he's right? Don't have the imagination to do that. I'm not that crazy. The person who defends him most is her, but even she can't pretend he's right. She says we have to listen to our father even if what he says is lunatic, he can't help being the way he is.

"She condemns him plenty, but she blames me for doing it, and she does both with that soft-boiled look in her eye, like liquid. When I want her to look at me, she's looking somewhere hollow at the back of his thigh. He was floating as he leaned off the edge, gliding easily into a living bed of liquid that embraced him. He felt empty, released from weight, purified. There was no limit to how he could move his limbs. Without friction, without any point of impact or change, Marc had passed through the surface to something more real, a world where the air was alive.

"Didn't I lose control a moment ago? Did I make a mistake? But that can't be. It was only a thought too tiny to feel, too quick to understand. Listen. I don't feel wet and have no problem with breathing. My breath is as quiet as a thought."

Light flowed in waves of turquoise blending into bands of transparency. Marc felt it flowing through him, washing and cooling. Changing shape as they flew, sparks of liquid glare raced from the distance past the surface of his eyes and kept flying, as if his mind went on to a great distance behind him. Inside and outside were gone.

else, or her eye is melting into itself. She sees me only as something to use against him. The only one who listens to me is Marc, and he's just a toddler, even younger than his age in relation to the world. Maybe I keep him that way. Anyway, I've got to separate myself from the parents. That's what draws me out here, the idea of freeing myself for good."

Ira looked around and saw that the water was smoother, rising and falling in ight-stained ripples. The low roar of the surface had quieted to a whisper, a heaving hush. The shore was gone. He was inside the sea's reach.

"Should I be bothered by that? Pretty hard for me to find my way to the beach. Hell with it. I feel exhilarated (but there's something cold down there). This is where I'm going. Glad it doesn't bother me. Let them worry about it. Jersey City is out there somewhere. I'm on my way. The sky goes all around the earth, and so does the ocean, meeting itself, going into itself, and here I am in the middle of this bay, the middle of the sky,

"Ira says we have gills, and I've heard there are children who can breathe under water—they're called water nixies. Must be too light and delicate to be burdened with the struggle of breathing. Maybe I'm one of them and didn't realize it. That's why I had to go to those nose and throat doctors. If I am, boy, I'll amaze everybody. The parents will be proud of me and Ira will give me credit for doing something clever. I'll be famous. Girls will look up to me. Gail will come to see me."

He looked up. "Up there it's ghostly, like the back of a mirror, seen from inside. Nothing to fear behind the mirror, and that's why I feel happiness swelling in my chest. But the surface is full of waves and stirrings. A field of milky light swirling in wrinkles. These movements of the water, can't be seen within the pool, but only on the top where the water ends. The surface is filled with so much brightness that if I could pass beyond it, I'd go to heaven, to shining paradise, float into the sky, into pure light. But it's impossible. I can't even with everything passing into me."

He dropped his right arm back into the water, and for a moment had a frightening sensation of trying to support himself while leaning on nothing... but then he paddled with his hanging arm, building up his own resistance, and swung his left around to turn into a swimming position. Soon he was drawing himself forward easily by a one-armed breast stroke.

"That would teach them a lesson, if they think I'm dead. Even he would have to see the significance of it. Right in his face. No matter how much he ranted about her craziness being the cause of it all, he'd know deep inside he was to blame. I made it clear. He'll remember how he called me spoiled, a jackass, a wrongie. He'd have to stop talking while he stood over my coffin.

"And she would see that my feelings really were there. It was always a joke for her, something I didn't know enough about to talk, my feelings for her. Now she'll take me seriously. In her reach the surface. Yet the light down here is also magic."

Marc felt, "I can see the inside of water shifting and swelling. Rays of illumination are curving, wavering, and weaving into each other. They dance around a swaying shape, a cave toward which I feel myself drifting. Beams of light cross each other to form an intense, twisting radiance that burns a hole in my head. The light in this cave is more alive than ordinary light. Ordinary light is fixed in shapes and pictures, but this light can change and shift without a limit. Like a dream, it can change into anything as quickly as a thought. Can you see it, Ira? It's beautiful. The water is streaming in my head and my thoughts are flowing outside in the pool.

mind she'll be looking at me, saying she's sorry for the rest of her life. I'll be done with that parade of shadows."

His mother's eyes opened into a space of distraction that was stretched across the sky by the cry of a seagull and then turned into the creak of a swing. "I'm only here with that little jerk." He looked at the pool and was surprised to see that the side of the pool that Marc had been sitting on was empty.

"Now I'm sinking deep into the cave, my mind pouring into its depth, and it's clearing and opening and lightening and softening into a sky. A great holy sky spreading itself in rich, glowing emptiness with a few light clouds clearly detailed against its serene expanse. I have reached it. I am delivered.

"I am really here. My worries were mistakes, illusions. How tenderly the sky holds itself. There are arms around me. Peace has opened itself to me. It was only life that could hurt. Now I float in the sky of light."

Marc turned from the sky and saw Ira, breathing heavily and smiling at him in a shy, earnest way over the bottoms of his soft blue eyes. Then some of the elation left Marc, for he realized he would have to go home again. Yet he was still joyful, to think that he had given Ira a chance to be a hero.

"Did I drown?"

"Just about, laddie," said Ira. "Why didn't you call for help?"

"I didn't know anything was wrong. It seemed nice." He wanted to say more than nice.

"You must have blocked out the danger."

In the distance beyond Ira, still jerking on its chains, Marc saw the swing from which Ira had jumped to rescue him. The right side twisted before the left, the left before the right.

Ira held Marc's damp, heaving shoulders along his arm and tasted the memory of Marc's cold lips on his. "I didn't know what the hell I was doing, but I did," he thought. "When I saw he wasn't there, I wondered if I should bother, but I did it all very rationally. I saw him missing at the top of the forward swing and swung back and forth once, pumping against the movement of the swing to slow it while building my energy for the leap. After the swing went back again, I used its forward momentum to hurl myself onto the ground and forward, then grabbed the fence to stop myself, spun and ran to the pool and dived. Could never have moved ahead so swiftly if I thought about it, yet I was dazzled by the wonder of it. It wasn't me. Some high-minded cuss. I kept repeating, "This is it. I can do it. It's my chance to do exactly what's right. I'm free of all that doubt and bitterness. I really mean something.' I didn't feel the surface.

"Under the water I saw him looking relaxed, asleep. I got beneath him and pushed him up with my feet on the bottom and rolled him over the side. Before I knew it, I was holding him in the sun, thinking, 'What should I do?' I pumped his arms. Put my mouth to his and I was stuck. A little water dribbled from his lips and it tasted sweet, but I didn't know whether to inhale or exhale.

"So I drew back and his mouth opened and he was breathing. Seems I'm pretty good when I'm not me. And Marc has finally done something worth doing. The kid shows promise. But how can I handle taking so much control of him? It only aggravates the way he's more like something I made than an item of his own. Hard enough to speak for myself without having to speak for both of us. Being God is a pain in the ass."

5

THE CLIFF

1955

Anxious to do everything for their sons, to enfold the boys in safety and hope, the parents made a point of getting an apartment across the street from a gigantic park, but this border of the pastoral had its sinkholes. Bronx Park brought one up against limits, so that the escape and imagination that the park offered were not quite possible, a metropolitan mirage. But they might reward those who were sappy or greedy enough to believe in them.

Bronx Park East was (counting parking) eight lanes wide, and after that, and a sidewalk with benches, there was a stone wall topped by an iron fence. About five feet above street level there, the park reclined and rolled in soft slopes, interspersed with bushes and groves. To avoid walking a block to the entrance, the boys soon learned to climb the fence. They did it by first stepping on the green wooden seat and back slats of one of the concrete benches beside the wall, then grabbing the fence to pull themselves up to the top of the wall, then using one of the periodic stone abutments to lift themselves over the spikes of the fence. It helped the interlopers that they both had long legs. With one leg on either side they became someone else by doubling themselves. Did one become the other?

The fields of the park were laced by bicycle paths and edged by patches of woods, remnants of forests that had once covered New York. Marc, who had trouble making friends (even his cousins found him abnormal), liked to sit on rocks in these patches of trees, which were left untrimmed because they clustered in rocky or bumpy areas. There he would read books from the public library about pioneer boys, pausing to imagine that he was a scout in the realm of the Iroquois. In these novels the Indians were exalted beings whose grace and skills the whites could scarcely approach. When he walked through the woods, Marc would step carefully so that the snapping of twigs would not give him away; yet snaps resounded from no visible source. After about a block's length of this greenery, there was a wide submerged highway parallel to Bronx Park East, and a little beyond this was a high fence of metal wire. On the other side of this fence lay the Botanical Gardens, which went on and on, as if there were no limit.

Though there were quite a few cultivated areas and buildings, most of the Botanical Gardens was straight forest. Here, where the sunlight was flecked with leaf shadows, Ira and Marc went exploring and sometimes rock climbing. First, they passed under the wire fence by shimmying into a hole someone had dug, and brushing off the soil, sprang like thieves stealing into freedom. Then they went down a series of dirt roads broken by ravines and chasms that looked like the work of flooding. Here and there big trees had been knocked over, apparently by hurricanes. Some trunks stretched across the landscape from one elevation to another, like demented bridges. Occasionally, these boles were almost as wide as a man is tall, and their naked roots writhed into the air.

After a series of descents, walking and clambering, the boys reached the dull brownish-green waters of the Bronx River, which ran north. In places the river was too shallow for boats, but once they found part of an abandoned raft stuck to some rocks in the middle. They thought of wading out to it, but they might hurt or drench themselves in the river, which was more than two feet deep, with big rocks at the bottom. So, the raft remained an image of adventure in the distance. There was also a waterfall, and though it was only about four feet high and man-made, a straight ridge of dam that the water vaulted over uniformly, the boys liked to listen to its gentle roar and watch its churning foam.

The nearest bridge over the river was quite high, one of many signs that the river used to be deeper. To reach the bridge from riverside, they had to climb twenty feet of rocks, but the rocks were easy and step-like, though some of the rock surfaces on the other side of the river were too smooth to be climbed. The bridge was made of stone in a single arch. At its highest point, it was forty feet above the water. When the boys walked on it, they felt a hollowness reverberating under their feet that gave them an uneasy feeling, a sense that the bridge was shaking.

On the eastern side of the high center of the bridge, the side closer to home, was the top of a narrow straight tree that grew up from the edge of the river. One could touch a branch of it from the bridge, but when Marc tried to lean over the bridge's stone parapet and follow its trunk to the ground with his eyes, he found himself withheld by fear from staring straight down. Afterwards, whenever he went to the part of the river near the bridge, the tree rising near the center was a disturbing presence. It reached upward into a space that was absolutely outside of reality.

Mossy and weathered green, the bridge seemed to have settled into its place in the nineteenth century. Often the boys found structures that had been built in the area, perhaps before it was a park, and then forgotten. There was a round stone bandstand, lost in the woods and covered with weeds, its cement railings and stairs cracked and broken, the earth around it twisting and plunging as if to swallow it.

The boys had no comprehensive sense of what the vast area behind the fence around the woods was shaped like. There was a big greenhouse with tropical plants, but it was far away and hard to find. Once Marc came upon a pond in a green field with picnickers and swarms of tadpoles. They were cute, like muscular, oversized, dark guppies, and Marc wanted to take one home in a jar, but Ira said it would die. There were baby frogs hopping through the grass. They were hard to catch, maybe because Marc was afraid to hold them. One of the people drinking Kool-Aid on their blankets said, "You've got a way to go to be a scientist, my man." In later months, he looked around what he thought was that area several times, but he could not find the tadpoles, or even a pond that looked right. Maybe they only came out a few days a year at breeding, and the pond was a temporary flood. Blades of grass had stuck out of the puddles of water in which they swam.

Now it is late in the afternoon and the two boys are crossing a field in which a stone platform is mostly buried, maybe the foundation of an old house, but quite flat and evenly rectangular. It is cleared of debris as if someone cared for it. After this, there's a gentle, rising slope scattered with small trees. Ira goes ahead beyond this slope and soon calls to Marc: "Yo ho! What have we here? It's the perfect cliff."

Marc finds him standing on the side of a low mound of solid grey rock with a large expanse of open air looming behind it. Going to the crest of this mound, Marc sees that one could not climb down over the top of it because it is so smooth and round, like a bald head, with nothing to hold onto. The cliff is quite high, though the bottom of it is a grass slope, so that the cliff does not reach to the level of the ground below. On the left of the mound, it falls away too steeply to be climbed, but on the right, there's a possibility. The boys go down to a flat area on the right of the mound and look at the rock formation.

The face of the cliff is rounded, bulging outward from right to left and curving inward from top to bottom, so that the steepest part is near the top. There are quite a few ledges, outcroppings, and crevices in the rock, but it's hard to tell if they are deep enough or close enough, especially since the bulge of the cliff makes parts invisible. Once they got to the grass, about forty feet below, the angle would grow milder, and the grass seems smooth, so that they could probably roll down to the end of it. Even the stone on the lower part of the cliff does not seem steep or difficult. But it won't be possible to know if the top of the cliff can be done until they climb it.

"I don't think we should do this," Marc says, "It's too difficult. You can probably do it, but I can't." He remembers the time when he got stuck, until Ira came to help him, on a ledge that was only five feet from the ground: "I could feel it then in my stomach, that I'm not going to be a hero at rock climbing, and the shame made it worse. Am I a coward? When Marty pushed me around a few years ago, I couldn't fight back, couldn't even see why I should hit him, what good it would do."

Ira says, "Poppycock. This here is easy street. In sooth, you've got a charming choice of places to step with style, depending on whether you want to waltz or tango. Just follow what I do and I'll be nearby to help. Stick with me, baby, and you'll shonuff end up in the room of men." To Marc, his words run together into an exhilarating soup.

Ira starts out, moving more sideways than downwards. Before each move, he stops to see what would be the best way to do it. Then he does it slowly and with emphasis, so that Marc can see not only what he is doing, but how easy it is. One time he retracts his move and does it over to make sure that Marc can see it clearly. It is clear but strange, as if a film were reversed. Nevertheless, Marc takes a deep breath and follows laboriously, thinking, "I can do this if I follow him carefully, and then I'll have something to be proud of." And then in a moment he feels free: he is a hero, seizing the opposition of reality with his conscious limbs. Yet this feeling seems artificial: everything that precedes it seems to melt away.

"Good show," Ira says, "Everything is copacetic." But he says this partly to cover up the fact that he's concerned: the step before him seems difficult. "Hmm," he thinks, "this will be a bit of a stretch, but I'd better not stop long or junior will start *kvetching*." Holding an edge above him until the last moment, he reaches two feet to his right and a foot downward to step, letting go with his hands and bounding onto a ledge about sixteen inches deep, and he grabs a good handhold about four feet above it. "Voila," he says, and this is deftly done, but Marc doesn't think he wants to try it. Even to Ira, it feels unreal, as if bravery were a dream.

Now Ira looks ahead and realizes that the next ledge is somewhat further away than it appeared to be from his earlier position. How did that happen? He scans around him in all directions, but nothing else seems to lead anywhere. He considers going back to his previous footing, but as he stretches in that direction, he realizes that it will be difficult because it's harder to move upward than down. He can't get a grip on the spur of rock he held onto to swing across without getting up on his toes, but that gives him little bounce to lift himself off. The easiest thing to do is to stretch ahead to the next ledge, but he can't see whether this next ledge is followed by others, for the bulge on the face of the cliff conceals what is beyond it. He leans his head back and sees a further ledge beyond the one ahead.

So he makes his leap, and finds himself on a ledge about fourteen inches deep and twenty wide with a handhold to his left that is not very solid because the rock does not give him anything pronounced to grasp—more like a ball than a wedge. Now he can see the further ledge, but it does not look good—only about a foot deep and the surface of the rock around it is too smooth. The stone goes in and out, but it doesn't do so sharply. Ira searches at every angle, but can't find a useful configuration. It's as if the cliff were slowly shrugging him off. A ripple of anxiety passes through him.

"What's the matter, Ira?"

"I have to think about this, Marc. Maybe you should go back to the flat part while I decide the best way to handle it."

Because he's two steps behind Ira, Marc can't hope to reach him with his hand, so he quickly decides to turn back. Being spread on stone makes him shaky if Ira is not radiating support. He assumed that the older brother could handle situations. When he gets to the flat part, he lies down and leans over the edge. He can see Ira's left side.

"What's going to happen?" asks Marc. "It's going to be getting dark soon. Maybe I should go get a cop or a fireman?"

"Hold on, my lad. Nix on the coppers. I'm not giving up. There's probably a way to be found out of this by logic. I can let go with my hand for a while to rest it if I stay still; and then when I use my hand, I can move my feet some. I just want to think about it carefully to be sure I use the best possibility." He looks for some detail of the rockscape that he missed.

Ira appears to be firm and relaxed, but Marc seems to be getting more and more agitated. He kneels on the flat rock and touches his forehead to its grey surface, which is cool and slightly curved inward. "My brother is lost," he thinks in faltering waves. "He's in an impossible position. I remember once when he ran away from home; the parents were so *verblunget*. Mom called Dad a murderer and he said she was the one who spoiled him. I suppose he has to take risks to be a man, ahead of me. Isn't there some way I could help him? I wish I could go reach him, but I'm afraid. How could I get all the way out there? Maybe over the top I can see him better."

He climbs around and goes over the brow of the cliff, lying down on his belly and squirming over the curving stone to inch his way down to where he can see Ira's head about five or six feet below. So close that if Ira reached up, he might almost be able to touch his hand. But as the surface begins to tilt more precipitously, he begins to panic:

"My God, there's nothing to hold on to. All I can do is form a kind of suction between my body and the curve of the stone. But that won't mean a thing if gravity kicks in. How can I pull him if he's heavier than I am and I can hardly hold myself? I'll fall on him and knock him down."

Quickly the pressure of his fear drives him back to his kneeling position on the flat part, so that at once his dazed nerves are not sure whether he has lain out on the rock or only thought about it. "Why didn't I even let Ira know I was trying that? What a coward I am." He begins to sob quietly, heaving as if praying to the stone. When he lifts his head, he sees that twilight has begun, and there are dark wet spots on the rock.

Ira faintly hears him crying and decides to cheer him up by increasing the volume of his own thoughts, reflecting aloud in show-business mode.

"Boyoboy. Here I am on the rocks. Spread iggled. I could almost reach up to that point up there on my right and swing across that way, but it would be a trifle tricky. In fact, to be precise about it, I could only do it if I was in a movie, and there's no projector. Hooboy. Maybe you should give me some flying lessons. The more I think about it, the less I seem to be capable of action.

"Thing to do is definitely to think about something inspiring. Well, lessee now. Leave us ponder.... The old man getting a heart attack. His eyes getting wider. His mouth pulled open at the sides. It's hitting him like a sledgehammer in the chest. He turns on the radio and starts singing. Ixnay. If I think about something too nice, the old man in the sky will be after my ass. Oughtta think about something constructive. Sailboat on the sea? Moonlight on deck. Not dynamic. Whatsay chicks? We have a girl in my class, Irene, who makes all the guys in the class pee in their pants. Her cheeks and lips are gorgeous and her face also looks good. Did you ever have the feeling that you wanted to go, but you wanted to stay? Ever have a woman's vagina around your neck?"

Marc hesitates and says he doesn't think so. Ira says, "Aha. So you must have been one of those asshole babies."

Ira hears Marc gasp with hilarity and he feels better. He shifts his feet to relieve the cramp in his calves. He hears a voice coming through that must be good, though it is only the shadow of words. It is not clear whether he is saying this to himself or aloud, whether he thinks it or it thinks him, but Marc hears or speaks it. He must have gotten himself in this situation to hear this voice if there's any reason, so he ought to listen to it muchly. It tells him where the truth is.

The truth that must be his friend, is here, here where he can't hold on, up against impossibility. Not hanging on but moving ahead. As he loses his grip, it'll hold him more. Didn't he always suspect that to protect himself is bullshit. It makes every part of life false. Now he possesses himself in reality. Only now, when he's separated, can he feel the love he could give people. He thinks to himself, "Sounds good, but how good could it be if I'm only trying to impress Marc? The only one who can hold me, and he holds me by his weakness."

As Marc hears this, he feels as if he were hearing his own thoughts, and he feels more than ever that his brother is in danger, a hero against the world: what Marc wanted to be, what he wasn't because he couldn't go far enough to be lost.

The shadow voice asks Ira if he ever got the feeling when he was walking down the street that he wanted to grab the people he saw there and hug them. Hey, let them think he was crazy. Everybody's got something in them that wants to give love, to make love, to be in love, inside love, all the time. You have to learn to hold it back to deal with what they call reality, and this holding back is murder, it kills you. Hardly ever do you get to release it. But when you're here, locked in this struggle against this rock, you feel as if you're pushing against something that makes you ache so that you're really alive. The loneliness exiled in him, which was really the source of his existence, was finally getting to speak. He'd opened all the doors inside him. He could feel every bit of him working, all this power. This situation was not something that happened to him. It was something he did. All the rest before was stuff that fell on him. But he was in control of this. Whatever his mind wanted was here. He had it.

Marc is listening to what Ira is thinking and watching him. But curiously, he is watching him from the back. He sees the back of Ira's head, shoulders, and arms breathing against the rocks as he speaks. Marc knows it is impossible to see Ira from this point of view and so, to disperse the image, he gets up and goes to look over the edge at the top of lra's left side. And he asks, "If you're in control, why won't the rocks cooperate?"

"The rocks are doing exactly what they should do, which is to make it as hard as possible for me, so I can find more of myself." Ira turns his head as well as he can to look down in back of him. "If you think you think I'm wrong, man, look at that," his strained head gestures towards the base of the cliff.

Marc wonders why Ira repeated "you think." Or did he? He looks down and realizes that the declivity is bigger than he had noticed. It is almost a valley. The grass inclined at the base of the cliff progresses by soft stages to milder and milder slopes. It curves gently downward for a hundred feet until it becomes an easy sliding meadow. And in the distance is a group of structures that looks like part of a little town. The white wooden houses and the road between them seem clean and neat. There are old-fashioned street lamps with curved, frosted glass shades with points on top beginning to light the evening, and lit windows with white curtains in them. The meeting of day and night casts a bluish-grey aura over the whole scene, even over the grass.

"It's beautiful," says Marc. "It would be lovely to get there." It occurs to him that if they lived in this town, they would really be alive, really American, have all they hope for, speak all their thoughts, be at home, with furniture that belongs to them.

"We will eventually. One way or another, we'll get there."

"I'm glad we had a chance to talk," Marc says. It's not the kind of thing Marc usually says. He is always failing to be considerate to other people, always saying stupid things and missing the chance to say something nice. So he lights up with joy to realize that in this situation with his brother, he can finally say it. The evening is strangely pleasant, as if one can forget the unresolved problem, as if they could stay like this indefinitely. But then Marc realizes with a pang that Ira's muscles must be aching—aching as if they would never stop.

6

THE ROOF

1956

"You're so much younger than I am," said Ira. "More chance to change. You can revamp the whole kit and caboodle." There was a sudden crash of metal against metal and the elevator they were in came to a stop. Ira wrenched the folding metal gate open as he continued, "You just need to be *systematic*. Don't have to be a creampuff all your life."

"I like to think a person can change," said Marc. "It's at least an interesting idea." Though he had done it before, and wondered when the results would appear, it was still an adventure to go up on the roof with Ira.

The stairway leading up from the sixth floor to the roof had steps topped with a dull white stone, less worn than the lower stairs of the building, but still slightly curved downward and rubbed smooth in the middle. Both of the young men stepped heavily, for each was carrying a dumbbell, and Ira was carrying a paper shopping bag. The wall of the stairway, like all of those above the first level (which was maroon with a fake masonry surface), was painted dark blue-green with a raised surface of swirls and points, as if it were a miniature stormy sea.

The door to the roof was plated with grey metal and had no latch or knob, but a counterweight kept it shut in the wind. Ira braced himself and pushed it open with his shoulder and the weight rose on a faintly squealing cable. As if walking through a frame, he stepped over a three-inch threshold into a bleaching glare and held the door. Ira knew that this threshold was to keep out rain, but it would not occur to Marc until fifteen years later, when he would revisit the roof alone. Once Marc was outside, Ira moved the door to a position where it was almost closed, then let it close the rest of the way with a low, rumbling slam that reverberated through the big space around him.

The roof was covered with mats of tar paper that was heavier than linoleum, but not as hard. This surface had been baked and frozen so that it formed a wrinkled crust frequently speckled with air bubbles and craters, and occasionally scattered with pebbles and pieces of dull broken glass, often partly buried in the tar. In places there were puddles of pebbles that formed patches of gravel, so it seemed likely that the roof was once covered with these. The sky was an empty pale blue, and the sun was so bright that there was pressure to look down, and even the black tar seemed an ashy white.

Marc and Ira took off shirts and undershirts and slung them over an empty clothesline. They were both tall and slim, but Ira was solidly built, with squarish, well-shaped muscles, while Marc's body was soft and undefined. Ira's blue eyes were stern and full of effort in his handsome, well-proportioned face. Marc's darting green eyes, his narrow head, and his pointy nose resembled a sea bird. Ira looked more European and Marc, more Semitic.

"In order to remake yourself," Ira said, "you have to want to change. You have to understand what you are, what you were, and be ready to throw it away. If you like to be as flabby as you are, you're going to stay that way."

They came to a hut-like enclosure in the middle of the roof, the top of the elevator shaft. Ira went up a metal ladder of a few steps, opened a little metal door in the side, put one foot in, and began pulling out a black barbell with red iron collars that was concealed there.

"Well," Marc said, "what I'm worried about most, I guess, are my hipbones being so big, but I can't change that." He helped Ira to carry the barbell.

"But you can, my boychick. If you tighten up and fill out in the right places, you'll look like a real he-man." He ducked under the clothesline. "But first, heh heh, you have to suffer." They carefully put the barbell down. Ira went to the paper bag and took out an old blanket, which he unfolded onto a relatively smooth area. Then he put the bag, which contained a bottle of water, in the shade of the elevator top.

"They've been laying Aristotle on us in school," Ira said. "He holds it forth that a rational man has to delay pleasure. We all start out wanting immediate joyfulness, but we have to learn to wait in order to get lasting satisfaction. The more difficult something is, the better it is for you, if you survive. It makes you stronger."

"Well, maybe, but that sounds like a drag. If you keep waiting for pleasure, you'll end up forgetting how to enjoy yourself."

"But if you haven't got reason to guide you," Ira picked up the heavier dumbbell he had carried up, "then where are you?" He began doing curls.

"My reason," Marc said, "somehow tells me that I could spend years lifting weights and developing a magnificent physique and I'd still end up doing exactly what I'm doing now, which is to say, wandering around in terror and dismay." He began to curl the lighter dumbbell.

"But you'll change," Ira insisted, lifting his weight. "I mean, what are you? You may think you know your identity, but it won't stay the same. Would be unhealthy for you not to change. You're only thirteen. What you are is made up of a number of things, including your unfortunate body and your appalling mind. Now of these two disasters, the one you can definitely remedy is your body. And if you change your body, you'll change the way you think." He put down his dumbbell and breathed out heavily. Marc put down his.

Hard with sunlight, Ira said, "You think that you're a mizzabobble wretch, and you've got a point there. But there are other people inside you waiting to come out. You remember the story about Looiyoo that I told you years ago, the one where he killed the monster, but lost the girl?"

"Yes. I think that was the last Looiyoo story." Marc realized that he saw no point in killing the monster if you lose the girl.

"Well, I said then that you're always trying to do two things at once?" "Yeah," said Marc. "That stuck in my mind."

"Well the only reason you can want all these things at once is that there's more than one self in you. You've got all these other selves going on while the one you think is your main one just ignores them. So when you're doing one thing there are extra guys inside you doing other things. Let's say you're angry for some strictly kosher reason. But you also have a baby in you throwing a tantrum. And you've got other fellas inside you who are afraid or sorry, but you can't admit any of this because you need to be sure that you've got a reason to be mad. Each one of these feelings has got to have its own person if it's going to speak for itself.

"Or you could be enjoying yourself hugeously, but all the while there's another guy inside you whispering, 'What's going to happen tomorrow?' And when did you ever enjoy yourself without feeling guilty? What basis would you have for pleasure without guilt? In fact, when you have a good time, what else are you doing but letting yourself indulge in feeling sad? You're just letting all that feeling out. This is probably true of everyone, but especially of a melancholy *vans* like you.

"This self-division and multiplication goes on in everyone all the time. In fact, no one's life could stay awake without conflict, which is why squares like you are so dull. Your personality is the conflict, not any of the little wish-people that make it up. The pleasure isn't you; the anger isn't you; not even the *tsuris* is really you, and that's why you enjoy it so much. What you are is the interaction of all these things, so if you want to be reasonable, you have to keep track of them, to control them. They could come creeping up on you."

Marc didn't understand much of this. "Here comes reason again," he said. "Do you think it's reasonable not to talk to Dad?" Though the sun was shining furiously, the hot air brushing against his bare skin tingled with an eerie chill.

"Ohman," Ira said, "that's eminently reasonable. It's profoundly sagacious. Nothing could be worse for my mind than talking to him. When do you hear of a reasonable man going out and talking to a pig? Conversation means turning around with someone, but if you do somersaults in a sewer, you're bound to get messed up.

"In fact, a conversation could never be held with him, because it means going back and forth, but he just keeps going forth. He's like what they call the first cause: nothing can change one comma of his little mind. It's like an eternal law of the universe. When you talk to someone like that, it keeps torturing your head for days afterward, like a sadist slowly pushing your brain through a meat grinder."

Marc saw the pink strands of meat coming out of the little holes in the meat grinder at home like sagging straws. Now they would be grey, glistening, broken coils of brain flesh. He was disturbed by what Ira said partly because of how true it was. He looked east across White Plains Road. The edge of the roof was a wall about three feet high topped with rough brown ceramic tiles that curved from the outside to the inside. There were mostly private homes and row houses in this direction, and some vacant lots associated with adventure. In one of these he had joined a boy named George who used a ramshackle wooden hut as a shelter for abandoned kittens, swabbing peroxide on their infected eyes. But the elevated subway ran across the field of vision two blocks away.

"If you can change, why can't he?"

"Because I can control myself," said Ira. His blue eyes looked determined. His body, doing reverse curls, gripped itself in bulging strength. "But he's old and crazy." The dumbbell clanked as it rose, as it stopped at the top, and as it fell.

Off to the right, on the other side of the el, was the home of Jackie Gordon, a girl with a button nose who wore pastel blouses with their collars up. Marc had a crush on her all through the sixth grade, but he only said a few lame words to her and she ended up going out with a friend of his who was more aggressive. But Marc liked to walk through that neighborhood dreaming that he might see her again. He imagined meeting her in the evening when she came out to put the garbage in the can. She would remember him, be amused and touched by him, and invite him in.

Ira was meditating on Tammy, whom he had gone out with almost two years ago. They had stopped in the hall that led up to her parents' apartment and she had turned on the stair above him. "Isn't this the way they do it?" she said, and she put her lips together and outward, closing her eyes. She was beautiful, too beautiful to be before him so suddenly, thrust in his face by life. The corners of her mouth and her eyes were laughing. She stood on her toes and all of her magic body concentrated on pushing her gorgeous lips toward him. Her lips, bulging with infectious vitality, were distorted, swollen. He wasn't moving forward: wasn't sure he could do it right. He said to himself, "This is the moment of my life. This is my deliverance." It sounded splendid, but why did he have to say it now? He felt ice on his ribs, felt his throat constrict.

Marc thought of the pretty block of private houses on the other side of White Plains Road where Jackie lived. Marc had visited a classmate who lived on that block. Everything in Victor's house was like Victor: neat, smooth, amiable, and rational. When Victor had shown him his stamp collection, Marc, while mulling them over, had put a few of the most impressive stamps in his breast pocket. He felt that Victor could afford everything, and he wanted to take away some of this purity with him. But a few seconds after his crime, he looked into a high mirror and saw that Victor was watching him and must have seen him steal the stamps. He felt paralyzed, as if he would disintegrate if the news got out, even though it had.

Neither he nor Victor were able to mention the theft, but he knew when he left that he would never see Victor again—as much from his choice as from Victor's—and that this was more important than the stamps. He soon threw the stamps away. Whenever he visited people, he did something wrong, broke something, said something embarrassing, gave offense. He condemned and attacked anyone who welcomed him.

As Tammy paused before Ira, he thought of Barbara, whom he had kissed on the cheek after class in junior high. She had smiled and hugged him, but afterwards, he had turned ironic and remarked that she smelled funny, chasing her away. She said, "I'd rather think about how good you are than what's eating you." She was understanding, but he couldn't relent, until she was gone.

Now, with Tammy, Ira realized that he was waiting too long. If he put his tongue in Tammy's mouth, she might be offended at this sloppy, spit covered intrusion, but if he didn't, she might think he was pitiful. And how does one put a tongue in a mouth? Do you try to force the lips open with your lips or do you jab your tongue into them? It was hostile to stick your tongue out at someone. "I haven't had much experience," he said. Her eyes smoldered open in anger and the brightness glancing off the center seemed to flare into his heart like hot glass that sticks to the skin. Now he was doing push-ups and he felt the ghost of that pain in the ache of his muscles. "I don't think I want a beginner," she said, and she turned and went up the stairs. He followed her magnificent figure energetically bouncing away from him. He went in and made small talk with Tammy and her parents, but his connection to Tammy had ended on the stairway.

A week later, he tried to approach her outside their high school. He waited in an alley off the path she went by, planning to apologize, to explain that he adored her. Her vigorous walk made him recognize her when she was still a block away. But as she got closer, he felt a tremor, and then his whole body began to shake, so that he had to step back into the alley and let her pass without seeing him. Then he was relieved, even in his agony, and he wondered if he had come here to do this, to retreat, picking a place from which he could hide. Now he had reached the limit of the number of push-ups he could do. His arms were trembling and he collapsed panting onto the blanket.

"That was great," said Marc. "Forty-two. I'll never be able to do forty-two."

"Well now, some of us is cool and some of us ain't. Your advantage is that you get to appreciate me, but I have no one to appreciate."

"I wish you could tell me," Marc said after a few minutes, "how to handle girls." "That's a hard one. It isn't easy to put into words. The main thing, I guess, is to act like you know what you're doing. Remember that the girl wants you as much as you want her. But she doesn't want you to be too pushy. It's best to be cool and wait until the time is ripe."

"Mrnmm. That sounds useful. I'll try to remember it."

"Nifty. Now what can you tell me?" Ira started doing sit ups, giving Marc a chance to talk.

"I don't know what I could tell you. You're so much older." "Just don't tell me any more to kiss the old man's ass."

"Well, you seem to be taking care of everything real nicely. I mean, you locomoted yourself through high school with style and grace, and now you've plunged into college over the summer. It's tremendous that you want to be a writer. I think I do too, must've got it from you. I don't know what to tell you about that except to tell the awful truth and stick to your guns." This wasn't much and that "stick to your guns" was a phrase of his father's. "I wish I could be as strong as you."

Ira kept pumping, the glare blazing across his closed eyes as his trunk rose and fell, his mind ramming itself into hard thoughts. "Miss Connolly was like this cluck over here, telling me that I'm fine. Some counseling that was! All those lights and worried people trying to speak at once. When I finally tried to set her and the rest of them straight, she told me I had the wrong attitude, shouldn't come to her group anymore. I suppose I overdid it: 'What's the use of my reacting constructively when the guy's a maniac? He never hears anything I say unless he can hold it against me.' I was jumping around and my hands were shaking, and anyway, she could tell I was trying to make it with her. Her radiant crystalline eyes. How could I explain to her? The last thing she'd want to hear would be the truth about her kind of comfort, and my kind of pain. It wouldn't allow her to do much business."

His eyes and skin scorching, his stomach churning with strain, Ira collapsed and lay back on the blanket, lost in roaring pulsations that seemed to be enclosed by nothing but a sense of floating in space. "The pain in my mind is the pain in my muscles, so I'm really in my body, with my body," he thought, "almost the way Miss Connolly said I should be." Then he smirked, "Heh heh, even if my body is nowhere, dead alone. But then I've got company of a sniveling sort." The pain and gasping receded and the roof scene came back. He smiled at Marc: "You can be as strong as me, if you try."

"I've got big doubts about that. I've had things smoothed out for me because you went before, to show me how to handle the disasters of reality."

Ira lay back glistening with sweat and heaving. "Well, if I ever did anything for yez, I hope you'll remember me if I need you."

Marc's assurance on this point lent him a certain flair, borrowed from his brother, who borrowed it from Fats Waller: "Believe it, beloved."

While Ira rested, Marc walked around the perimeter of the roof to see what he could see. In the middle of each side of the building was a square inlet, a courtyard. These divided the large square of the building into quarters. The brothers were on the northeast quadrant of the building, toward the back. Marc looked down into the yard below, which was outside and one level beneath their living room window on the first floor. No one was in the courtyard. Directly under the roof on this side lived a redheaded Brenda whom Ira had once had a crush on. But they never went out, had hardly spoken, and she was now with another guy. Then Marc walked to the front for his favorite view, across Bronx Park East.

When he saw the park from this angle, he remembered how he had flown his model plane into it. The plane was a big rubber-band-powered P-40 Flying Tiger, olive drab with teeth painted on the cowling. After spending weeks putting it together out of strips of balsa wood, pieces he cut intricately out of balsa sheets, and stretched tissue, he was impatient to sacrifice it, and it hardly lasted longer than it took to make. As soon as one of the wheels broke irreparably on landing, he took it up on the roof. He taped a firecracker with a long fuse to its tail, wound up the propeller, aimed it, lit it, and launched it.

It did just what it was supposed to do: flew in a straight line across the wide street, curving slightly upward along its path of decline. The cracker went off with a jolt and the plane went on to land about thirty yards into the park, wrecked after its longest flight. Now Marc followed the line from the roof to the field where it landed. This supple curve of air was easier to pursue than the steep plunge of the tree by the river even though the roof was higher than the bridge.

The people in the park were neither close enough nor strange enough to hold Marc's attention, and his eyes soon passed beyond the fence to the mysterious realm of the Botanical Gardens. The river was not visible because it was a recessed area. Even the top of the bridge was not visible from here, but he thought he could identify a clump of trees that was hiding it. Mostly it was the tops of trees that he saw back there, with a few slopes, hedges, and greenhouses that he could identify, usually in the relative foreground.

He scanned carefully across the area in the distance on the right side, trying to locate the cliff where he and Ira had gotten stuck a year ago. It was such a big cliff that he hoped he might see some part of it, or the little valley behind it. The place where he and Ira had shared strong feeling and come to understand each other. But the landscape in the area that should have been likely didn't seem to have any particular changes in height. Moreover, he could dimly see some of the buildings of the West Bronx in the distance. It made him a little uneasy to see how the Botanical Gardens were enclosed by the city.

The cliff must have been hidden by the slope on this side of it, yet he didn't see anything like that slope. Maybe they had wandered farther north than he had realized, so that the cliff was now far off to his right, where the forest extended all the way to Westchester. He was not clear about how they got there.

He saw his tears on the grey stone, Ira's shoulders against the rocks, the soft grass curving gently downward toward the neat little houses. It was his most penetrating image of Ira, his vision of his brother's soul. Maybe Ira could explain it. He walked back to Ira, who was getting ready to press his barbell.

"You know, Ira, it's really funny. I've been looking in the park for the place where we got stuck on that cliff, and I can't find hide nor hair of it. You'd think there'd be a sign of something so big."

"Which cliff is this, bro?'"

"The one where you started from the top and then found that you couldn't get back and couldn't go forward. You were stuck on this ledge for a long time."

Ira looked serious, knitting his brows so they almost met: he had a few hairs in the space between them over his nose. "When was this?"

"About a year ago, maybe a year-and-a-half."

"I don't remember any such cliff."

"It sloped off to a sort of little town in the distance."

"I see," said Ira. "A town in the middle of the park." He hoisted the barbell, which made conversation difficult.

"Well, there were just a few houses," Marc said. "Holy shit. I must have dreamed the whole thing. But it seemed so real. I looked for it in the park a few times and wondered why I couldn't find it again. I asked people where the big cliff was and they looked at me like I was daft. But actually... I can only remember thinking about this lately. So it may be that I dreamed it recently as what happened in the past. It's puzzling."

To himself, Marc thought, "My God! So that explains why I never found out what happened to him. It means I'm really worried about him. Yet I still can't be sure that he isn't denying something that actually happened because it embarrasses him. Can't believe that I dreamed the whole thing at the cliff. After all, I can't see the river from here, but it's there. There were way too many details for a dream. He may be lying, but I can't ask him about that any more. In fact, the details about the scene at the cliff were overloaded, as if I knew his thoughts or God's point of view. To believe that actually happened makes me crazy. Well, I'd better avoid that and stick to apparent reality, to what we can agree on, that we're sane. What happened to me didn't really happen."

Ira's face was red as he pressed the bar, and his neck muscles and veins stood out. "He dreamed that I was trapped on a cliff," he called out to himself impetuously. "It never happened, unless I'm even wackier than I thought, tutti fruiti! Marc must have invented it because he wants to kill me. This is too much. I hang around here with this nincompoop partly because I can't keep friends of my own age (that bastard Gornstein!). Partly for Marc's sake I stay in this Paunch and Judy show—and his idea of social intercourse is to tell me his latest fantasy for getting rid of number one son. He's always wanted to get me gone: hit me in the head with a hammer when he was three and doesn't remember it. But this latest routine is the straw that humps the camel."

Ira finished and put the barbell down carefully to avoid banging on Brenda's ceiling. "And yet," he thought, "it can't be denied that he means well. But he doesn't know what the hell he means. And he sure as shitting doesn't see me—only his dreams of me."

"This is really weird," Marc thought. "I mean if I find out something that happened to me in the most solid way was a dream, I have to consider that what is going on now is a dream. So where can a line be drawn, and which dream is reality?" He didn't articulate it, but he felt welling up in him like a bubble in the airy sunshine a feeling of delirious fascination. He sensed that the possibility that the present was a dream was enormously attractive, like the butterfly of beauty he could never hold on to.

Ira spoke decisively: "You haven't had too much truck with this stuff called reality, my joyful boyful, but some of it is about to come sashaying your way in extra-large."

"What do you mean?"

"I've been thinking about it for a while, and I've decided to move out."

"Oh. I don't know if that would be a good idea. The parents will have a royal shitfit. You've just turned eighteen. How could you support yourself and take care of school and everything?"

"I couldn't do it worse than I've been doing it here. You have to understand that when I hear him singing that diddle diddle diedle dee stuff, I feel like I'm drowning in excrement. Lots of folks live alone at this age. Wouldn't have to be a crisis if the parents weren't permanently hysterical. I know for me, it may be a little harder than it is for some folks, but it has to be done. Living here now for me, it's like I can feel the whole building pressing down on that apartment. It feels fatal what they do to me, do to each other. Like a spear with barbs in it that stick back so that you can't pull it out again. I know it by heart, but I can't understand what it means at all. It's like science fiction." Lying on the blanket with his eyes closed, he thought for a minute, then spoke again.

"You have to realize that they live in a world of spirits. I know more about this than you do because they spoke Yiddish more in Newark, but even I only have hints of what goes off. You've heard them mention the evil eye. They live with these curses, these possessions, like drapes of lead hanging in the air. And everything lasts forever. It's not like you're mad at someone and then it's over.

"The feelings are attached to your soul for good. A spear isn't enough for it, cause a spear just sits there, but this is alive. Imagine a vampire has bitten into your brain, into your hopes and dreams, and the fangs digging and gouging. It doesn't get dull from doing it over and over: it gets more irritable. A burning Nazi kiss, an enemy singing in every penetration of that pain exulting in the intimacy of your pang." His voice seemed to implore and to wonder if he were really saying this.

Marc, sitting on the blanket and facing away from Ira, was slumped down. His brow was contorted and his eyes were pressed shut like Ira's, but his mouth was open and gasping with the onset of terror, his breath pushing out dread. He felt that Ira saw the truth on an inner level that he couldn't confront. Though he sensed that Ira's vision was unbalanced, he blamed himself for avoiding such powerful, incandescent forces. To keep Ira from seeing how horrified he was, he asked, "Where will you go?"

"I'll get a room on the Upper West Side, where I can be near CCNY."

"It's not safe."

"Sure it is. There are thousands of students living there from City and Columbia. I's gonna mingle wif da Ivy League types, give myself a spot of class." He put his palm on his ribs.

Marc said, "This will be devastating to Mom."

"She puts up with him. Let her put up with the consequences." Ira lifted the barbell to put it away.

"When do you think you'll leave?"

"In a month or two, when I get together more money. Just be sure you don't tell the parents about my plans."

"I won't, but this won't help my physical development."

"You're the only one who can help that, and you haven't been doing prodigiously with me around. I'll leave two dumbbells, counting you." He finished stowing the barbell in the elevator top and walked toward their camp.

The sun was beginning to decline into the west over the park, now a lifeless stage set. Ira and Marc drank some water, folded the blanket, picked up the dumbbells and the bag, and staggered toward the door to the building, feeling the sweat on their skins. Ira hauled the door open and stepped over. Inside, everything was dark, and covered by the blurred anti-shadow of sunlight, as though they were blind. They felt enervated, but their bodies felt lighter, so that they seemed to have to press down on their feet to touch the stairs. It was like entering a pressure chamber, a submarine, sinking deeper.

7

THE WEST SIDE

1958

She wore a tan suede coat with sleek lines and a free-form silver earring that was a work of art nestled amid delicate wisps of her blonde hair. Her blue eyes, clear as the sky, were filled with calm regret. Was it regret that they were free from care, would never, no matter how hard they searched, be able to find trouble? She would not find it in this case, for Marc, who was standing two inches away from her, would never give voice to the line rushing through him: "Gosh, you're amazing." And then the door of the subway car opened, they got out, and she went south while he went north. He had been more successful with Gail, the little girl by the pool, and had understood her better.

    The Broadway station at 96th Street was an island shaped like a boat, with round columns along its sides. On one of these dark green columns, someone had painted in black, "Bird Lives!" Marc recognized it as a reference to Charlie Parker's death, three years earlier, from which some people felt that the world might not recover. Almost sixteen, Marc was beginning to become aware of hip culture, so that these first trips to Manhattan on his own cast a spell of yearning over him.

    To his left, the Thalia was screening *Les Enfants Terribles*, and a few blocks south was a bookstore that had the whole line from

Grove Press in the basement, books in which revolutionary ideas were inseparable from the secrets of sex. Going north, he passed a newsstand featuring copies of *Evergreen Review* and *Jazz Review*. He stopped and looked at a menu posted in the window of an Indian Restaurant, which affirmed the existence of something called mulligatawny soup. The smell of the place inebriated him. He passed a bodega with papayas and cuchifritos, a music store with Monk and Mingus.

The streets were filled with Puerto Ricans, Negroes, and Asians who, like everyone else around here, looked more self-possessed than anyone he had ever seen. There were students and professionals in sandals, dungarees, loose hair and dark glasses. A plump girl in braids and a peasant skirt looked at him so fixedly that he had to look down. A new world was coming into existence that was so beautiful, it hurt to look at it. Marc turned and went a few blocks west until he came to the basement entrance of a grey stone building. Ira was waiting for him there with two big boxes and his barbell.

"I've been working on the moving," Ira said, "and this is the last stuff we'll have to take." Marc carried the barbell, which had only a few small plates on it and was handier, while Ira took the boxes. They went north and then west until they came to a narrow building in poor repair, not far from Riverside Drive but high above it. Here they went up four flights of stairs, stopping for breath at the landings, to reach a large apartment that had been divided into about seven separate rooms with a shared kitchen.

Someone had taped a picture on the wall above the kitchen table, the cover of a black and white magazine the size of a comic book. The picture showed Lenny Bruce looking earnest in a field full of discarded plumbing as he swung a sledgehammer to smash a toilet bowl into pieces, and the title above it was "Stamp Out Help." A cheerful-looking young man with thick eyeglasses and unkempt hair was sitting at the table in a threadbare maroon bathrobe. As the brothers passed, he said to Marc, "Would you care for some mustard?"

Marc and Ira turned down a corridor, and as they came to Ira's door, Marc said, "The place seems lively. I hope your roommates are good." The place was dumpy, but he would have wanted to live here if he could, in the mystery of the new situation and the new people, in the freedom of bohemian life, far from the parents.

"They aren't roommates. We each have our own room. They're students, though not always studying much. Some are good and some are not so good. At least I don't have that crazy lady after me who kept the other place, with her damned cats that would get into my room and jump on me when I was trying to study. Her cat would know when I made contact with a book and pounce. Here we mostly just keep to ourselves." The room was featureless and neat, with yellow walls. The best things about it were a desk and a bookshelf.

"I hope," said Marc, "this place works out better than the others." The only window looked north at the tops of some big, airy trees and other apartment houses. The branches of the trees were constellations of leaves without visible support. On the left of the view were the highway and the upper reaches of Riverside Park. "You know, I'm sure, that the parents told me to tell you to come home. They say that the fact that you're moving again shows things are not working out."

"You can't be on their side and on mine, too. You're working for them, trying to hook me. If you don't know it, that only makes you more pitiful."

"No, believe me. I've been getting it from both sides. I tell you their side, then I tell them yours. Right now, this is what they want me to say: that you claim you want to be free of them, but you're always asking for money. You want them to pay for your defiance. It might be better for you to come home and save up for a while; then you can be in a position to be really independent."

He was afraid to withhold the argument of experience, even crazy experience. But he felt guilty that he was compounding the argument of the parents by presenting it more effectively than they could themselves.

"I'm independent now," Ira said, "because I'm determined. Those savages know better than to mess with me on my own turf." A phrase passed fleetingly through Marc's mind: "What turf?" He didn't say it, but Ira thought, "My boy is munching on that one." Ira forged on: "Going home, now that would certainly wear down my independence. I'd be like a stag surrounded by hounds. I once read about a hunt, and it said that when the dogs start moving in on the stag and tearing pieces from him, the hunters can see him crying. That place you want to drag me back to is custom-made to destroy me. My destruction is its ground plan. It has the shape of my wounds. Every lie, every cruelty that goes on there sticks right into my center because it's launched from inside me."

"That suggests that you can't leave them."

"Honey-child, I have left them. The few bucks they occasionally begrudge me add up to less than my room and board at home would cost. If they want to help, why can't they use all the money they save to actually help me do well?" He opened the two boxes. "I have a new life: Ira Glogover, Feature Editor, *The Observation Post*. I'm getting new friends. There are some sharp people with City's paper, including this girl who's not only smart, but gorgeous—Marcy." He was taking books, papers, pots, and barbell plates out of the boxes and finding places for them.

"The friends I had on Bronx Park East were conditioned by that environment of displaying brutality: they were vicious cretins. Now I'm going to relate to people as I really am. Of course, I'm not a politician; can't wheel and deal, can't take advantage of people. But I do rock-solid work, and people have to appreciate that. I've had a string of ace quality stories."

"Fine stuff," said Marc. "That piece about Townshend Harris and John Wayne was a hum-dinger." He found his brother's articles pedestrian, but he was proud that they were in the City College paper, and he wasn't qualified to judge feature writing. Yet he was bothered by Ira's statement that he wasn't a politician, which suggested that others were.

"Of course, I want to do a lot more. A student paper job is only a beginning. But I'm rolling. I can feel strength running through me." He took a few steps in a strange, energetic, prancing walk he had, with excitement shooting and trembling along the sides of his back and out of his arms and legs. He concentrated intensely, as if trying to push himself through a heavy door. "When I'm away from those cruds, the life force comes up and propels me like a flood. I've got to stay clear of all that bizarre crap."

"Well, but really...." Marc began.

"Tell me to be reasonable," Ira said. Marc stopped talking because Ira had anticipated him. "I know all about that game. I taught it to you. I liked it when it seemed to lead to change, but if you hang on to it, you shonuff gonna find yourself hamstrung. Strung in ham. At this point, when I need to go forward, rational rules are a trap for me, like being put in the stocks.

"Since I got off that merry-go-round at home, I've taken off my blinkers. I can see a whole panorama. It's like becoming more alive and getting extra senses. I can see people's thoughts. Think how important that is. I understand what people's words really mean, even when they aren't aware of it, I fathom behind their skins." He sat leaning his forearms on the back of his only chair and faced Marc, who sprawled on the simple bed.

"I see," said Marc. "Like someone will come up to you and say, 'Isn't it a nice day?' and he'll really mean, 'I'm better than you are.'"

"Yeah. Or someone could say, 'I want to help you,' and really mean, 'I want to hold you back.' Everyone goes around reciting scads of horse frockey that's conventional, but it's more than deceit. They've got all these feelings that they can't possibly express; they'd explode if they admitted it. They may hate somebody so much they could bite their tongue off; or they may want love so badly that they'd scare away anyone who could give it to them, or maybe they're just lost in dreams, like you. Ira tilted forward on the back of his chair, supported by his knees on either side.

"They don't know what they're saying, which is what they really are and is much more than they imagine. Some joker will say, 'The train leaves at three o'clock,' and what he really means is, 'When will my suffering be over?' But he isn't aware of it, so he goes on suffering. Or a girl could say—in the lightest little voice, looking hard at nothing—she could say, 'May I have your pencil?' and she could mean...."

He paused and looked in Marc's eyes with a cheerful, bright expression that was half earnestness and half irony. He was thinking, "I wish he would understand me, yet I enjoy puzzling him. But what could she really mean? Is he looking at me, so seriously, with admiration or pity? He must see me from the parents' point of view, as someone who lives in birds' nests, with no foundation, nothing to rest on or settle into. He spends his days rubbing up against the old man."

Ira settled his chair and spoke: "She could mean something she has no idea of, something she could never imagine. She could mean, 'The shining light in my eyes is burning me to ashes.' But she doesn't know it, you see. That's why she's looking so hard. She's trying to find out what it is that she's saying. And so I think, 'It would be easy to tell her, and how could she deny it?' But don't kid yourself, old man. She'd resent it plenty. She'd never talk to you again—as if she ever did talk to you."

Ira looked at Marc again, exhaling as slowly as he could. "All these messages stand out clear for me now that I'm on my own and mixing with different kinds of people; I can hear a person saying a lot of different things at once, like a passel of radios gabbing away, and I can tune in any station I want. It gives me this hugeous feeling of power to know things other people don't know that I know about them, and even things passing through them that they don't know at all—like this secret chorus I control.

"I guess I learned the basic idea from the parents, because no matter what they say, they always mean pretty much the same thing. Always telling each other how much they hate each other. She says, 'That'll be fine,' and what she really means is, 'I can't take this at all, you scum bag.' He says, 'Yiddle diddle dee,' and what he's really saying is, 'Drop dead, bitch.'"

Marc said, "We'll have to give the old man credit for being more direct than that."

"Yass, won't we? It really is to wonder what the old boy wants. If I died, he'd wake me up just to explain to me how wrong I was. Yet he must want something else that he doesn't know. Whatever he wants is out of this world."

"I remember once," Marc said, "standing in Zimmerman's looking at Father's Day cards. I was hesitating for fifteen minutes over this marvelous card I wanted to get. It said, 'You've been just like a father to me.'"

Ira smiled. "Did you get it?"

"Naw, I chickened out."

"That's the trouble with you. You're going to spend the rest of your life trying to make up your mind between two possibilities."

Marc thought, "'And how are you going to spend the rest of yours?' That would be saying something, but I can't say it because I'm afraid. And reasoning makes me more afraid. Afraid that I'm wrong or right? Don't be so sarcastic. He may do well. The outline of the window seemed to drift across the wall. "My older brother, who saved me from drowning when I was a tot. I remember when he taught me to ride the bicycle. The grass on which I had to fall seemed softer because he was with me. But he's waiting for me to speak."

"What two possibilities?"

"Well, my darling boy, there's you and there's me. How's that for possibilities?" He looked at Marc and wiggled his eyebrows up and down. "We were asshole close. So what assets did we have between us? There's your set, which I feel it incumbent on me to describe as a colorless one, like watered down dishwater, to put it mildly. The little boy who's careful for himself, the product of the parents. You never had to resist them because I resisted for you.

"Now me, I may be strange, but I yam what I yam, as Popeye would say. I've made a choice, taken responsibility for myself. I'm in no danger whatsoever of turning into you. But you may have to be me whenever you want some excitement. Face the fact: there's no known cure for normality. Try as you may, you'll find yourself being sensible, so you're doomed to be my parasite for the rest of your life." His face bunched into an acrid grin.

"You lose track of me," Marc said, "when you think you know me."

"But you don't know me at all."

Marc felt that he did, but he said, "That's because you came first."

"I not only kept you company, but I was a trial run for you. Bad as they are, they were worse until they had experience; like blind men feeling up an elephant. I had to wade through manure to make a world for you."

"Well you know, they like you more than they like me," Marc said, "They're convinced you're better looking, smarter, and a mensch. They worship you."

"What you worship is what you sacrifice. I'd be a heap luckier if they liked me less. I was always supposed to eat endless food. Sitting with those damned cold eggs, and her standing over me with the strap. I had to work hard, sit in shul with those stinking old men. Stand up for one of them against the other, stand up for the other against the one. When I couldn't take it, it was a cataclysm. When my foot was bad, I was a cripple; when I talked back or didn't embrace their idea of truth, I was a gangster. It was his term, but she supported him. I was always hanging by a thread over an abyss."

"Yet in their own way, they tried to help you," Marc said. "Would you be smart without their *mishegas*? Remember they went through awful hardships when they were young, and it distorted their minds. They have all these weird superstitions, prejudices, crazy ideas. But the truth is that they're fanatically dedicated to you. There's nothing they want more than for you to do well. They'd give their arms and legs."

"What percentage is there in this for me? What difference does it make to me that they like me on some level that I'm never going to reach? A long time ago every detail of their idea of me was rubbed into me like salt into a wound. For me to go back to that warped fantasy world would be annihilation. If you mean what you say, kiddo, then you want me to give in, to give up when I'm finally near the chance I've been struggling toward for scads of years, the chance to have a real live life. No one else I can explain this to, and you can't hear."

"But remember that when I'm with the parents, I defend your right to be on your own; and then I have to listen to him ranting and her shrieking."

"Sometimes I wonder if this business of being caught in the middle isn't a trick you play on both sides—a way of getting control for yourself in your own weaselly way. No matter which side you talk to, you always put yourself in a position to be self-righteous, just as righteous as they are." He started to his feet.

"But look," Marc reflected, "I can't agree with them that you should come home; and I also can't agree with you that you, well, shouldn't forgive them, should be so absolutely opposed. So this is the only thing that I can do."

"You should think about what you can do. You make it sound so simple. You don't have a choice, so whatever happens, you're not responsible. A real convenient arrangement, but it's skullduggery is what it is, m'boy. You make a definite choice by refusing to choose. For your own sweet sake you become responsible for everything. You're doing it all, on both sides, got your finger in every pie." He was pacing in a bouncy way and turning rapidly. Now he stopped, looked up, snorted, and sat down.

"Look here, punk, that idea of playing against both sides comes from the parents, from the *plotz*ing pressure to agree with him that she's evil and to agree with her that he's dreadful. You contradict yourself nonstop, so you only have any integrity or existence insofar as you can tell both of them they're wrong."

Marc nodded deeply, sinking his neck between his shoulders as he leaned his elbows on the mattress and closing his eyes like a vulture in a cartoon. Ira looked at him with sneering conviction, but a thought occurred to Ira that he couldn't speak aloud or hold in his mind. It was Marc's side of Ira speaking: "And if they're both wrong, then where are you, brother?" Rather than face this question, he bounced back to his main argument against Marc.

"But you can't tell either of them that they're wrong *nohow*. Soon as you suggest that he might be less than perfect, you become part of the demonic plot against everything good. And you can't tell her she's wrong because she feels so right. She's always putting him down, and we're always wishing that she would do it in a more extreme way. Not much foothold in blaming someone for not being nasty enough. Ain' I right?"

"Mos' definitely, but this may not be all bad." Marc imitating Ira's voice. "I mean, if I deny both sides, it can make me pretty sharp, cause nobody can take me in." Later he realized that he was enjoying being involved in an intelligent conversation. Now he felt that such active thinking must be helpful, would have to show that Ira was doing well.

He avoided focusing on the level on which he was taking the lead from Ira in arguing. A few months earlier he had had a hand-grasping contest with his father, something he did with friends at school. He was surprised that he crushed the old man's hand easily. He felt a spurt of exhilaration, but then a whiff of panic, as if he'd stepped off a ledge.

Ira said, "Well it's a boost to be aware of all sides of your mind. It makes you more than you were. But how far can you take it? I mean, how long can you keep on saying, 'The more confused I am, the better?' There comes a time when you've had enough, can no longer benefit from getting it coming and going."

Marc felt what he said too sharply to argue. "What about my other point? If you know the parents are sick, why can't you forgive them?"

"Forgive," Ira said, "You're pretty ambitious for me, aren't you? Well, I'm not particularly interested in holding a grudge against them just because they happen to be numskulls who are possessed, but I have to defend myself. They're my parents; it's only natural for me to slide into wanting to believe in them. How many years I spent wanting that. But some fantasies are deadly. It's excruciatingly important for me to remember, for my own protection, that they're out to destroy me."

Marc knitted his brow and looked at Ira searchingly. "Well," Ira went on, "they work to destroy me. Lots of people have been destroyed by folks trying to help them, whole countries. Slaveholders believed they were helping Negroes. The parents can't stop gnashing on my nerves for a moment. They're like piranhas who have tasted blood: you can chop off their heads and they keep on chewing."

Marc tilted his head to one side. "Well you're not being fair to compare people who are trying to help you to piranhas."

"When were they fair to me? I can't afford to be reasonable to them. Got to try to be fair to the one who can use a chance to grow."

"I guess you're right," Marc said without conviction. "But when I listen to them, I'll start to worry again." Ira shrugged stolidly. "Well, anyhow," Marc said, looking at his watch, "I notice it's almost ten and I have to go." He picked up a book. "I've been thinking about reading this guy. How is he?"

"Kafka? He's great. The most realistic writer ever."

"What does he have to say?"

"He says that people are suckers, that they put up with authority all their lives until it finally wipes them out. They have this deep urge to give in, to let themselves get mashed. It's really part of their being conditioned by society to be good boys. If you stop to cogitate, the first purpose of any social order has to be to teach its sons to kill themselves. If they can't do that, they might as well throw in the towel, 'cause they have no way to carry out wars, not to mention getting folks to work hard. That's why religions are built on the image of the son being sacrificed. Anywho, our friend Kafka is constantly suggesting that if these poor clowns would only strike out at what's devouring them, they could be free. But they never do: they just keep taking it. It is to laugh. Lots of yocks. I'll walk you to the way of the broads."

Ira seemed uneasy about having said too much, and Marc was bothered by these wild words. Yet Marc was also impressed, and implanted with the idea of Kafka. Thinking about what bothered him in his brother, he was unable to separate the likelihood that Ira was unhinged from the likelihood that he was smarter than Marc. They walked quietly through the darkened, turning hallway and the empty kitchen to avoid disturbing the other boarders. No one seemed to be around in the apartment or on the stairs.

Outside, the cool night air lightened them up. As they walked east, Ira said, "This veritably knocks me out: all those lights in those windows, all those invisible people busy living their lives."

Marc looked up and spotted a green ceiling and the top of a high bookcase. All those books! "Yeah. I'm also attracted to other people's windows. I suppose it's because we didn't feel at home ourselves; yet I guess most people could feel that."

"But think of it, lad," Ira said, pointing to a window with a gauzy curtain. "In there could be someone dreaming about someone he hasn't seen in years. Maybe he's happy to remember her or maybe he can't remember her. Maybe he remembers her in fear, but even that connection leads him into a different world. He could be awake or asleep, but he has to be dreaming about that someone. What else could he do? May be dreaming about someone he's never met." He pointed to another window, dimly lit. "Maybe people are making love in there, still dreaming. Or someone is writing a poem with a desk light." A glaring window—"maybe someone is beating someone with a strap in there, and terror is pulling their eyes back into their heads. It could be something so beautiful or awful that if you saw it, you'd never escape from it. It's hard to accept that you'll never see whatever it is, but still, it's stupendous to know that those possibilities are out there."

Marc said, "I never thought of it in words, but I guess I feel that way too. I've always tended to be fascinated by those windows. Maybe there's hope for me."

"Oh sure," Ira said, "You've got a crackerjack chance of becoming a peeping tom." Then, after a few seconds of mirth, he said, "You know, I think the real reason we like to look in these windows is that we imagine there could be a welcome for us in there, a home. We could step through a door and there could be winsome cheer. We would find open arms, a love that we could understand and hold. We would really be alive, instead of sliding from one doubt to another."

They had reached the glare of Broadway. A man with a wet face, wearing a torn jacket, was fishing through the trash in a big wire basket. "I'll see you in two weeks," Marc said, "You take good care of yourself and try to prove to us homebodies that our worries are wrong."

Ira lifted his head a little, and Marc thought, "I can't tell whether that means he understands or he's offended. Which should he be?"

8

Falling, Apart

1959   1962

It was 1959. "Look at all those windows up there," Ira urged. "In each of those apartments, people may be happy or sad, in despair or in love." He thought, "An apartment is a place where people are apart. I put this better to Marc. This girl makes me nervous. Look at the bright side: they all do."

Marcy thought, "What those people up there are doing is their own business. But I'd better not say that. He's making an effort, and he's got looks and brains, whereas most guys have neither. I should do what I can to encourage him even if he is weak." She said, "You're a thoughtful person, Ira."

"Do you think so?" he asked.

It was 1962. Marc and Carol had barely noticed each other in their circle of biology majors at CCNY. He was interested in literature, and she in classical music, but both were bio majors because their parents wanted them to be doctors. Otherwise, they would never have met. Before he went to the pre-Thanksgiving party in Brooklyn where he got to know Carol, Marc had been told by the hostess, Ann, that there would be a girl there who was interested in him. Running into each other in the group, passing a few remarks about classes, news, books, and music, Marc and Carol were almost friends before they knew it—or before

"What do you think?"

He thought to himself, "'I think we are in rat's alley where the dead men lost their bones.' No, don't be so cute. She asked a reasonable question." He said, "I try." If he lost his voice, would another voice speak?

Marcy tried to communicate: "I've worked hard at learning to be considerate, Ira. It not only helps people around you to know how they stand in relation to you, but in the long run, it also helps you to advance yourself. A woman trying to get into journalism has an uphill battle. She can't afford to make a mistake."

"Well, people are really impressed by your cleverness, Marcy. You should be able to make it fine." To himself, he said, "Wisecracks don't count."

"Thanks, but I've found that brains aren't everything. They can actually hurt if you're a woman."

He thought, "They can hurt if you're a man, but I'd better not say that. She might misunderstand, or she might not."

Marcy said, "You've got to use your ability to relate to he knew it. But then, what did he know?

Marc lay along the back of a deep couch while Carol sat in front and he looked up at her from the side. "Dostoevsky and Kafka," he said, "have proven that every possible basis of happiness and anything that anyone could consider of value are all illusions. Whatever you believe in, say religion, love, or art, you have no way of knowing whether what you believe is true. You can't know what the person you love is thinking. She, or he, may have thoughts the opposite of what you imagine. If you write something, you'll never know if anyone understands it. Their idea of your work might shock and depress you. Even if you're angry, you may want to teach someone a lesson, but he'll never learn what you want to teach him. You can't communicate anything of your own thoughts. The more you think you know about another person's thoughts, the more you're kidding yourself." As he said this, he had a flash of recollection of the story Ira told him of Looiyoo's attempt to people, to be careful." In his mind, Ira added, "You've got to control people, make them wait on you, torment them, if you want to succeed. But this sour stuff will get you nowhere, as the old man would say. I should act cheerful."

They had reached Marcy's apartment house and he complimented its clean, smooth elevator. He was glad she had no parents to deal with. The living room of the place she shared with a girl friend had two big windows at one end. A set of glass shelves in front of these windows contained a large variety of miniature cactuses. They perturbed him, but while Marcy made coffee, he complimented some of the stranger ones and said obvious things about the movie they had just seen. Then they sat down on the sofa, brought together by the bright circle of light around a table lamp next to where she sat, like a space of shared knowledge.

Ira looked at Marcy and thoughts rushed into his head. "Now my life will begin. This is going to be love. How can it reach the truth. But his brother and his problems were far from his mind.

Carol said, "'Which of us is not forever a stranger and alone?' That's what I wrote in my Science yearbook."

"That's sharp," Marc said. "Well, so then there's no valid reason to live. I mean people just kid themselves along because they can't get up the courage to face the truth."

She said, "But there has to be another kind of truth than logic, which always ends up negating things. Big whoop. It may be no more than mental masturbation. For me, it's easy to see the good things of life, things that are beautiful."

"But how do you know they're beautiful?" he asked.

"You feel they're beautiful," she said, and she looked at Marc with large, dark, almond-shaped eyes. "They make you happy, so they must have value. Looking at a sunset, for example, with its pink and blue and yellow streaks and spaces, can fill you with wonder. When the sky changes color, you get a glimpse of the fact that you're miss? Such a lovely girl—she's like a Greek goddess, Athena. She's taken me to her place and we're alone. In this moment, here, after all these years, I feel real happiness coming to me, filling me up. I don't even want to go on, don't want to do a thing. It's a shame I have to try to be sure if it's real. Feeling it should be good enough. I'd let it be fake if it would last. (Yet there's a chill and a voice that says it's bullshit, but I don't want to hear it.)"

"Her lips are like begonias the color of pale raspberries that are breathing," Ira thought, "Her nose is as straight and clean as a geometrical figure. Her eyes are as soft and smooth as pools of honey. (Shouldn't they be kind?) Her forehead, her cheeks, her chin all flow together in delicate, graceful perfection—but now she's waiting for me. I don't know what to tell her. How could I possess the truth?"

contained in something beyond your conception, and it makes you see that life could be more than it is. Things like that seem to me to make the value of life obvious: it will always give you more to imagine...but not always, and that's what worries me. I think of life ending, that we're constantly moving toward death. I can't bear to realize that someday I'll stop existing, that I'll become nothing. It's so final."

Marc felt a moment of panic: "Could she expect such a hopeless creature as myself to respond? After all, the idea that life can always give you more to imagine was contradicted by the fact that you're always moving toward death."

But then he realized to his surprise (as if it were given to him from somewhere else) that he could respond. "Is Ira guiding me? Can I have anything but illusion?"

(What speaks between the two brothers—Marc, who has every answer, and Ira, who has none? Marc cannot live without the truth that Ira cannot live with. The illusory nature of life, the truth of intelligence, is a trap for Ira, who is afflicted by it, but it liberates Marc, who takes it from Ira and evades it.)

"Marcy," Ira gasped, "You're so beautiful. Your features are exquisite. I feel so lucky to be going out with you."

"Thanks Ira, it's been a pleasant evening." She was thinking, "There's something strange about him. He speaks so deliberately, as if he were stopping to plan everything he said. That haunted quality that attracted me to him is frightening up close. I don't want another emotional man, haven't quite recovered from Harvey. Why doesn't he move instead of gaping and talking? It would probably make him feel worse to ask."

Ira leaned forward and tried to impend, feeling the energy flowing through his shoulders, feeling as inevitable as he could. "I find you overwhelmingly attractive," he breathed. "I'd like to make love to to you."

Marcy thought, "If he grabbed me, I might resist, but give in; but I can't come out and say we should when he's so insecure." She said, "Well, I think we should wait a while for that, Ira. It's only our first date.

Marc said, "Well, I'm not bothered by the thought of dying. To see it as unfair is egotistical. My feelings will be carried on by other people after I'm gone. They'll feel and think the same things I did, or parts of those things. We all have the same feelings. So all that will be lost will be my own particular identity, a selfish concept. I can't help clinging to it, pretentious wretch that I am, but it's not something I should value. Can't pretend it doesn't depend on someone else.

"Besides, if your time is limited, the only thing to do is to make the best use of it you can. It's not logical to spend your time worrying about it. I dismiss problems from my mind once it's clear there's nothing I can do. They only subtract from the time I have."

Carol said, "But how can you be sure what you can do about a problem if you don't try? You might think of a way to help if you gave it time."

This idea had occurred to Marc. "Well," he said, "You can't try everything. There are some

People should become friends before they give themselves to each other. It's a serious thing to do. I don't feel I know you very well. Of course, we've seen each other at the paper, but you haven't been socially involved there. You should speak out more at the office. I think that Walter is taking advantage of you."

"I don't want to talk about that retarded bastard Walter" flashed through Ira's mind. But he tried to keep his body loose, exhaling slowly, so Marcy wouldn't see that he was disturbed. He tried to calm himself with logic: "Her clichés are only the surface shell. I have to be patient. There must be something underneath. A girl will resist 'cause she doesn't want to be taken easily. I should say something true and nice. Maybe I'm only numb because I'm excited. I should believe my pain is pleasure."

"What I feel now, Marcy, is that I'm suspended in a dream of transcendence, and that this dream must not end." (He thought, "That sounds unreal. Gotta explain.") "You see, I situations where you have to use reason." It struck him that he was not able to answer her argument that reason could hamper one by denying possibilities one does not understand. But he moved on to talk about a Monk record he had brought to play. Like his father, he tended to focus on what others didn't know about. Carol appreciated Monk because she played piano. She got in some rounds of her own by demonstrating a few modern dance steps, bending and stretching into worlds unknown to him—the worlds of dance and a woman's body.

Marc talked to Carol for three hours at the party and for two on the late subway ride from Brooklyn to the North Bronx. She was three years older than he and they had both gone to Science High without meeting. "She's beautiful," he thought, seeing the harmony of her soft face, "though her nose is too wide. And she's talking to me and I'm talking to her, and it feels easy. Must be because of her."

They agreed that they liked each other and would meet the

Stealing: A Novel in Dreams

grew up in a very unhappy home, and all my life I've felt"—he paused and felt an excited sense of opening into the unknown—"that there was something wrong with me, that I was on the edge of existence. But now, being with you here, it's so lovely. It's like heaven. I have this deep feeling that I've finally found what I'm looking for. I'm actually here, undeniable. I can't bear to give it up. Just give me one kiss." "Okay," she said with a puzzled smile.

She was thinking, "He's sick. I've got to get rid of him eventually. He picked the wrong person for a nurse mother. I haven't the strength." She had opened a button of her blouse heating coffee for him and he could see the creamy tops of her breasts.

Ira moved forward welling with elation. As he grew close to her mouth, he felt the tiny, mysterious tingle of her breath on his face. Then his upper lip touched hers, and she was cool and soft. His chest convulsed in rapture. His hands were on her arm and shoulder and he breathed a soft moan and following week. They kissed when the time came to part, and though she did it externally, he felt her lips like a sigh of flesh waiting. After Marc left Carol in the West Bronx and got off the subway to walk home across the park, he ran up the incline at the end of the deserted station. Then he found himself skipping and bounding along the moonlit paths beside the highways that had been cut across the Botanical Gardens. These were now so reduced in scale to him that he knew the old cliff must be a dream. Excitement coursed through his limbs in gestures like Ira's, opening and closing his hands spasmodically. He sang to himself some lines from an old spiritual that he'd heard on an Odetta record:

> Free at last, free at last
> Thank God-a-mighty I'm free
> at last.

A week later, back from their first date, Marc and Carol made small talk with her parents, who he thought were superb compared to his, for an hour. At 11:30 the paragons retired pressed both his lips to hers and rubbed them slowly. His fingers caressed the upper edges of her breasts, lightly, thrillingly. And he pressed his tongue against her mouth, but her lips stayed firmly shut, and he felt them hardening. So he held them with his mouth and moved his fingers onto her breasts.

She turned away and said, "No. I'm sorry, Ira, but I can't start anything serious with you out of pity or because you force me. I had a guy recently who was very emotional and unstable, and I realized that I just couldn't take it. I need a man with a certain amount of control. Maybe it's because I had an unhappy childhood, as you did. I'm probably being irrational, but right now, I'm really afraid of getting into another affair like that one."

For a moment, staring ahead of him, Ira tried to collect his thoughts. Then he realized that he was so dazed that he couldn't. "Please," he said in a high voice, "just give me one chance." (He thought, "What chance could she give me that wouldn't be and left them in the living room on an old, worn couch.

"I can't believe I'm here," he said, "You're so beautiful."

"Am I really?" she asked. Her nose and hips were too wide for most people, but not for Marc. Her skin was soft and smooth, and her eyes were big, warm, and intelligent.

"You're just gorgeous," he intoned. "I've never been so relaxed with a girl before. You're as sweet as sunshine."

A wave of yearning passed along his throat.

"I enjoy being with you," she said, "and you're pretty gorgeous yourself." She was tickled by his inexperience, which helped her to relax, and she found his awkwardness cute.

Marc swayed his head to the side and downward, feeling Carol's words wash over him. Then he yielded toward her and embraced her. Light and fluttery as a leaf freed from the ground by a flood, he kissed her neck, her cheek, and her expecting lips, and found streaming in his chest a knowledge of freedom. He pressed his tongue to her pliant lips and she opened

Stealing: A Novel in Dreams

giving herself away?") "It seems so unfair to me. Once I was too shy; now I'm too aggressive. It... how could it be wrong for me to have too much feeling? It's terrible, like a puzzle that can never be solved, as if there's no way I can do what's right."

Marcy sighed. "I feel for you." Her eyes were shining with the beginning of tears. "But you shouldn't exaggerate the problem. You're a handsome guy. There will be lots of women for you, and in time, you're bound to mature. One day you'll look back on this and laugh. But I'm sensitive, like you, and I know what won't work for me. I have no choice about using judgment. These things have to be done in freedom and hope or they turn into...something oppressive." She decided not to say, "nightmares."

"So," Ira seized her words silently: "No freedom or hope for me." He stood up, feeling clammy sweat on his limbs and cold waves of dread washing across a great empty space in his torso. Grim thoughts seemed to slither by him at a distance. Everyone in the world

them, and moving to her slow rhythm, he licked the insides of her clear, innocent lips, her tongue. She opened further and drew her tongue back and he felt himself going into her, surrounded by her. It reminded him of something he had forgotten, the way he saw space open up under the pool when he was a child. Now what he had been worrying about for as long as he could remember was being washed away, away.

Then Carol opened her blouse and Marc saw the tender expanse of her cleavage. He had seen many pictures of breasts, but had never had a good look at them attached to a living woman. He reached a hand forward as if in blessing. His fingers floated in the zone between them, which was like a veil made of the delicate film on the top of custard if it could move with life. Then he fondled her left breast, thrilling to its softness, and asked her if she could take off her bra. He remembered Ira's precept that she wanted him as much as he wanted her.

could make love but him, even educated fleas. It was inevitable that he should pick a sick girl. Maybe he made them sick. He could pick a hundred more and they'd all be sick. He said, "I'd better go." "Well," said Marcy, "before you do, is there anything else I can do for you—except make love, that is?"

He wanted to say that she had done enough already, but he shouldn't throw away this chance, this beauty. "Well, let me look at you for a few minutes." He was hoping she would see the feeling in his gaze. Yet part of him suspected that this intense feeling was the main thing she objected to.

"Okay," she said.

So they stood there, little more than a foot away from each other, and he gazed at her harmonious, unscathed face. It looked like a different face in this light, less sophisticated, more simple, more like a child, but still perfectly beautiful. And whoever had her would have hundreds of such faces in different times and lights and situations, and they would almost all be divine. And it

Carol seemed nervous about taking off her bra. "I really do want to get it off—never have liked being trussed up in a bra. But there's a problem. Promise you won't laugh."

"Sure." Marc wondered what could be so bad about them. Were her nipples cross-eyed?

Carol reached back and took off her bra, then dropped it on the coffee table and lay back on the couch. Her breasts were not big, but they were pretty. Marc wondered what was supposed to be funny about them. There were a few hairs around the nipples, which were a bit bumpy, but delectably pink, and well-shaped in a modest way. Marc did not want assertive nipples. Then he noticed some diminutive wounds on the lower parts of her breasts. "What are those?"

"Well," she said, "I was nervous and had pimples, so I tried to get rid of them by squeezing them. When you do that, they sometimes get red. I felt awful when I saw what a mess I had made, and realized there wouldn't be time to heal. You don't think it's too disgusting?"

Stealing: A Novel in Dreams

would be wonderful to melt his cheek where her neck met her ear. And if he kissed her smooth eyelids, he would feel the light flowing into him. But now it sank into him that he had lost her, and he would be ashamed to see her again and to remember her. It swept over him and before he could stop himself, he grew angry with an anger made up of terror: "Don't you have any womanly feelings?"—a line his father might have used.

Marcy said, "My womanly feelings are my business."

"I didn't know we were talking about business. No wonder you always sound like a goddamned business report."

"Please, Ira, let's try to talk nicely to each other. It's important that we stay friends."

"I've heard that 'friends' bit before. It's what women tell men when they want to hurt them badly and…don't mind using a callous cliché to make their cruelty obvious." Ira's voice was getting shrill, and he was horrified to notice the hysterical tones of his father.

She gave an outcry of exasperation and pain. "So that's

He grinned at her anxiety: "I think it's esthetically superb, with interesting overtones of sadomasochism. In fact, I'm an old pimple squeezer from way back. Indubitably my favorite sport. Me and my brother Ira, we used to have contests popping them. The object was to see who could hit the mirror best from half an inch away." Carol burst into a high pitched pretty giggle. He was touched that she should worry so about him. It made him feel sorry for her, and compassion made him more excited. He fell on her gasping, rubbing his body against hers, and began to moan, "Can we have intercourse?"

"My parents would hear us making love from their room. This couch is unstable and it creaks. But I could, uh, give you a blowjob."

"Well, okay, but what could I do for you?"

She opened his pants, found him ready, and blew him. It was excruciatingly, excruciatingly good. Then she sat on his lap and embraced him while he stroked her, one hand in front and the other behind. She told what a girl's friendship is worth, and that's what happens when a girl doesn't want to be...required to get laid by every man who dates her. I'm afraid you'll have to go."

"All right. I'm not going to impose on you." Stung by her words, he grabbed his jacket and headed for the door, slipping a little so his foot stamped. "I hope you're happy with what you've done to me. You'll be getting dividends on this little transaction when you see the results."

"It's a cheap trick," she cried out, "to make me responsible for your self destructive urges." Before she could finish her sentence, he was on the other side of a slamming door.

Marcy jerked her head to look to the side, wheeled around, and plunged onto the couch, sobbing. "I wanted to help him," she thought, "but he has such an awful, bottomless need. I'm not strong enough to handle it. I could use a little pleasure. I'd fall into the abyss and destroy myself, and I wouldn't be able to do any good. I don't even know whether he

him what to do, and he mostly obeyed her. With some sensitivity, he discovered that he was skillful, or she let him think he was. Never again would he stop taking orders from her.

Feeling her intimate parts, his control and her response, he felt more powerful than he had ever felt before—the power of being free from power, her miracle of love. Spaces opened around him to great distances filled with joy and life.

That night, slumped over a seat on the bus home, feeling sore in his lips and in his groin, Marc decided to marry Carol. When he told her the following week, she said that she wanted to have his children. He said that the children would be gods, and that he wanted a large number of them. They waited two years to marry because their parents enjoined him to finish college first. With Carol's encouragement (she was insufferably right about everything), he changed his major to literature, did well, and got his B.A. in three and a half years. Reading *Great Expectations*, Marc noted that Herbert Pocket asked Pip

Stealing: A Novel in Dreams

was too aggressive or too passive. Was he speaking to himself or was he right? Maybe I'm a person who'll never find love because she doesn't deserve it."

Ira pressed for the elevator, but it sounded eternally slow. He realized that he didn't want anyone to see him in his agitated state, so he turned to tramp down the stairs. But his knees were wobbly, and a floor below, he collapsed onto the stairway, heaving and shuddering: "No freedom and no hope. I've passed into a world of shadows."

if he had ever noticed that "the children of not exactly suitable marriages are always particularly anxious to be married?"

After they had been married for six years, Marc was thinking one day about the party where they he and Carol had first connected. He mentioned to her that Ann had told him before the party that a girl coming was interested in him. Carol responded that the girl had been Leah, not her. For no reason at all, Marc and Carol had come together and were doomed to be happy for the rest of their lives.

(Has this action been completed? Can it be found between the two times, the bad dream and the good? Perhaps the action is the formation of two beings, a living one and a dead one, who can only speak through each other. This runs between us through the years, the current of life that feeds on what is lost.

Who is speaking in this action? Who can claim to be the voice for both? Perhaps I, who have always been here, informing Marc from the beginning, become audible at this point, when time has broken down and Marc and I have passed into irreconcilable worlds, and can only speak to each other from outside of our minds. I am the meaning of what he says that he does not know, what he says aims at.

We used to collect these EC comics that scared us sick, *Tales from the Crypt*. They were told by a witch or a demon speaking from a dungeon or a burial vault underground. The art was luridly graphic about torture, monstrosity, decomposition. The plot would often involve a character who saw some nightmarish scene, in a dream, a painting, or a distant room, and ended up being sucked into the nightmare and caught in it.

I have been swallowed by this story, which cannot be told unless I tell it in the form of the undead. Maybe I became a ghost and my story became a horror story—one that concentrates on the taking apart of our body—when Marc fell in love with Carol and I was cut off from him. Then I was cut off from myself, my mind was amputated, and the story I had to tell became the story of someone else, of him.

Notice how pompous he has become, using words like "superb" and wanting his children to be gods. He thinks he's found freedom by enslaving himself to a woman. But would he have enslaved himself so joyfully, or would he need such shelter, if he didn't suspect he was betraying me? Could he love her and allow me to continue living?

Maybe I'm crazy, huh. Maybe someone else can break his heart the way I can. Carol can only swell it up. His heart gushing with feeling and ideas. Where does a blessing end and a curse begin? They are intertwined in an embrace forever. So each is always the other, alternating with the expansion and contraction of the heart, its endless breaking.

My parents, putting a demented mask of kindness on a curse, would say to each other in Yiddish, "Hang yourself on a sweet rope." From the crypt in which the screams echo, I curse him with sweetness. May he be so desperate, so lost, that he will never be free of it, this shining heart that he holds in his opening hands. The heart that I found only in dreams, my own heart. My bliss too great to be contained in facts. The song of joy that exalts us.)

9

The Best Yet

1959

This is the best yet. The room is tiny and bare, but that's peachy. Did you ever hear of a peach with a hairdo or a necktie? This is the student's unadulterated chamber, and I'm your stalwart student. That Richie asked me downstairs what my major was and I said English-I'm gonna be cultivated and find the answers. That literature can tell you how to live. He didn't seem impressed. It's deeper than journalism. Don't think I'll be talking to the folks around here much, but that's swell. I's'll be *au privave*. Uncompromised. Clear to myself. The best is the truest, with no deception. My stripped down self, on a shelf.

All the drawers of the plain chest, painted brown, are empty and clean, their contents defected, resurrected. They could receive the furnishings of a new planet, but they aren't quite void. Just a small infection of affection. At the back of the top drawer one garment reclines. A pair of girl's cotton panties, simple and trim in form and ivory colored. I can smell them. They're not stained, not new, but in decent condition with a smooth finish. The smell is considerable. Where does it come from, the front or the back? I try smelling front and back and there's no difference. The same rankness. Might be a general womansmell perfume, 'cause it spreads itself too vibrantly to be natural. Don't they sell tubes of womanstink in magazine ads? These knickers may be artificially enhanced, undrying, undying undies.

Must've been left by a guy who kept it for a fetish, whether or not he got it from an actual girl. She'd want it back unless it's too dirty, cast off. Hard to believe a woman would leave her hogo behind. Guess he couldn't bring it to his new place. Maybe he left it rather than ditching it, to give comfort to the next guy here, companionship for those lonely nights. To share a pillow. To let someone know there are people who care, but it may be an insult to a lad who can't get the real thing, concealing scorn.

Probly a nice gesture, so the room is furnished after a fashion, a sort of maniac manna. But I wouldn't want to be creepy enough to use this *schmatta* for kicks. Yet I don't see how I could meet anyone at this point. The girls in this building seem to be taken—Karen is with Pete. And the ones in class seem to be expecting moves I don't have. Gotta read the last chapters of *Sons and Lovers* for tomorrow. Keep away from the nasty somewell of those pants.

The light on the table is almost the right bright and the seat is low enough. The words skitter by, entranced with yearning anguish by the death of Paul's mother, transfixed by his impulse to kill her…I feel satisfied to understand the reconciliation with Dawes and the abandonment of Miriam. This is what Paul has to do. If only I could do it.

My eyes are happy to touch the beautiful words, but it moves too quickly. It's over and I'm no longer in the knowable world of the book. Back in the room with the aching, insidious chest of drawers drawing. Paul says he is lost: "whatever place he stood on, there he stood alone." So I could go through his passion for his mom, his defeat by love. But he's written by a genius. Is able to pass beyond his mother, Clara, and Miriam because he possesses their love. Believes in the force of life: "he would not give in." His survival lives on the strength of fiction.

Whom do I have to write me? The multiple voice of the old man who kills absolutely everybody. I have God in hum form. I have

Joel, who the others can't compete with. Mom, who holds me off for Joel's sake, can only pretend to know me. She certainly tries. She started the book because I told her it seized me. But she says Paul has to get over his attachment to his mom. Yet where will he be without her? Nowhere. His involvement in her death can only claim her for keeps. Mom wants to give me the strength of her beauty, but she doesn't have it herself. She's only advising me from the past, from a tradition that's a trap. Yet to give up Mom is to succumb to Dad, the devil to her deep blue sea..

And Marc, who wants to advance at my expense, writes me in reverse, putting me down by telling me I'm okay, my opposition doesn't matter. They don't have the force to resist Joel's attack. Can only participate in it by showing how I fall short. So my vacation in bookland is over, and I'm back in the outside world that's not so inspired, or inspired the wrong way. Just a hint that's malodorous, malevolent.

What are you waiting for? Pretending to live sensibly, your precious defense that keeps life away. I'm not going out. Went to the bar and only sat there. Second time I tried to talk to that Aileen, who didn't seem very bright. The booze made me sick and everything turned green. I couldn't find what to say except that she seemed slow on the intake, and she pulled away looking sad.

Was that drawer open a half inch? Does that mean that I wasn't sure I should close it? Or did it move, huh? Maybe that reek's strong enough to move furniture. Those thrilling threads are throwing off persuasive whispers of aroma. They barely murmur, "Oh, don't think it's us!" Spirits of beauty or disease? Can I step through the screen into a movie that can't be seen, that's all darkness?

I pull the drawer open and the panties seem to stir as they settle into their new position, as if they were responding with a tiny tender wiggle. Not so often I get this close to a woman's inner feelings. The fifth degree of nowhere. Supposedly in the imagination, which has delicious advantages over reality, in the past that can never stop because it never existed, her wet sex dripped on it, soaked it, it clung to her crotch infatuated, it wiped her crack with slow, close strokes that reached into her the more she bent. So it pressed its absorbent lips to her holes, folded into her in endless contact blending.

Now that I hold her close, she breathes her sultry scent into my face. It radiates gently up into my nostrils, washes across my mouth like the shared surface of the lightest kiss, speaking: "How can I meet you in such a ghastly scene? What a pathetic wretch. For my own sake, I need strength, not misery. Insofar as I'm here, you're dragging me down aching with shame. How could I be touched or moved by something so revolting? What happiness could I find if I can't help?" Does she really want to help? In what reality?

This is what she would say if she were really here, her sorrow for me. An actual person would compromise, falsify the vision, break each moment. She's closest to me here in my dream if I call her Flora because she smells like the richest flowers.

Flora clings to me with the resistance of empty flesh embracing the sensitive tips and inner surfaces of my fingers as I stretch her waistband yieldingly open to expand the moaning chamber of sordid smell within her. The way to get inside her is clear to me. I know what I'm doing before I know it. (No time to think of the danger of disease.)

Before I know it, I surround myself with her scintillation by pulling her over my head. Guys do it: maybe the guy who left her for me intended it. Her waistband fondles my neck and chin casually, as if touching would help her see me, and seeing could relieve my anguish by her sweet consideration.

Now I'm in the half-dark, the light stained by the membrane that rubbed against the moistness between her legs. My head floats in the buzzing odor of her juices. My prick is throbbing as I grasp it and slide excitingly over it. I am in possession and take on leisure. I can imagine further, and want to expand my powers by learning what I possess, what it really is, to know myself by knowing why I am here now.

But now I know what it is. My efforts to avoid the truth are nada. It's the fuming stench of her bottom, the most powerful smell is from where she sits, where she shits. Why does this intoxicate me so? I could never ask her. Ask who? Someone who has disappeared before I ask. Who could I hope to find with my head in the toilet but myself?

The darkness reveals the answer that light had hidden. The pungent odor evokes the festive rampage of my desecration as a tunnel of vision leads down to the past, to the dreadful demon. My father stands in the bathroom, wearing only his undershirt. He has one foot on the edge of the bathtub and his back is to little Ira and he's giving himself an enema. He speaks in a cheerful, exultant voice: "You don't have to be shy about it. It's good for you." He mocks me for being prim enough to object to his comradeship. That was the first time I was upset by a rear end. I was told that I should be man enough to accept it. The monster that turns my heart to stone, that what excites me is what horrifies me.

Flora has flown. Fickle like all her sex. I was right at the start when I figured I couldn't use these panties. The smell has gotten stale. Take them off and stop blinding yourself. It's ridiculous, pitiful for a man to look for love by putting dirty underwear on his head. I don't think I can stay in this place where I degraded myself so far. Got to keep moving. I can't throw Flora away and I can't use her. Maybe the last guy felt the same way and the next one will. Passing the torch. But I don't even know where it came from.

Just before I left, I heard that a guy would be moving into my room. Decided to leave him a dirty pair of my pants to cheer him up. David said I smelled like roses. They were too tight, itchy. If I washed them they'd only shrink. Wish him joy.

10

THE PICNIC IN THE DESERT

1960

Marc walked down a long, narrow, straight corridor. It was dimly lit, and its high grey walls and uneven floors were damp. Reaching a tall door set with a number of locks, he rang a jeering buzzer and waited. Marc visited Ira every week or two, and much of the time, Ira seemed to be in a new place. He had dropped off the weights at Bronx Park East, where Marc assiduously neglected to use them. When Ira finally opened the door for Marc, it sounded as if it had not been locked.

Inside the door was another dark, narrow corridor, but this one twisted as if it couldn't make up its mind. They passed a tiny room with the door open in which a middle-aged man in a bathrobe was lying asleep across a cot. Marc observed to himself that his brother's neighbors seemed to have declined from friendly students to withdrawn deadbeats. Ira's room itself was narrow and grimy, with two windows that faced a wall. It was not small, and it had a high ceiling, but it had a strange triangular shape, and there was very little furniture in it; most of Ira's things were in boxes.

The room had a sink with dirty dishes and utensils in it, and Marc decided to look benevolent by cleaning them. He picked up the sponge, and found that it was saturated with a transparent, glutinous slime that had an acrid odor. He tried to wash it off, making the tap as hot as it would get, but though he rinsed the sponge several times, rubbing his hands in the goo, it remained viscid. He felt that it would dirty anything more than it would clean. Finally, he cleaned the dishes with his wet hands, trying to make them squeak. "There doesn't seem to be anything I can do with this sponge."

"Then there isn't, as they say in the old country."

"Maybe there's something in this closet that could help?" It was a wardrobe or upright chest rather than being set in the wall, and it was made of dark, dull, heavy wood.

"I wouldn't recommend that you go in that closet."

Marc stopped moving toward the closet. "I don't see how you can live like this."

"Call it a bare-assed minimum."

"You haven't been doing your schoolwork properly in more than a year." Marc decided not to mention that Ira had not had a piece appear in the paper in the same time. "It seems to me that you may have to come back to the parents."

"Are you trying to break up my happy home?'" Ira held up a pornographic magazine that was on the windowsill as if it couldn't go in the wardrobe. "Trying to rain on this permanent picnic. Odd's bodkins, if you mention that novel notion again, my beamish boychick, it will be my solemn duty to give you the bum's rush. Hmmm." He scratched his head and looked sideways. "How best should I proceed to demonstrate my right to exist? What will make me credible? Obviously, the thing to do is to impress you with some high-class scholarship." He took a paperback from a ledge.

"You see here the crowning work of one of the great minds of this century. You have my permission to applaud at any time, especially while I talk. Too bad I haven't got a laugh track—the laughs I get are out of sight. Folks have taken to greeting me with an awed hush that must betoken reverence. Never mind that this joker here was a particularly sick comic who liked to mess up people's lives, or that his story was the story of the destruction of the Jews." He held the book towards Marc: *Moses and Monotheism*, by Sigmund Freud. "My pile-driving research has uncovered within this very volume something of inestimable revelatory value (dig it!) for both of us, namely an extremely accurate description of our dearling daddy, may he rest in peace."

Marc was shocked to hear the traditional formula applied to the living Joel, but couldn't help chuckling.

Ira said, "Honor thy fatter and mutter." He seemed agitated, and as he held the book open, his eyes looked first to his right and then to his left. Marc thought it was a gesture of distraction disguised as acting out reading from the right, perhaps disguised from Ira: "Reading backwards, Siggy sez here that the chosen God Jahve was a volcano god, a clear reference to the old man's rhetoric; that he was an uncanny demon that demanded human sacrifice." Marc felt another stir of unease at hearing the unmentionable name of the Elohim. Ira said, "Seems Moses was an Egyptian who got the idea of monotheism from his people and needed a figurehead or scarecrow to make it stick but good. Shame Moe hadn't yet developed Larry and Curly to complete the trinity."

Ira opened at a dogeared page and read a line: "'A rude, narrow-minded local god, violent and bloodthirsty.' Now that's what I call hitting the nail on the head, or is it the point?" Ira was misusing a typical line of his dad's. "A profound articulation of Joel's universal qualities. You can't use language without using his language because the purpose of each word is to carve out a definition. It doesn't rate, mate, if it doesn't eviscerate."

Marc's abdomen heaved with a silent laughter that was almost nausea. "Pretty wild, but what does it get you as gospel?"

"It gets me free. Means I possess my own soul. I don't have to belong to some old sadist forever."

"But Ira, how will it work to possess your soul if your life is a disaster?"

"I used to think you were on my side, but it's more and more obvious that you're working for Jahve."

"Don't be silly. You know I'm very attached to you."

"When you pick your nose, you're very attached to the snot on your finger, but only until you can get rid of it, and certain stuff can be hard to scrape off your shoes completely. You can be very attached to that for months."

"You shouldn't talk like that, Ira. For you to talk as if I'm your enemy makes me feel awful. It's nothing at all like how I see you."

Marc took twenty dollars from his wallet and put it on the bed with half a shrug. Ira had not been able to keep a series of office jobs and had fallen back on vending beer at Yankee Stadium. He did other sports than baseball, but it was March now, and Marc did not understand how he got along. He seemed less substantial and his color was sallow.

"Swell," said Ira. "Let's play cards"'" They spent increasing amounts of their time together playing poker, rummy, or their childhood favorite, breece. Once they had played breece for comic books, with piles of comics stacked up around the table. These represented articulate wealth, though the ones they risked were not the ones they cared for (which ended up disappearing anyway). Now as they sat on the bed watching the cards turn, they knew they would not turn up anything exciting, but they felt enclosed by a ritual that echoed with harmonies of the past.

Later, feeling more relaxed, they took a long walk on Riverside Drive. Marc was seventeen now, and allowed to stay out later. The night was clear and fresh as they descended the moonlit slopes of the park toward the Hudson. At first it seemed to Marc that they were sharing the mysterious night air, that the strangeness of this uninhabited landscape of ghostly trees and parapets would bring them together. But when Ira talked, he was more sardonic than ever, and Marc realized that they were walking in two different nights.

They sat on a bench as close as they could get to the river. The surface was smooth and luminous, looking like an expanse of milk. The river, withheld by a damp ledge of stone, framed by an elaborate scaffolding of bridges, lights, and buildings, seemed stagy.

Marc said, "It looks like there's a low mist on the water, but it's hard to tell 'cause it clings so. If you look at it closely, the little movements of it are more like the rolling of clouds than the sweeping of waves. You can't see the water move, can you?"

"No, I can't, and my eyesight is better than yours."

"Even that ship over there seems to be standing still." Ira said, "It's probably anchored."

"It looks stately, like a movie." Marc remembered that Ira had once said that he was in a movie. "Or did he say it?'" thought Marc. "Maybe I only imagined it. When you worry about someone a lot, you make up different versions of the person, and you grow uncertain about which version is the true one. If the person is unhealthy, there may not be a true one." He said, "With nothing moving, it feels like we're in a hole in time."

Ira said, "Perhaps time is a series of holes, a chain of holes plunking along to separate what is constantly going on at once. We keep doing what we've always done, but at the same time we're doing something in the future. We have to use the present to keep the future from the past, to keep them from getting lost in each other.

"Now that we're not so close, we're not in the same time frame anymore. Maybe this means that what we hear each other say or see each other do may have happened already or it may be coming later. Do you understand me?"

Marc said, "Not quite, but it seems suggestive, worth thinking about. It shows potential for a writer."

"Well maybe you'll understand it someday. Or maybe it'll be just as well if you don't. I'm not sure I do. Not sure I want to. Fortunately, you have quite a talent for misunderstanding."

They were embarrassed and puzzled, but felt uplifted by having shared something. Yet the conversation drifted away, never having been in touch. After a while, they got up. As they walked south beside the glowing river, Marc looked up and saw a diagonal path worn in a large field of grass that ascended at an increasing angle toward a high cliff hidden by foliage dark with night. It occurred to him that the path couldn't be seen from the cliff. He felt like following the path, and wondered why he was struck by it. Several days later, he realized that it reminded him of the cliff he had once dreamed about.

11

TO THE SHITHOUSE

1960　　　　1961

"Where are you going?" she asked.

"Where I came from," he answered, trying to be elated, clever. "How much?"

She said, "Ten dollars for twenty minutes."

Not a bad price, but expensive for him, all the bills he had with him. But she was enticing, with her big dark eyes and her tall, curvy body. She would have to excite him. He shouldn't start badly by being indecisive, so he gave consent. As he walked beside her to her room, he determined that he didn't want it to be just a trick. He wanted to have some good feelings, something tender.

Sunday at noon, 1960, Marc was draped backwards over his father's recliner when the phone rang. His feet were hooked over the high top that leaned far over. His legs hung down the back in reverse, and his stomach and diaphragm rested on the seat. A platform that lifted up for the feet when the chair was tilted back was strained by supporting his elbow and the science fiction he was reading. He was getting too old for this position.

A minute after the phone rang, his mother shrieked. He almost threw the chair over backwards (it teetered for a second) in his struggle to

So he gave her the money in advance, to get the money out of the way, to pass beyond it to the truth.

As she undressed, however, the woman kept asking for more money, saying she could do special things to turn him on. She was concerned not with what she had gotten, but with what she could get, surplus profit. He insisted over and over that he had no more money, and when he finally held open his empty wallet, her coolness increased. She finished undressing and lay back wearing nothing on a low bed under a mirror. Her body was good looking, but cold and immobile, and he was annoyed at how she had nagged him about the money and forced him to reveal his financial impotence. The emphasis of his voice saying "I don't have anymore" reminded him of how he used to say, "I don't want anymore" when his mom fed him. And this girl's classically beautiful features reminded him of Marcy, but he tried not to think of that.

She said, "Loosen up and relax." She thought, "I'd like to give him a break, but I have to extricate himself quickly so he could get to her.

In the parents' room he found his mom lying flat on her back on the double bed moaning, "Oh, oh, oh, oh, oh, oh." Marc was too appalled to think about the orgasmic aspect. Meanwhile, Joel tried to get the facts straight over the phone. Ira was in Bellevue and wanted to get out. To do so, he needed responsible people to come down and sign for him. Deciding not to take a seventeen-year-old to such a terrible place, they dressed as quickly as they could and left. Joel said, "I hope you're satisfied with the fruit of your years of work." Judith was stonefaced.

When Ira arrived home that night, he was pale, unshaven and mute. He mostly lay asleep or sat in impassive silence for a day and a half. Marc lay parallel to him at night and wondered what was happening to him. Marc wanted to be generous and dismiss Bellevue as an accident, but when he thought of Ira, he couldn't help a tingling in his bones. He perceived his brother as (perhaps) a dormant get through this life right here. A sensitive boy is less work for mother. Why should I put out more than I have to? He might make it in life and I might not. If I try to help him, I might end up with something really weird. If he tells me his troubles, it's not going to get him off in twelve minutes. If I waste too much time, the boss might hit me. This clown here should try doing what I do. Can't afford to look pitiful more than I have to."

Staring at the prostitute on her back, Ira thought, "I was blocking it by being too tight," and he tried to loosen himself so the energy could flow through him, but there was no energy, only a vacuum. He tried to imagine her opening her legs, taking him in, moaning, but it was like a statue moving. She didn't suggest fantasies. She seemed as still and massive as a dead body. He could get himself up by rubbing himself, but he was too embarrassed. She would think he was a creep, so it wouldn't work.

"Is something wrong?" she asked, underlining the obvious.

host from *Invasion of the Body Snatchers* or *The Puppet Masters*. What pod was planted in him? What kind of alien being had entered him? What was he metamorphosing into?

On Tuesday Marc got back from school to find Ira sitting at the sewing machine in his father's old bathrobe, shaven and seeming more alert. "I feel considerable better now," he said. "You don't have to worry about that happening again. I wasn't really sick, but disappointment got me down and I needed a rest. Actually, I never got a drop of rest."

Marc said, "You can rest here."

"May not be too good for me to rest here. Anyhow, Bellevue was of value to me 'cause it shook me up." He paused and smirked listlessly. "It showed me there may be worse things than the parents. You wait for a long time in a room with a lot of folks who are standing around, leaning against the wall or sitting on the floor. Turns out they can't trust these lads with chairs that can be swung. They have doctors there that

"Could you use your hand on me?"

"That costs extra."

"Well, hell, that's unfair. I paid your price and you won't give me a chance. It makes me mad."

"Look, buddy, it's not my fault you aren't ready. You should have remembered your boy scout oath. You don't want to get nasty now, 'cause I can call a guy next door who takes care of nasty types. So just relax. How does this get you?" She turned over on her stomach.

The idea of her rear end was tantalizing to Ira, her softest part, her secret, smelly place, but the actuality of her ass seemed stolid, even frowning in its upside-down position. Moreover, he was still angry, and she had a cruel looking scar high on her left buttock that made him queasy. He felt an ache of pity for her pain and humiliation, her refusal to degrade herself somehow must have given some bastard an excuse to cut her. This explained why such a beautiful girl cost so little.

She said, "You can kiss me there if you want."

It might have turned him on, but the cool way she said can cure things you don't have. It's easy to see your head when you're holding it in your hands."

Marc asked, "What's it like over there?"

Ira's eyes focused on something that wasn't there. "They give you a mattress in a big ward with thirty-nine others, and two bathrooms. people screaming, yelling, "Help me," cursing, wandering around asking for things. Sometimes they seemed to ask for sex, and that bothered me. But most of the time I couldn't tell what they were asking for. Maybe they couldn't. Folks strapped to their beds, staring. People never far away jerkng off or shitting or vomiting. You could hear it and smell it all the time, like air, like silence. It's like your nerves are rubbed clean.

"At night, when you lie in this noisy, bubbling stew, trying to sleep in it, you're not asleep and you're not awake. Then you wonder if sleeping and waking are only covers for this, covers that have been around for a long time and are barely long enough, soiled, wearing thin.

"You're drifting with nothing to cover you, nothing to hold

it made it seem ironic, seem like an insult. He tried to move toward her body, but felt locked. To show feeling for something so callous would be degrading. She would be laughing at him, thinking he was a homo. He got close and detected a faint, stale smell from her behind.

The smell was tempting, but he reacted against it. He remembered Flora. It would be like eating shit.

He fell back, his head and shoulders sagging, and said to himself, "I'm caught between two shames—shame of the body and shame of loneliness, and shame of the body is stronger.

"I feel like my bones are made of Jello. I'm shivering. I was a fool to give her the money in advance. I couldn't wait to let her know that there was something wrong with me. I hoped I could get to learn how to handle prostitutes, but I'm getting worse at it. I couldn't afford to do this, and I spent my money on nothing but grief. It's too late to do anything in the few minutes left of my twenty. All I can do now is try to get out of this without falling apart. But onto—sinking into it, getting lost in it, that there's no skin, no separation between you and it. And they make you feel like you belong there. I saw a guy who didn't want his 'medicine' and they held his jaw open and forced it into him. That place wouldn't be good for you if you were the healthiest man in the world."

Marc was thinking of the musician Lead Belly, stuck in Angola prison, where the prisoners would sing, "Angola, Angola, where the lights burn all night long." He said, "You must have been strong to take that. I don't think I could handle it."

"Strong, yes, I guess what I learned is that you have to be strong, though it seems I've heard that before. Yet you know what Mom says: sometimes a person can be too strong."

"Oh, I don't think you have to worry about being too strong," Marc said, and he put his hand on Ira's shoulder. But then he wondered how he meant that.

Ira shrugged his hand off and smiled with half his mouth: "Look here, *vans*, am I strong or am I strong?"

the worst part of it is my desire. It's still there, like a watermelon in my chest. I can't separate it from shame."

Ira looked at the woman, who sat on the bed dressing. He felt sorry for her as he hadn't felt sorry for Marcy, though Marcy had suffered, while this woman was mainly amused by him. He knew that her life held little hope, and he thought it must be horrendous to offer your body to a stranger and not get any response. "It wasn't your fault," he said in a flat tone. "I just had a bad day."

She muttered in a perfunctory way, "You'll grow up more."

He thought, "A kid I'm not. I could tell her I've had some good things with women, but she doesn't want an explanation, and it wouldn't be true. I didn't hold on to the few women I might have had anything from. When you aren't getting any, it's hard to believe you ever did. But what I had wasn't so great—could be described as a couple of fumbles. But it was better than this. Hard to think of anything that wasn't better." As he

Marc had a sinking feeling as he realized that he'd said the wrong thing. "I tend to hurt people when I try to be nice. Maybe it's because I'm really nasty, but it's more like I'm too wrapped up in myself to consider other people. I'll have to hold my thoughts back around Ira."

Ira was released with the proviso that he obey the orders of the psychiatrist in charge of the case. This doctor wanted him to stay at home, but he objected so strenuously that he was allowed to take a room in a quiet corner of the West Bronx. He was strictly required to report to the parents once a week. On these occasions, he was sullen as a prisoner and said little, mostly to Marc. This behavior was logical in that it kept the old man from exploding, an accomplishment.

Alone with Marc, Ira spoke of the need to be strong, to have presence. "People judge you by what you look like." He had a long mirror in his room, which was upstairs in a little wooden house kept by a sympathetic walked away from the building, controlling his tendency to tremble, he felt his sides pressing his body together, forcing his chest up into his throat, making him stoop over.

Ira was afraid he'd have trouble with the subway, but he didn't have to wait long for the train, and late on a weekday night he found a car with only a few people in it and sat near a corner facing the window so no one could see his face.

In assuming the pose of the subway loony, he managed to amuse himself by sitting stooped and twisted, holding his head in his hands, staring out the window. "Now this is riding in style," he proclaimed.

Yet as he sat watching the grimy ribs of the tunnels flying toward him, lashing him with their lights that served only to illuminate darkness, he felt fear blowing into him. "My God," he thought, and realized he was not entitled to this exclamation. "My reaction is only in its early stages and these lights and darks hurling themselves at me are attacking me because

old lady. In front of the mirror he practiced walking so that his feet were firmly planted on the ground the way a strong man's should be, striving to impress himself on the earth. The lady was angelic to put up with it. He worked out furiously with his weights and began to look formidable, even menacing.

When Ira visited, he tended to be suspicious of the dense piles of food with which he was confronted. He rejected most of it, saying it tasted funny or bitter. He inherited his dad's pickiness and obsession with diet.

Joel made an effort to restrain himself that was impressive in its way. He had learned years ago to speak to Ira in the third person to avoid offending him when Ira wanted no contact with him. Joel used the third person more consistently now, and he would try to smile in Ira's presence in a way that looked meek rather than sardonic, and to use innuendoes rather than direct statements. He had developed a kind of refinement.

of what they are in the simplest literal sense. The future is what is coming at me irresistibly."

When Ira got to his triangular room. he sat on his bed and exclaimed, "What shall I do?" At first, he was inclined to hold his head in his hand and say, "Oh my God," but both of these gestures had been corrupted by use so they were only acts he was putting on. His hand on his head, even his palm on his forehead, seemed to grip, to wrench, to abrade; and the sound of the word God frightened him.

In fact, his suggestions were often framed as amusing, light-hearted quips, which he thought they were. "I'm positive Ira's going to keep on visiting us 'cause I know he's too smart to go on the wack path again. He's had enough of those guys in the white coats." Another time: "Maybe he doesn't eat his food 'cause he misses his buddies over there in Bellevue." He pronounced "Bellevue" with three syllables. Sometimes, when he felt particularly inspired, he would slip back into improvising in the second person: "Boy, you really want to make money for the doctors. I can see you have big plans for those blood suckers. You want to get each one a fancy sports car, maybe two."

Joel regarded all doctors as criminals. This didn't keep him from using them when he had to, but it justified his not paying them. He regarded everyone as a criminal unless they showed weakness, in which case he felt affection for them as patsies.

Once when Marc was out and the old man was gnawing away, Ira sprang up and glared at him. Joel, reverting respectfully to the third person, said, "Now if that doesn't look crazy, I don't know what does."

Ira struggled for a moment. He felt physically unstrung, but morally impelled to hit his father, so he said, "You bet it does," and gave the old man a half-hearted punch in the arm. He was disgusted at how weak his punch was and how weak Joel's arm felt.

Stealing: A Novel in Dreams

The idea hurt Joel more than the impact, but he said to himself, "If I make a big production of this, it'll make it worse." He stood there holding his arm and looking darkly at his son. Ira kept saying to himself, "Serves you right." But he was stunned and felt a ghastly hollow in his chest and burning in his throat. Hitting his father had made the old man human, and Ira found this unbearable.

After a few minutes, he muttered, "I'm sorry, but you'd better leave me alone." Then he sat down and held himself still. Both father and son were trying to pretend that nothing had happened. But no one could think of anything to say and Ira's small fingers twitched. He stood up and thrust his hands in his pockets. Then he said, "Well, I guess I'll be toddling along," and slipped out.

Joel said, "That's your blue-ribbon son that you raised your way. Quite an accomplishment."

"I never thought I'd see it," said Judith, "but I'm not the one who egged him on."

They were dazed and tried to gain security by blaming each other, but each suspected that the real problem was beyond them. An hour later, Ira called and apologized and they made him repeat that he would never do it again. He was obviously afraid of being reported to the doctor. The parents decided not to tell Marc.

The post-Bellevue Ira was losing weight, and the preoccupation with feeding him evoked memories of childhood, when the parents crammed food into the boys, Mom standing over them with a strap, forcing them to eat cold scrambled eggs, congealed and grinding. She was convinced that the boys were tall because she forced food into them. Cousin Ernest was the ideal, certified to eat ten slabs of rye bread every day.

One evening when Ira refused hamburger because it had too much garlic, the parents made him chicken. He refused the chicken as soggy, so they looked for something else. Digging into the ice of the freezer, they found lamb chops, but Ira said they were no good because they had grey spots from being frozen too long. Finally, they got him tuna, but he wouldn't eat it because it was too dry. Judith said, "This is impossible." Joel said, "What are we going to do?" Ira said, "You'll do what I want."

The concrete image of the wasted food was unbearable to Joel, and when he heard this unhappy mandate, his ability to keep from accusing Ira faltered. In a shrill tone he yowled, "Do you have to be such a jackass?" But as he said it, he noticed that the charge was absurd for someone sick, so his voice broke into shudders on the last word and he heaved a few times and convulsed into tears.

With his pitiful, high-pitched wail, the forward movement of the scene stopped and the light in the room started glaring. Marc had never heard Joel cry and it was years since Judith had, at the death of a brother. The situation was so unusual and dreadful that Judith and Marc also started crying, tears welling from their blurred eyes, groans welling from their sinuses. And then to everyone's relief, even Ira was caught up in the rhythm that was wracking them. He began to blubber fitfully, carried by their throbbing, as stiffly as a corpse bawling at its own funeral.

They leaned against the walls and cabinets of the kitchen and cried together, gasping, heaving, and reeling in a chorus of lamentation. At the edge of the vibration that was churning them together, there was a light feeling, a feeling that this was working better than anything they had tried. They all shared it. In the bright room suffused with waves of sobbing, they felt more in touch with each other than they could ever remember having been.

Marc said, "Can't you see we want to help you?" He was trying to take advantage of what they were sharing, but this tended to slow down the crying by putting things into words. Soon they were shaking into a last few rounds of sobs, gasps, sniffles, and sighs. Joel said, "Why don't you listen just a little bit?" And though he said it as gently as he could, in a faint little voice that was pathetic, it had an overtone of insistence that revived the conflict and dragged them further from what held them together, what spoke in them all. Before long they were quiet, and then they went back to the scene they were playing before. Ira was persuaded to have some tuna, but after a few bites his red face hardened and he said he had had enough. They all had an inkling that their problems would've been solved if only they could have gone on crying forever.

Ira let go of his head and slumped to his side with his head lolling on his shoulder. "Holy shit," he thought, "Sanctimonious feces!" He searched for a secular expletive. "Good grief! Great Koogamuga! Good lawdy, Miss Clawdy! I might as well laugh. What the hell am I going to do with this? I suppose I should learn something from it, but what could be learned? When they stick a knife in your heart, you learn to take a knife in the heart. I could learn to curse, learn to hate women, learn to kiss ass, learn to give up. It's all a bunch of evil shit that I should forget soon as possible. But how much can you forget before you're lost in the sea of your forgetfulness. My God. Holy shit.

"What should I do?" he thought, "What should I do? Wait. I know. I'll write. That's it. The poem I wrote to Barbara—not that good, but it made me feel better. Depression can drive me to creativity. I've done

Two weeks after the foodless meal, Marc visited Ira's place and found him more animated than he had been in a while. Unfortunately, this tended to be a bad sign. They exchanged stories of CCNY, where both were English majors.

Marc was doing well, but Ira had taken a semester off. Under the circumstances, Marc decided to make fun of the school. Passing along items from his circle of friends (Ira now had none), he compared a series of professors to animals: Magalaner to a marmoset, Waldhorn to an ostrich, Mercier to a honeybear. His imitations were hits with Ira, who grinned and paced the floor of his little room energetically. Then, as Marc went on with his monologue, Ira walked to a shadowy corner of the room and stood facing the wall. Marc thought he was stopping to absorb the happiness he was feeling.

Ira thought, "What I feel now, is it connected to what came

it. But what to write? Dirge. *De Profundis.*" He found paper and a pen, feeling lightened by a sense of purpose, but suspecting that he was only putting off reality with words.

He looked at the pen. "It has a tiny hole to let in air, like my fishing reel, yet that's for oil. But I should write. If I write it won't be only of death even if I write about horror, because I'll be writing it, living in my words. From the depths I call. Call to whom? Marc might want to see it. He talks about living in words. But I can't show him this: he's young and his image of me as self-destructive is bad enough. Besides, there's nothing to show.

"It would be ridiculous to make some sort of symbolic abstraction out of it, and I don't feel up to making a joke out of it, like 'The Miller's Tale.' I'd have to write about it as it was. I got trapped in a room with a cold woman and it was my own fault, my own choice, and not the first time. I was torn apart by the darkness and dirt between her legs, between her ass, too weak to take what I can't do without.

before and will come after, or is it part of another scene in another place and time?'"

As he stared at the wall and touched it with his fingertips, Ira saw it as a door before him, with soft yellow light coming out around the edges. He remembered a moment when Barbara had touched his hand and he felt himself melting. "Behind this door a mother is preparing a meal for children. I have it in me to be the father they are waiting for, a yearning that tells me I'll find them someday. So I can feel that I'm a real person and can level with Marc, can be this by doing this."

With joy bounding in his limbs, he turned to Marc. Then he felt uneasy about what he had to say, but then he was saying it: "Listen, I want to explain to you what's happening. I found out the truth about the food the parents give me. I wouldn't believe it if I didn't see it myself. They're putting something in my food. You can use the word doctored or the word poisoned. It's the same thing."

Marc was shaken by the flash of how far away his brother's

"Who wants to hear about such stuff? Even I don't want to. No one would sympathize. It's disgusting. Everyone says 'Holy shit,' but no one wants to see a turd with a halo on it. I can't write now. I did it once when I was sad, but I didn't plan it then. I can't do it when I want it too much. That's the second time tonight. The inverse proportion of desire to its attainability."

Ira sank down on the bed. He was too depressed to masturbate. "I can't have fantasies about a girl I know 'cause I don't know any. The pictures in the magazines have become too familiar, only ink on a page, and I used the money I could have gotten more with. That leaves me with fantasies about possible pictures or about women I lost. Those women in those pictures are posing not for me but for the gangsters who control them. Whatever I could find to think about is blocked out by the image of her on the bed. And that's the worst because she was beautiful, lying there. And the more lovely she was, the more grievous. Because I failed.

thoughts were, in an alien world he could scarcely imagine—yet somehow he knew it. "That's ridiculous. Why should they want to poison their own son's food?" Ira hadn't foreseen this reaction.

"Why do they do anything? To keep control over me. Why do you claim to be so naive? Go ahead, look surprised. Say something cute. Tell me the medicine they give me is to help my mind. I bet you can say it."

Marc said, "The medicine is supposed to clear up your mind."

"Then I must be taking it in the wrong direction. It seems to me to be slowing me down, blocking me out, cutting off my mind. But who am I to know what's happening in my mind? Any jerk with a diploma knows more," he insisted, to make up for a sense of having said too much.

Marc hesitated. "If you aren't taking your medicine, Ira, you can be excitable. You should be careful you don't do something wrong."

There was a pause in which Ira seemed to withdraw. He

"Maybe she was too beautiful. Maybe maybe. Maybe her asshole is what I wanted, or her shit. Maybe I'm a faggot after all. Maybe I need to be fucked if there's no difference between shame and desire. If I want what's most disgusting. Ugh."

He felt something pushing up his diaphragm and realized he was throwing up. He got to the sink with it and told himself good things instinctively while he was doing it: "Well, this shows that I'm not a homo. At least I didn't get it on the floor. I'll feel better when it's over, and I'll be tired enough to go to sleep, a sort of visceral orgasm. But what do all these hopeful thoughts mean? They must mean I'm puking. So much for optimism."

He rinsed himself off, took two aspirins, and dragged himself back to the bed. Though he was afraid of bad dreams, he tried to lie straight and sleep. He felt weightless but weary, and he hoped to drift off. "I should feel heavier," he thought, "then I could sink into sleep, but my mind can't finally said he would be careful, but he said it a moment late. Marc was pained that he had to make such calculations, but he felt something threatening. The visit ended in a shadow of embarrassment.

Marc told the parents some of what Ira had said, feeling that it was more important to Ira's well-being that he level with them rather than side with Ira. Perhaps the parents, without letting Marc know, told the doctor. Maybe the doc decided to increase Ira's dose and to order him to stay at home, and maybe he said this to Ira a few weeks after Ira mentioned his theory to Marc.

Maybe. At this point Marc no longer remembered the remarks about the medicine or thought that Ira had any reason to be mad at him.

Early one afternoon in June, Marc and his father were setting out to get Marc a suit. Marc had gotten good grades at City, while Ira, his mind ravaged by conflict and Thorazine, would need years to graduate. They saw Ira coming down Bronx Park East almost a block away.

get away from this pain, like a sore tooth. Why should it hurt me so, that I couldn't make it with that nasty whore, that I'm not a real man? It's because I'm afraid that I won't be able to live as a person, that I won't be born, that I'll go back into the parents. But I've had my times and this is just bad luck. Making love to a prostitute is so cold that I might be a better person for not being able. This will pass. All I need is patience."

Lying in bed, Ira thought, "There's too much tension in my stomach. I've got to turn over so I can press it against the bed. But lying on my stomach makes my shoulders and neck tense when I bend my head, and my *tuchas* is up. The paper said that if you lie still and rest, you'll get the benefits of sleep, but I can't lie still. The aspirins are making me float, but my mind keeps working and I can't stop fidgeting. I remember when I swam for Jersey City—I felt something dark down there that gave me a chill. Maybe the reason I felt it was thinking was that it was part of my mind, and it's always been there, waiting for me."

He was striding strongly, planting his feet on each successive square of the pavement and thrusting his rigid body powerfully forward. His weightlifting was about to come to its fruition. As he got closer, they saw that his brow was clenched in concentration and he was seizing the air with his fists the same way he was seizing the sidewalk with his feet.

Joel said, "He's angry. Look out."

Marc said, "Don't worry. It'll be alright."

Ira was hurtling himself forward, like a train, and Marc felt an inrush of fear at something so unstoppable growing rapidly closer. At the same time, part of his mind remained detached and distracted itself for a moment by playing with the word *loco-motive*.

Ira's body crouched before Marc now, pulling energy up through the arms, the shoulders, the collarbone, to the base of the skull, and out through Ira's fierce, staring eyes. "I'll show you," he said in a deep rasp. He was shaking with rage. "This time," he thought, "the violence will be real. No more pussyfooting, backing down. All I got by putting it off was a noose that grows tighter."

Marc could see that Ira was attacking him, but Marc had no idea how to fight and didn't see any point in it. What could he accomplish by beating Ira up?

Ira swung and Marc put his hands out and said, "Stop it, please." But he wasn't blocking effectively. He was stooping and looking down at the sidewalk, which puzzled him by seeming to be tilted. Ira hit him solidly in the mouth with an uppercut. It shook him cold and split his lip. He felt numb and shocked, and when he looked up, things were whirling.

Marc was observing the scene from a chamber deep in his head, far from the action, which appeared on a screen in the distance. He felt guilty for having withdrawn: if only he could fight like a man, the situation wouldn't be so out of control. But he couldn't imagine the impulse to fight, couldn't grasp that he could do Ira more harm by not fighting. He stepped back as Ira swung. But Ira charged forward, hitting his shoulder and punching him in the cheek, just below the right eye. Marc looked down and saw the sidewalk covered with blur.

Then Joel stepped between the boys and said, "Come on. Cut it out now." Ira glowered, "Out of my way, old man. I'll kill him."

Joel said, "If you want to hit someone, champ, why don't you hit me? You did it already."

Ira pushed Joel and Marc into the street. "I will," he said, but he didn't hit Joel, only shoved, and he was unable to get around him. What Joel said about hitting him reminded him of remorse over the earlier blow. The old man and the young clinched for a minute, but Ira couldn't stand the physical contact, and he fell back with a furious stare. Marc moved away, leaning against a car, and put his handkerchief to his bleeding lip.

Judith came dashing out of the building and said, "Stop it now." Her voice had a

Through the early morning, as Ira hoped he was

threatening edge to it, barely holding back a scream that would be heard by most of the building. Ira stood his menacing ground for a few minutes while his mom said, "You should be ashamed of yourself," and his dad said, "What do you expect to accomplish?" Then Ira stalked into the house, saying, "I'll kill him. I'll murder the bastard."

Once they had ascertained that Marc was not seriously injured, the parents went with Marc to sit on a bench in front of the park and confer about what to do. They were all panicky, and united unusually by their agitation.

"We should have him taken away to some nice quiet place," Marc said. "He attacked me for no reason." As he spoke, he thought, "I'm betraying him because I'm chicken. That's how he'll see it. But that's distorted. I'm only facing the logic of the facts. It takes a strong argument to get them to spend money on anything, especially doctors." Then he asked, "And what was that you said about him hitting you, Dad?"

approaching sleep and knew he was not, he heard an extra hum under the drone of the city's night, a ghostly cricket. After an uneasy while, he was able to make it out and to realize that it was closer than he thought. It was inside. It was his father lilting:

> Diddle diddle bumchick,
> Dumchick, bumchick
> Diddle diddle dydle diddle dee

"It seems to be coming from the closet. How long since I looked in there? Is it four days? Little scary when time isn't clear. I realize that the chances are there's nothing in that closet. There was nothing last time I looked. But I thought it better not to try it." What if he should open the door to find a decorated chamber, a tabernacle? What if his father's chubby figure, covered with gold cloth and magenta jewels, was to grin out at him with the light streaming from its joyful eyes?

Now Ira stopped moving, although he was uncomfortable, because he felt that if he moved, he would call himself to

"Well, he punched me in the arm a few months ago, but it wasn't serious." He was thinking, "A king's ransom this is going to cost."

"How serious does it have to be?" Marc asked. "He wasn't done hitting me when you interrupted him. And thanks for that, Dad. It was brave of you." Joel turned his head to the side to belittle his bravery with a dismissive "Aaah." He was a hero.

"But," said Marc, "he said he'd kill me and he didn't sound like he was joking. He has to have professional help, but not a place like Bellevue."

"All those places are terrible," Judith said. "The state hospital is a snake pit and the private hospitals cost sky high. And how do we know it will do anything but make him angry?"

In a half-hearted way, Joel said, "We should wait and see what happens. He might get better." It was almost a question, quite unlike him.

"You want to save money," Marc said, "but he's getting worse. He's become really the attention of the figure who might be in the closet. So he lay still and sweated. Yet he felt that this being could see him, and even read his thoughts. "What can I do to keep my thoughts from him? Think about something else, liven things up. Letsee, a cheerful subject, something innocent so I'll stand clear of the charges, whatever they may be. Well, there's Marc and then there's Howdy Doody. May be best to combine them both for a double whammy: 'What time is it kids?'"

A chorus of children answered, "It's Howdy Doody Time!" and out came Marc as a puppet with freckles painted on his hard, glossy face. He said, "And keyuds, I hope you'll remember to drink two healthy glasses of fresh milk every day!"

Ira said, "Gee, Mr. Doody, you sound an awful lot like my daddy! But could you tell me now what I should dooo? I just don't seem to be bouncing and beaming the way I used tooo!"

For a moment it seemed as if Howdy's face could move somewhere other than his dangerous. If he stays around, he could kill somebody. And then what will be saved?" They looked at his split lip and swollen cheek, tension in their eyes.

"I have the number from a friend," Judith said, "of a man in Long Island who's supposed to be good, Schreber, but he's very expensive. I'm told Ira would have plenty of privacy and they use the latest methods."

No one had an alternative, so Joel went a block away to a phone booth and called. They waited outside, afraid to enter the apartment.

After less than two hours, during which they found little to say, a wailing ambulance arrived. Two men in white uniforms got the key from Joel and went in laden with parcels and two long metal poles. Twenty-two minutes later they came out with Ira on a stretcher bound up in a straitjacket. Ira was saying, "You fucks. You fucks."

Marc sat beside Ira in the ambulance as it drove through the bright green park. He had trouble convincing himself up-and-down mouth, but his exclamations continued their enthusiasm: "You know I'm on your side. You can free yourself. I learned it from you. To accept life, you have to realize that no one wants to hurt you. We want you to be happy."

At first this sounded appealing, but then Ira thought, "Great. If no one wants to hurt me, then I'm hurting myself. Not a happy thought. Hurting myself into oblivion may not be something I can take responsibility for, or even come close. Why should I accuse myself to clear everyone else, when everyone else seems to be wheeling and dealing, making sure they profit by my disintegration?"

Then the puppet stage faded until all he could see were the strings.

He was back in his bed, the only place he had a right to be. As he lay numbly hushed, he thought he heard words in the low, voiceless thrum of the demon closet. "Relax, honey. Enjoy yourself and feel sweet. I can wait for your skin, for your meat, for your heart." And Ira that Ira would not burst out any second, even though the straitjacket was reinforced by heavy canvas straps holding him to the stretcher poles. The contours of the cloth were swollen and bulging as if something twice as big as Ira were inside it, but they did not move. The unnatural tension of a tidal wave frozen in place. The parents, slumped further forward, could not hear.

Marc said, "Ira, believe me. I'm really sorry. It was a hard choice to make. We all felt ourselves pushed into rushing ahead. The fact is you weren't getting better, and this way, you can get better. You must know after all this time that I love you and want to help you. They'll take good care of you where we're going. These guys on the ambulance are just for emergencies. You'll have your own room. It's an excellent place. You'll be okay soon."

He felt it was trite and stupid; a good thing Ira wasn't hearing him. He tried to lighten up. "In fact, it's so expensive we can't keep you here long." But this hopeful line only generated the silent echo of humor that thought, "It would be seriously nice if I were asleep, but I'm not. I'm awake. I can't wake up."

When a little light appeared before five in the morning, he cautiously got up and went out. It was a relief to be in the air, and he felt surprising energy. He took the subway south to 23rd Street. "I need professional help," he thought. "There's no place else to go. They'll take care of me." He walked east. People were staring at him, knew what he was doing. Bellevue was an endless brick building with a big round white arch over the entrance.

Outside was a guard seated in a sentry box, an outpost in the war against insanity. The guard was a light-skinned, overweight Negro. Ira asked, "Is this the admissions part of Bellevue?"

The guard said, "Yeah, this is it. But listen, buddy, if I was you, I'd have a think before going in there. You may believe you have trouble when you're only in trouble, and it might not last. Life is plenty hard in there. Like as not you'll be wanting to get out before you can. Freedom may be terrifying, but it's yours."

falls flat. "Please don't worry. Don't let it bother you. You can be mad at me if you want. I suppose you think I'm doing this to get even with you, but that's not the way I feel at all. I'm doing this, we all are, because you need help. I wish I were braver and could handle you better, but it's obvious that it's no good for you to be this wild. You're going to a nice place in Long Island, a place where people get better quickly."

Inside himself, Marc heard Ira's voice saying, "You coward, you're doing this to control me. You betrayed me like a fish takes to water, and what you're doing to me now will never end." And he said to himself, "Yes, I hear you. Look in my eyes. Let me take some of your hatred. I'll hold it, keep it, won't forget it. But what could I do for you if I took all the abuse you could give me? Finally, we both have to follow certain logical rules. It's a drag to have to follow the old tyrant Reason, but it's likely a disaster not to. All I can do is stay with the best I can see by the light that I have. What else can I do?" and he said to himself, "What crap."

Ira sighed, "What you say is true and good, but what's after me, you see, is something that I can't escape in any way but this. Here is where society tells me to go for help. At the most important times, I have to be rational." He thought, "Great! Using reason to prove I'm out of my mind."

Ira asked someone at the door for the admissions desk. "It feels good to be going somewhere. Do people have this kind of thrill when they get married? I'll fill out my forms for a loonie license. Here's a role I can't fail to perform adequately. A little practice making faces and I'll be a pro."

At the admissions desk, there was a pretty nurse with dark eyes. He told her that he wanted to admit himself because he was depressed. She warned him, as the guard had, and gave him a form. Then she told him that he would have to wait for some time until a doctor was ready, and led him into the next room, which was large and filled with people. He leaned against the light green wall to wait, feeling giddy. "Make a commitment. I feel better already. Now the

Ira's head was not bound, but it did not move. His eyes seemed to stare up at the roof of the ambulance, hardly blinking. His muscles seemed to be constantly straining against the jacket that wrapped his arms around his chest, without letting up for a moment. He gave no sign—not even a movement of the eyes focused on something a few inches in front of him—to indicate that he knew Marc was there or that he followed what was happening.

He only repeated in a low, deliberate voice, "I'm nobody. I don't exist. I'm nothing. Nothing at all. I don't exist."

eagerness that vibrates through my body is going to be satisfied."

(Now that I can no longer connect to ordinary reality, I take over the narrative. Marc is only a filter through which I stream. He collects my dirt. The illusion of continuous order must be dislocated to see the order in which to tell what is most real about our lives, how everything is connected to everything else. This is the disorder through which we speak to each other in words that seem to fail, so we realize that our separate identities were defensive illusions. Now that we have lost each other, we are joined.)

12

SAVE THE COUNTY

1961   1966

After a long trip in the ambulance, they reached the hospital in Amityville where Ira would be committed. From the outside, it looked like a posh country club. They left Ira trussed up to be tackled by the attendants and went to the office, where they struggled to arrange the admission with a supercilious executive nurse. The parents tried to bargain down the astronomical price, and Judith threw a fit—or at least temporarily loosened the controls on her hysteria. But they didn't get a break: the nurse said that if they didn't have the money, they could send him to a public hospital. She said they had great expenses. The place seemed modern and specialized in schizophrenia, so they relented. They came home by train, exhausted. Since no one in the family drove, they took the train back two days later to see Dr. Schreber.

In September of 1965, Marc departed New York to pursue a Ph D. degree at the best school that admitted him, the University of California at Berkeley. He and Carol got two rooms on Parker Street, in the back of a wooden house with thin walls and slanty floors. Marc was ecstatic about Berkeley. "It's fantastic," he said, "a town filled with young people making their own lives away from their parents—free to recognize the truth about their feelings and about the world. Enjoying themselves and knowing that it's right to enjoy themselves so they can reform the way people live. Once people have gone beyond repression and war, how can they go back?"

The doctor was a tall, slim, handsome precise German. He said that Ira was very difficult and that schizophrenics sometimes had the strength of three people. At this point Marc observed to the parents that they could never have handled him. The doctor said that shock treatments were necessary if they were to keep Ira without either heavy sedation or violence. He said that these treatments would not hurt and would put Ira at peace. They agreed to the treatments. The doctor said that he was glad to see that Marc was not like his brother, and could tell that Marc was not the same type because Marc did not have a feminine face.

(Ira and Marc were going further from their home than they had ever been and finding new worlds. Did these two worlds live by reflecting each other? Marriage and the asylum were polar ends of a system that depended on them both.)

Above Marc and Carol lived Skip, who was blonde, and George, who was black. Friends of these guys were visiting constantly, especially girls. Marc, who worked so hard that he only slept about three hours a night, spent long stretches in the apartment grinding out papers. He was often alone because Carol had a job for the Alameda County Department of Welfare. Sometimes, as he would work, he heard someone who seemed to be building something upstairs. It was a steady hammering, and sometimes the carpenter seemed to hit his or her thumb and there would be a protracted scream.

The noise from upstairs seemed so strange, and Marc was so drowsy, that at one point he wondered if he were dreaming. It took him weeks to realize that the noise came from Skip and his girlfriend Karen making love. Then he counted and found that they sometimes did it seven times a day. When friends were visiting, Skip and Karen would occasionally step into the bedroom, and the loose, rickety bed soon would begin banging against the wall.

"How do you feel today, Mr. Glogover?" Dr. Schreber stood elegantly in the doorway of Ira's room. He looked as if Ira could jump him, but it was probably a trap. Ira felt debilitated and he knew there were attendants just out of sight in the hall.
"Awful."
"But you have calmed down."
"I calmed down because part of my mind was washed away. If you kill me, I'll be even calmer."
"Nothing was taken from your mind. You may forget a few things temporarily, but you may be sure that they will be back. Do you in any part of your body feel a pain as if a bone were sprained?"
"My right hand. The fingers."
"Can you move them?"
"Yes."
"I will look at it if you promise not to strike me."
"Don't bother." There was a pause.

Marc and Carol never saw the neighbors in front, who entered on the other side, but they heard them because the side entrance to the back apartment was right near a ventilation shaft from the bathroom of the front one. The neighbors argued in the shower. He said, "No matter where you go, you'll always play the same roles you learned from your mother." She said, "You force these roles on me by your rigid behavior, then you blame me for them." They were a high-class version of the parents, and reminded Marc of how good his life was with Carol.

The pattern of their life together was laid down on an early date in a restaurant on the Grand Concourse. Carol lived on the other side of Bronx Park, an extension of the Botanical Gardens. In Jahn's they shared a hamburger and he told her to have the last delectable bite on the plate, but she said he should have it. Their main activity was trying to please each other, and their typical arguments consisted of each asking to give more, to do more to make the other happy. It was a utopia, but filled with potential for laceration—not only because the competition to bestow bliss involved selfishness, but because it led in Berkeley toward the need to give each other the freedom to be unfaithful. And the generosity was more hers than his.

Once he had a talk on Mosholu Parkway on the other side of Bronx Park with a friend who was a junkie at the time, though Marc didn't know it. Morris said that junkies have an absolute attachment to reality because whatever mayhem may happen, they *have* to get their heroin. Marc and Carol could attack and betray and denounce each other, but what they could give each other had them hooked because it was beyond belief, like religion. They couldn't imagine they could possess it, the heroin of freeing themselves by making each other free.

In the apartment beside Marc and Carol's on Parker Street lived a student named Rose. Friday and Saturday nights, when her boyfriend would visit, she would scream and cry out, "No, Roger. Don't do it! Anything but that. Please stop!" At first Marc worried about whether to rescue her, and blamed himself for not having the courage to knock on their door. Then he realized she did it week after week.

"You are looking good, today, Mr. Glogover."

"Hoo, boy. Do I look more appetizing from the door or from the ceiling?"

"I assured you that the treatments would not hurt you."

"They did something worse than hurt."

"Whatever do you mean by that?"

Ira lay staring at his knees.

Dr. Schreber said, "Mr. Glogover, I am here to help you. If you can tell me anything about your condition that could assist me in understanding it …"

"Look, Kraut, I know who you work for and exactly what you did to me."

"It is no secret for whom I work: your family, which is concerned enough to pay me a large fee although they cannot well afford it. As for what I did, I described the treatment to you, but you were not conscious when it was administered."

"Part of me was, my head."

"What did this part, as you call it, perceive?"

Ira held back for a moment and felt tension building. Then he burst out, "You shoved your dick into my mouth hard and squirted into my brain. I'm not being ironic about this. This is real."

"That's absurd. I was in touch with my assistants during the entire procedure."

"I don't care how many assistants you were touching. You wanna hear, right? Right? Honey you must've been real excited, 'cause you shot your juice into me quick. You like that slippery grey matter, heh? I want you to know I felt it all. Your drugs didn't stop me. My conniptions didn't stop me. I could feel your foreskin rubbing back and forth in my brain, your hot scum washing away my memories."

"It's unfortunate that you cannot use your fine intelligence to help yourself instead of imagining in such a fantastic way that things are worse than they are. I had no contact with you during your treatment."

Ira said, "I suppose you're not working for my father either. He just happens to say the same thing. That I like to screw myself up. But I'm not screwing myself, Jah ... Joel, you're doing it. You're doing it!"

"I am not Joel. You are getting better and will continue to get better. Do not alarm yourself with bad dreams that may have no relation to reality and may soon vanish." To himself, the doctor said, "He will need more treatments than I thought."

As he left, Ira called out, "Nazi. Go tell the lampshade that you just gave it a shower."

The woman underneath was a belly dancer who liked to bring men over, play Edith Piaf, and burn incense. Music and aroma would come wafting up through the floorboards around one a.m. as Marc was trying to interpret imagery, and Carol, who had to get up early to visit her clients, was trying to sleep. Carol had a lot to do, and she cut corners. One night he said to her, "Shouldn't you put on a diaphragm?"

"It's okay," she said, "I don't need it. I had a period only ten days ago." Twenty-five days later, they found out she was pregnant.

Ira fell back and looked at the wooden rafters of the ceiling. Then he remembered the opposite corner. There was a dark hole in this corner of the ceiling, and Ira divined that it contained a camera observing him. He turned himself to a habitual position from which as little of himself as possible could be seen by this corner.

A minute passed, and then another, and Ira felt again the familiar weight of time in this fish tank designed to take away his mind. The room was decorated self-consciously to look simple, rural, and wholesome, but the floorboards were warped, reminding him of *The Cabinet of Dr. Caligari*, which ends with the hero discovering that he is in an asylum, and that the evil doctor he wants to expose is his keeper.

Marc and Carol's most serious problems came from a group of bikers who lived in the house next door. Marc was constantly delirious with worry about his work, but he felt this as a privilege, something he craved. These guys—varying in number from three to maybe eight—seemed to have dropped out of the university en masse and settled down to a life of noisemaking competitions. The driveway was so narrow that they lived about six feet away. They had parties at which they wore Viking outfits: bearskins and pointed helmets with horns. The parties went on about five days and six nights a week. Motorcycles were constantly roaring in with cases of beer strapped onto their racks.

Marc screwed up his courage for Carol's sake early one morning and went over to the bikers to tell them to be quiet. One of them picked up a fifteen-inch Bowie knife and asked what he wanted to do about it. Marc backed off and said that his wife was pregnant and needed sleep. They said they would try to be quiet, but didn't.

Marc got earplugs, but even with the plugs, it was still hard to sleep or read John Gower with the Rolling Stones swaggering full blast or a bike being tuned outside his window. He could feel the floor vibrating.

Separated as if by a glass enclosure from the active part of himself, Ira reflected, "What do I have to cling to? My life belt is sadness, grief over my own murder." His muscles tensed sporadically and he tried to calm them. "I have to try to be clear about the disgust of knowing that the old man's organ is replacing my own, my own being. That those feelings, images, and ideas that I have had, that I might have had, in the past, in the future, are being wiped out before I can communicate them, before I can even know them myself.

"I don't know what they were, and it'll get harder and harder for me to figure out what I knew. Maybe it was like the feeling I had when Barbara was sweet to me, or riding down the hill on the bicycle in Newark, or when I ran to rescue Marc. But she's forgotten that she forgot me and he's out to get me. And when I have nice feelings, happy feelings, I have to learn that they're going to be shocked, smashed, raped, twisted, electrocuted. I'll never recover those lost selves. They're somewhere in outer space, trying to talk to me, withheld by the old man.

All I can remember is the sadness of losing them. And even the sadness will be taken from me, as lost as my foreskin. All I'll have will be the pain of this moment. And the old man will make me take it again and again, and say that I like it to clear myself, even believe that I like it, like the lowest prostitute." He gazed at the artificial furniture designed to be innocent and heard the artificial silence that was a commercial for normality.

Some of the neighbors called the police to complain about the noise, and the bikers quieted down while the cops were there, but they resumed their ruckus a half-hour after the fuzz left. A few times after this, one of the bikers went out on his back porch around two a. m. and yelled at the neighborhood. "You motherfuckers! You want me to shut up? I don't give a shit what you want!" Marc took this as a positive sign because it showed that the bikers were not just fun-loving guys, but sick people, and that no one could deal with them any better than he could. The bikers got worse for a while when they got a set of drums; eventually one of them stabbed another one seriously enough to disable him for a week, and after that they quieted down somewhat.

Two weeks after his shock treatments ended, Ira, who was now more subdued and apparently less intelligent, was transferred to a state hospital in the Bronx. He was not about to be released soon, but the private place was too expensive. Though he had wanted to leave Amityville, he had much less privacy in the new place. He was surrounded by groaning, whining, threatening, and incontinent men whom he was pretty well able to fight off physically, but they got to him anyway. There was one whose saffron face was wider than it was high who sat with such a sly smile that Ira sometimes imagined this one was controlling his mind without speaking.

Despite the bikers and other hassles, Marc and Carol loved Berkeley. The landscape was so soft and the people were so free that it seemed the rivers of paradise were running through their bodies. There were so many cultural events that were revelations, mixing art and politics. Art was politics was making love was expanding your mind. The people who mattered to them would share private ideas and feelings in public, kiss each other in the streets, and give each other things without expecting anything in return. They were showing off their kindness and tolerance instead of the traditional mode of showing off cruelty and chauvinism. They were filled with light by the feeling that they were changing the world, singing silly songs to themselves.

Ira had refused to see Marc in Amityville, but here in the huge Bronx hospital during a Christmas break, he finally spoke to him. The first thing Ira did, as they stood with the parents on the sixteenth floor, was to put his hand on the upper part of Marc's arm in a respectful way, stare at him, and say, "We're good friends, aren't we?" His hand felt like the image of an ordinary human hand on Marc's soft tricep.

In that simple gesture of comradeship they both saw themselves in each other, the same thing in two different positions. They felt the pride of their bodies as two tall, handsome young men filled with life, sharing a breath of hope. Yet at the same time they felt that they weren't really there, that the flesh they touched was only playing a role.

Although he said, "Sure, Ira, of course we are. I'm so glad to hear you say it," Marc couldn't help seeming uneasy. He thought, "I can't tell whether he means it or is being ironic. He may feel a lot of affection, or want to feel it. May be doing his best to smile, yet it wavers on the edge of a sinister grimace. At least it does to me, but maybe that's because I'm afraid of him—and my own smile may not be very convincing. A smile is not a smile in an asylum, where every gesture has to be calculated in relation to the desperate need to seem normal in order to get out. Maybe I mistrust his repentance because he's been a hero to me. I don't want him to compromise his defiance, but the daemonic heroism that inspired me is murder for him."

Ira thought, "Jesus, when I can use a little affection from this bastard, he's calculating every step. Better keep smiling."

When the time came to leave Berkeley and go back to New York for the summer, Marc and Carol packed what they could to make a Santa Fe train. Their friend Katka was coming to drive them to the station. They looked at their old broken-down bed, and they felt regret to be leaving this place full of excitement where they had discovered the freedom of a new world. They weren't sure whether it was the town's freedom or theirs, and really whether or not it existed. So they got on the slanting bed without a sheet and had one more for the road, fitting naturally into each other's happiness. Katka arrived right after they finished and they piled everything into a convertible, including six shopping bags rapidly filled with clothes and sundries, and raced down Grove Street to the station. On the train Carol, who was six months pregnant, found herself bleeding. She recovered, even though the three-day rail trip across the country was an ordeal. They tried not to dwell on the extent to which the freedom of Berkeley was freedom from Ira.

When Marc returned from Berkeley, he tried to be warm and cordial to his brother, who was back at home. He had told himself when he went West that he would see Ira over the summers. But now their bond seemed to be weaker than ever: polite, lifeless, and marked by apprehension on both sides. While Marc was away, Ira did two oil paintings of the kind in which you fill in spaces bearing numbers with corresponding colors. They were carefully done still lifes of musical instruments, loving cups, and watches against wooden boards, yet they still looked like paint. Marc tried to say something nice about them, but it was obvious that he wasn't impressed when he told Ira that he should try to do original things.

Ira was reading Jane Austen, which gave him a sense of peace; here again, Marc was hardly able to conceal that he thought her too conventional. Marc told himself that Ira must be reading this stuff to escape reality. Marc assumed that the revolutionary and visionary writers he loved represented reality. In fact, reality, a reality as powerful as life, was speaking to Ira at odd moments when his resistance to life grew strained.

A few times that summer Ira took two busses across the Bronx to visit Marc and Carol in the West Bronx apartment they were using for their sojourn. On these visits, he talked and played cards, and if the talk was often halting, it had its amusing moments. Ira was developing a comic persona based on his special interest group. "Us loonies," he would say, "get to talk to ourselves whenever we want. It's a privilege of the craft."

"You haven't been so happy in a long time, kiddo," Ira thought, or was it Marc? "You're stable enough to be playful. This means that you're getting better, making progress, feeling good, looking strong, or all of the above. Don't laugh. It's clearly the path that works best for you, for me. Wisecracks don't help, and don't give me that guff about how I sound like Dad. I'm you, and we wouldn't be alive if it not for Dad. Everyone sounds like Dad or you can't hear. Dad did the best he could with the paranoia life dealt him. You have to take responsibility for your life. Think in paragraphs, man, be continual." If Marc was thinking this, it may have emphasized the hopeful aspect of Ira's situation to avoid blaming Marc for deserting him, but Ira may have done the same. Yes. Brotherhood. Maybe the medication was helping.

Early in December, Carol had a girl—whom they called Sybil—and just before the new parents returned to Berkeley, Ira visited them to see the baby. He asked to be left alone with her, and Marc was a tad nervous about this, but let him do it without hesitation. Yet he watched through a gauze curtain. Ira went in, knelt beside the crib, looked at the sleeping baby thoughtfully for a few minutes, and kissed her cheek as gently as a butterfly. He thought to himself, "I feel so happy to be doing something normal, like a kid. A baby tells us that everyone can be saved."

13

THE NIPPLE

1964   1966

It took Ira a year and a half to get out of the hospitals, partly because he couldn't hold his anger in convincingly. When he did get out, he was a heavily drugged twenty-four-year-old child who had to stay with the parents. By the time Ira was released, Marc was married, so Ira, with no possibility of living on his own, had the boys' room to himself. The honey-colored furniture that had lost its luster no longer served two promising boys, but a broken promise. He struggled to finish the last few courses that he needed for his degree. Earlier, he had a B+ average, but now he got a few Fs before he managed to get enough Cs and Ds. He finally finished his B. A. after Marc had already gotten his M.A. Ira got his picture taken wearing a mortarboard, looking confident and handsome.

Early in his second year at Berkeley, Marc went to a reading by the poet Robert Duncan. Dancing beautifully on his words, in the airy hesitation of his rhythm, suspending his mesmerizing crossed gaze over the audience seated on the floor of Cody's Bookstore, Duncan described a man's breast as a delicate fountain of loveliness. A few weeks later, Marc dreamed that he was back in New York and had found Ira improved, wondrously improved.

Ira's degree didn't lead anywhere. Newspaper work was out of the question. He got a job in the post office as a sorter, but he had trouble handling the work. He couldn't keep track of the categories involved, the scheme, as heavily drugged as he was, and they fired him. He felt that they counted his record of mental problems too heavily against him. He embarked on a Kafkaesque process of petitioning to be reinstated through the civil service: filling out forms, going to offices, constructing defenses, and searching for hope in the ambiguity of dismissal. He continued this process long after it was clear to everyone else that it would not work.

One day, after Ira had been turned down by a secretary who seemed to be laughing at him, he thought about it (saving your grace) logically. "The poets all say (as junior would have it) that if you suffer, you'll get a reward. People need to believe this in order to be motivated to live. But looksee. For me now, all these years, there seems to be no reward, just suffering. I have to adjust to only suffering if I'm going to keep acting sensible without blowing my top—and put off reward way out of sight. What reward could I get from the parents that they haven't already given me?

"Yet ultimately, I have to believe that it'll lead to something. But how? In a future very far away. Maybe for someone else, maybe for Marc. The likeliest culprit, the one who gets all the happiness. But he has no idea what I'm up to, or down to. He's over there in the West Bronx, with his books and his wife, a sort of absentee landlord. But in the end, my suffering sho'nuff has to lead somewhere, if only because it can't go on forever, a logical fact without much tact."

One night in 1966 after another rough day—his claim that there had to be another channel of appeal had gotten only a raised eyebrow—around the time of Marc's dream, Ira dreamed that he was back teaching Marc to ride the bicycle. Marc was eight and he was thirteen and he started Marc out by holding the handlebar and trotting beside him on a wide flat field of sunlit grass. It was in Orange, New Jersey, and there was an orange billboard in the distance that read "Dad's Root Beer."

"Yes," Ira said in Marc's dream, "I can see now that I was driven by adolescent rebellion. It was all so foolish. I understand now, and it's such a relief to be free of all that bitterness. As I've grown older, I've come to my senses, realized that everyone is trying in his way."

"I'm real glad to hear that," Marc said. "Now we can both get together and stop worrying. I always needed you and depended on you. What are people born for but to be happy?"

With Ira holding the bars, Marc felt secure in Ira's dream. He watched the grass fly by. Even the air seemed to be moving quickly, as if the air were a river, the clouds alive. He felt strong because Ira was holding him, his solid older brother, as if he were living through Ira, an extension of Ira. Through Ira he was competent.

As he jogged along, Ira began to wonder why he was having Marc's perceptions. He looked at his brother, and the boy seemed happy, but impassive, looking expectantly ahead. "Does he know I'm having his thoughts?" Ira felt a need to speak: "Let me know," he said, "when you're ready for me to let you go."

Marc, on his bicycle, said, "Are you tired of running?"

"No," Ira said, "but you've got to learn to do it for yourself." He felt clear and light, as if he could trot forever. Then he felt something opening inside himself and he remembered that he had once been used to thinking with Marc, but that he did not seem to have done it for a long time. To Marc, his thoughts could be beautiful, wise, funny.

In his dream Marc was so happy that he let out a high, slow sigh, singing under his breath, and his shoulders swayed forward. He was moving toward Ira as Ira moved toward him. The hardness of Ira's face was gone and he looked into Marc's eyes with soft intention. Then they embraced. His cheek was on Ira's neck and it felt cool and firm.

   Marc held the softened strength of Ira's shoulders and sank into him and kissed his chest, which was clear and smooth and soft. Like Joel, both brothers had large breasts for men, and Marc gently took Ira's nipple in his mouth, a tender point of opening into the soul.

   Ira's adventures in these years were few, and he survived none of them without harm. He was refused a driver's license after testing, partly because of his record, and this decreased not only his mobility, but his identity. It made his life obvious without relief. One of his accomplishments at this time was to complete his fishing reel, which he'd won as a precocious twelve-year-old, by getting a rod. Marc, on one of his visits, handled the green plastic rod attached to the reel, and congratulated him, and then Ira set out to use them.

   In his dream, Ira was thinking about thinking with Marc so intensely that he was surprised when Marc said, "I'm ready." He looked at Marc and Marc looked at him and they both began to smile. Ira felt joyful, but it was disconcerting to look at someone beaming that way. He was afraid he might lose control of the bike and the pedal would cut into his feet, spraining his ankles and tripping him.

   Then Ira thought, "Why not be happy? If someone smiles at you, why don't you smile back? Why do you always have to be withdrawn, like a prawn?" So he smiled and Marc smiled, and their smiles were bright and natural, the white teeth of childhood, the innocent eyes like leaves, the same smile of brothers, looking at each other looking at each other. And they both knew that they were happy and were sharing this happiness. And then Ira slowly said, "One, two, *three*," and he let go of the handlebars.

In Marc's dream, Ira smiled and put his hand on Marc's head and said, "There, it's alright. I forgive you, nothing to forgive. I know you always wanted to help. A person isn't responsible for what he doesn't know about. We won't misunderstand each other again." Marc's right eye was closed against Ira's left nipple. He opened it and felt the soft protuberance of the nipple against his eyeball, and Ira felt the moistness of Marc's eye kissing his breast.

Ira got up at 4:30 and took the subway, followed by a two-hour bus trip out to Long Island, to do some salt-water fishing. He was by himself, his friends long ago moved away or lost touch, but he had heard of some guys using this route and had wanted to do it for seven years, dreaming about it in the asylum. There were closer places to fish, but he hadn't had luck with them. It was a nice day, and he smiled a little too much at the people on the bus, thinking, "Now I'm doing something good, getting better."

The pier was a straight road leading into the sea. As he walked it, he felt a deep reverberation through his heels that thrilled and frightened him. "Don't pay attention to the fear," he told himself. "It's irrational." He felt life springing in the muscles of his torso and shoulders. "I'm going on an adventure. Hey, even if it doesn't go that great, I'm trying. That's what Marc would say: We should live life when we have it, and not let worries about the future detract from the present."

As Ira let go of the bars, Marc pumped ahead and held his balance. "Look at me," Marc said, "I can do it. It's easy." Ira had an uncanny sensation that he could feel both his pride and his brother's pride. He felt both handles of the handlebars and he saw the front wheel penetrating the grass before him. And he also felt his own hands and feet running without effort. And the sense of consciously possessing two personalities at once, both filled with joy, flooded him with exultation. And he said to himself, "This is more than a human being could feel. It must be what God feels."

Marc pressed his temple to Ira's chest, hearing his brother's heart beating, and seemed to hear the words of a favorite poem echo in a soft, childish voice:

> O be a nurse to me and sing the old song
>   that where I dream,
> taking wrong for right and right for wrong,
> to find myself before some grievous sin,
> shit and blood draining down from the tree
> as if rot ate beneath the skin,
>   I shall come home
> having prepared the door and the key.

Five people, lined up with heavy gear in front of a barred window, were paying and getting tickets to take boats. Ira waited in line and reached an old man in a yachting cap with a white five-o'-clock shadow. When he asked for a ticket, the old man asked him for his driver's license.

"What for?" he asked.

"For security," said the old man.

"Well, I haven't got a driver's license."

"Well, I'm afraid you can't take a boat then—unless you got a fifty dollar security deposit, plus rental fee."

"Whaddaya *mean?*"

"I mean just what I say, sonny. And besides, you couldn't do much deep-sea fishing with that tackle."

Then Ira's bicycle, with Marc on it, began to lengthen or run to the side as a bead of paint on a piece of paper does when the paper is tilted. As if the perspective were being stretched out, the bike and Marc stretched as a streak across the field. Then the wheels of the bike became eyes, with silver radii of spokes sparkling around sky-blue pupils. And he heard a voice that seemed to come from the distance or from the sky, and the voice said, "Take me. I'm lonely. Take me." The voice came from everywhere, from all around. And Ira said, "I will, I will." He was weeping, something he hadn't done for a long time. Brimming tears from his eyes, he was weeping for joy, and he cried out, exultantly, from his throat, from his chest, from his belly, "Here I am. Yes, please."

In Marc's dream, Marc and Ira lay down beside each other in a sloping, sunlit field of grass and embraced from head to toe. Feeling his brother's skin sliding on his own, Marc realized that the feeling between them was growing sexual and he thought, "I'm turning into a homo, his dick will come to my mouth. He'll screw me. I can't let that happen." And he woke with a pang, regretting that he'd broken that blissful contact.

On the pier Ira knitted his brows and stared at the old man. He felt like exploding and cursing him, but he was afraid to. He dreaded losing control in public. Even trying to argue was dangerous. He had to drop his eyes shamefully under the old man's arrogant gaze. He tried to control his breathing. His cheeks were pulling his face downward as he withdrew from the window. "Good thing I can't cry anymore," he thought. "I'd better try not to think, try to get on the next bus so I won't be stuck here."
He sat in a secluded, shady spot near the bus stop until he was able to board the bus. He said to himself, "Although this is a difficult situation, I can control it." But he couldn't drown out another voice that said, "Sure you can take it. That's obviously what you were made for, to take it and take it. But what an asshole you were to think you could do anything right."
So he dragged his gear back on the long trip, alone and purposeless. The light seemed unnatural, and the bus wheezed foul gas. He took another pill so that the image of the old man gloating to himself in his tabernacle would not be so sharp. The others on the bus could all see exactly what he was doing there, popping his pill with his dry tackle and his empty box. As the pill began

to take effect, as usual, he had a feeling that something was being stolen from him.

In his dream, Ira heard ecstatically all these voices coming from all around him, and he felt as if eyes were watching him from all sides, holding him with their beams. Now he realized that there was a great chorus of voices that had been lost to him around the time he had lost contact with Marc and had his treatments. He had been living in deprivation without these voices, and now they had come back. He felt rich, restored. He wanted to tell Marc about it, and felt it possible to talk to Marc.

But Marc seemed to have exploded, and Ira felt as if he had caused it by not paying attention to Marc, as if he secretly wanted it. But where was Marc? He had to awake to find him and tell him that all these voices were back. Then he awoke, glowing with excitement that he had recovered something so incredible.

As Marc awoke, he had a strong feeling that his dream must be a positive sign, that it showed that Ira would get better. He should call Ira in New York or write to him and tell him what had happened. It seemed to him that Ira might react favorably, that the dream must correspond to some improvement or potential in him. Its recounting would show Marc's love and give Ira hope.

But then he realized that it would probably hurt Ira because of the contrast between the dream and the truth; and that it would sound sappy, even if he avoided indicating the disturbing sexual angle. He remembered that Ira was surly and suspicious in any discussion of his condition. He heard from Ira's viewpoint the words, "I dreamed you were well," and he felt a deep twinge. He was always doing stupid things to hurt his brother. He resigned himself to the fact that he couldn't tell Ira such a thing. In the early morning one can wake feeling that the world can be made new, but as the day goes on, one wakes further and further from that waking until one finds oneself drifting toward sleep.

After Ira returned from the hospital, the parents grew more manageable in their dread. He was sometimes sorry to see them so frightened, but mostly he was glad they could be controlled. When Joel told him what he was doing wrong, he would growl, "Shut *up*," with a strong accent on the second word, and after he had said this four or five times, getting louder each time, the old man would back off. Sometimes it amused Ira to say, "Okay, you're right. I'm wrong. You win." But this would not stop Joel, who would go on, "So why don't you change?" Yet he was no longer certain that Ira should be blamed for not knowing the answer. Ira could see that he was not happy to be right after all, and Ira wondered to himself, "If he didn't really want to be right, then what the hell did he want? He's like those guys in the hospital who want something, but don't know what."

Ira felt the warm consciousness of his dream drain out of him as he realized with an ache that he could never tell Marc about the voices he had discovered, though Marc was the only person he could tell. For Marc was on the other side of the continent and could not be forgiven. Ira was back in this room with the childish furniture and bad memories. The room where he had tried to stand fast while they twisted his arms into the straitjacket. The room Marc had escaped, next to the bedroom of his aging parents. He lapsed into depression and began to forget the dream. It seemed that there was no way that he could forgive his brother, but perhaps there was a way, difficult, but possible.

One of the things Carol went shopping for was a nipple for Sybil's bottle: the old one had split. Sybil, who was seven months old, was left asleep with Marc, but when he played some wailing saxophone solos on the phonograph, she woke early and was hungry. Marc tried to amuse her by holding her up and spinning her, which usually worked; but she was fretful, and the motion annoyed her. Her mouth made sucking movements, but there was no bottle. She started to cry, and he held her, rocked her, and tried to soothe her, but it didn't help much. Her crying grew louder and her face turned red. Then she shifted into shrieking spastically, and her face became purple. Marc was petrified: what could he do?

In deciding to go to Berkeley, Marc realized that it might be best for him to stay in New York because he was the closest one to Ira; but he felt that Ira had been alienated from him by what Ira saw as his betrayal. His attempts to talk seriously about Ira's problems pained Ira, so he avoided such talk. There seemed to be little he could say to Ira or do for him. Change for the better seemed so unlikely that action hardly seemed desirable. Moreover, Marc was afraid of Ira, and wanted to get away from the burden of his presence. If Marc had taken time from his studies to concentrate on thinking of ways to help Ira, it probably wouldn't have done any good. So he told himself, and so he went to the new world.

In his panic, Marc had an idea. He took off his undershirt and presented his right nipple to the howling baby. Sybil seemed to notice that the breast looked funny, but she stopped crying actively (though she still shook), and she soon plunged forward and put her mouth to it, which was enough to make Marc's nipple stick out. As she sucked, she quieted down, though she noticed that the nipple was small and she wondered when the milk would come. Marc felt proud that he could help her, though Sybil was biting him. This must be why God made babies without teeth, but even so there were some cutting moments. After a while, she got exasperated at the lack of milk and began to sniffle a bit, but he could calm her momentarily by putting the nipple back in her mouth to revive her hope. She hadn't really returned to serious crying when Carol got home.

14

PRESSING LIDLESS EYES

1966-67

Dr. Mendelson was not well-shaven, and this implied that he was profoundly concerned, more like an artist than an official. He was bald as a potato to emphasize his brain and to show that he suffered as his patients did. His bright yellow tie seemed like an accident, yet designed to make you sympathize with anyone caught in such a thing. Every thread of his classy but casual clothes, every atom of his being, was calculated to calm you, to help me. But this profusion of striving to soothe could enclose you, could amount to a trap. His hands were too still, his peacefulness part of a concealed effort to control. Indeedimo. He could pretend he wasn't here, but I couldn't. If I looked at him too closely, cracks might appear.

His furniture was tasteful, uh huh, muted and serene. Described itself in a murmur. Probably grey, but it was hard to tell in the hushed light whether it was grey or beige or light blue or pale green. It enticed me to stay there, whispering, "Wouldn't you just love to stick around forever, kiddo?" But I couldn't stay: "We regret to inform you that you aren't good enough, expensive enough." It was like the fancy parts of Schreber's place, the parts beyond where I was confined. Now with Mendelson it seemed I was closer to these parts, but I wasn't really. The wall was still there. Mos definitely learned the hard way it would be dishonest or nuts to give in to the temptation to pretend it was caused by anything but my ever-loving mind. Face the facts, Jack.

Mendelson asked, "You really think your father was trying to seduce you when he took you to see the Yankees? For seduction, the Giants or the Dodgers would make more sense."

He was trying to lighten me up, melt my resistance. Joel isn't a giant or a dodger. He's a small man trying to be big, to be a Yankee doodle dandy. I said, "He didn't admit it, maybe even didn't realize it, didn't even know he was concealing it, but every atom of his being was calculated to infiltrate you, to degrade you. He doesn't know it like an animal doesn't know the meaning of his actions, but that means he can't stop."

Hey, I was a star. Mendelson was feeling up my every word. The star of my own destruction. Could play the role better than anyone, but it's the role of a clown, someone who gives you pleasure by humiliating himself.

Mendelson asked, "What did he do to molest you after taking you to the ball game?"

"He put his hand on my rear end."

"Well, many fathers pat their sons there, not to mention daughters. It may not be necessary to see this as seriously harmful."

I said. "But the way he did it was creepy. It made me feel weird." His hand seemed to stop to become aware, to think of my softness. I felt there was something wrong with me. The feeling I shouldn't feel seemed to come from outside my body, but it was inside me like another mind hiding, waiting to expose itself. A vampire hidden inside, in my heart, drinking the circulation of my blood, so every movement of every part of my body was caressing him, feeling the wetness of his mouth."

When I was eight I saw him across the room touch Mom's rear end by the sink. Their backs were to me and I could see him fondling her roundness, moving toward her crack. She pulled away and glared at him in outrage. Darling little me had supposed love was romantic, but now I saw that it was a simmering infection. Then I turned away and looked at the Sunday morning sunlight in the kitchen. Tiny particles of dust were skittering through the glare like feelings that can't be controlled or known.

When Joel caressed me, I moved away and said, "Don't." Then I closed my eyes and saw the dust dancing in the brightness. It gave me a chill and I felt broken apart, like the pieces of me were bouncing in a void, the ball that bounces too quickly over the words of a song at the movies.

Mendelson said, "These unhealthy feelings are not central to you. You say they attack you from outside. The active force that makes you conscious makes you want to live. Don't let yourself be invaded by something that isn't really you, something that is against you."

I pulled back and saw in my mind a green woman with a cruel smile on her beautiful young face looking down as if she were on a cloud with golden eyes that were fearfully bright, burning with a dreadful glowing gleam of joy. She had what she wanted and the doctor's words were powerless against her. Yet I saw her from the side, couldn't see her from the front because she came from someone else's mind. Now her eyes were kind, flowing with pity, and this made me happy for a sweet moment, but then the happiness trembled into a fatal terror.

There was a pile of dolls, pale, naked and smoothly shining with lifelessness. I felt, if only they could come alive! But if they moved, they could turn malignant, infants who could talk and sneer, grinning, speaking fetuses. They told me that I was dead, that when I was born I had passed the border that leads from life to death. So death could be a blessing.

I said, "What's really me may be what I feel most strongly. My core may be something I can't bear." I closed my eyes and looked at the inside of my eyelids, a pattern of light without depth that was fading. It felt like I was seeing the other side of my awareness, my internal thought retreating toward the past. Seeing that the movement toward the future moves toward the past. That waking is falling asleep.

Mendelson said, "The part of you that can't bear it isn't really you. Your sense of yourself has to believe in itself to continue, to go on. What makes you exist has to be most real to you."

I said, "I may be kidding myself if I believe or make a belief that my survival doesn't depend on bondage, on being possessed. You want me to claim the greatest consciousness, but what you make me concentrate on, what you map out for me, are eerie spectacles from my childhood, nightmares that invade my mind, upsetting me insidiously." Isn't this myself as you and I see it?

Mendelson said, "These bad experiences abusing you from outside are buried in you like infected splinters as the source of your disturbance. If you examine them, you can cure the infection. If you understand them, you can see how irrational they are, damage built on misunderstanding. Your father seems to be an emotional slob, maybe somewhat crazy, yet he works hard to support you and you've given me enough information yourself to indicate that he wants, in his own diseased way, to help you. Everyone has his *mishegas*. You have to live with it. The way your parents live with you, put up with the sorrow they feel because they love you."

I was silent. Why should we continue hurting each other? To live with him is an affliction from which I may never recover, partly because my regret for their sorrow is burning me on fire. But what justifies him defeats me. I said, "The me he wants to help is an idea so twisted that it's light years from being my own." That's why I seem under your brilliant light to have no being but the infection of disturbance—my precious version of love, the sum of my injuries. The profile of the green woman lifted itself slowly backward as if to let knowledge sink in.

Mendelson said, "If your dad wants to help something he believes is you, you have a motivational basis there for doing everything you can to make him aware of the fantastic nature of his idea of you, from which you want to free both of yourselves by recognizing the decent side of his devotion. I've talked to him and he feels real regret at what he's done to you and wishes he could learn to do better."

I thought, "Talked about me behind my back. The green woman opens the mouth of a fish to show sharp teeth that penetrate flesh. And you're most certainly lying to claim Joel recognizes any part of what he did to me. As if you want to make it as obvious as possible that you're lying."

I said, "I've been with him all my life, and his wish to do better doesn't do anything to actual reality except jeer at it. It's like someone who never leaves the toilet wishing to be a highly cultivated angel. Religion is a masquerade to justify death, and his wish to be good is nothing but an excuse to justify his evil. The more he believes in it, the more harmful it is.

"This drive toward being better is a construction you impose or force on me. I used to play chess with my kid brother, who wasn't much good at it. What you and I say to each other is like a game of chess. Each move leads to the next, but this is a game I can't possibly win, 'cause your assumption of health entitles you to call the rules. You want to reveal my true self, but that self is manufactured by you. You can't pull a rabbit out of a hat unless you put it there."

Mendelson said, "That was an intelligent argument, but you shouldn't use your intelligence against yourself, so that it attacks the existence of yourself."

I said, "Joel says the same thing."

I thought, "What else is intelligence actually for? Did anybody ever get anywhere except by using intelligence to attack himself? Is intelligence ever anything else except attacking oneself? Sweetheart, you could learn from me, if you weren't such a dimwit—so pleased with yourself, so superior, knowing all, godlike. Hey, what if the creature attacking me is life, surrounding me, filling every moment, running away from itself?"

15
HAPPINESS

1967

"They're both asleep and I'm tickled pink I have time to talk to you. Shirley, it may seem like *tsuris*, but in fact its finer than anything else. The other stuff is what's cheap and flashy. You may say it's a nightmare, I say a holiday, and I'm not kidding. You know how I like to get *fapitzed* with jewelry and fancy garments. But as the Almighty is my witness, there is nothing more precious than to have someone who needs you without a doubt, even if he doesn't know it, which of course is the usual with men.

"Most people in my experience don't exactly love their work. At Blumstein's for weeks my fingers didn't heal because of the needles that stuck in them. The boss was always scrutinizing, the *mumzer gonif*, keeping tabs on me to see I made more hats. Most of them, the hats and the bosses too, I would call tawdry. I mean *takeh* tawdry. The hats looked like the bosses behaved, like what the girls called tawdry heartburn." Her lips took a wry twist.

The spirit of her elder sister likewise curled her mouth at the hatmakers' joke. Judith looked up to Shirley, though Judith was taller. Shirley's broad jaw seemed to give strength to the words carefully released from her finely curved lips. Judith was proud of how Shirley admired her and still couldn't believe that Shirley had died so suddenly of pneumonia many years ago. Maybe she should have warned Shirley not to go out in that thin grey coat. Shirley had been happily married to Phil, but still found time to sympathize with her catastrophically married kid sister. Shirley's mouth was so expressive and her eyes so telling in a restrained way that she survived for Judith in a form like the Cheshire Cat.

Judith went on thinking to these features, and feeling with them, since they were both inside her and outside, her sister's features commenting on hers, through hers. She was repeating what Shirley knew, but had to say it again to another version of herself: "Ira says in both places they picked on him. In the ballpark, faggot they called him. He finally couldn't take it anymore, was shaking so he couldn't use the beer can opener without making a mess. I got him to tell me when I saw him practicing on soup cans. The post office was more polite, letting him know *azoy* indirectly that he was weird. This was more dignified, but they found he wasn't up to their standard. The only party he could keep working with was the doctor. It doesn't exactly pay, but I hope it'll work. Of course Joel the expert is sure it won't. If only we could get that man and his spite out of the picture—but maybe Yoyel and I only exist against each other.

"Work you do to give life to someone is not ordinary work, no matter how difficult. I would've liked to be a doctor, and a woman can do it in her way. It would be nonsense to call it playing doctor—but the chance he might appreciate it is a gamble. Gamblers usually lose, but something keeps them going. It's the possibility of getting more. When you step up to the plate, there's always the chance you'll hit a homer, though you usually don't. All our lives we kept going with the odds against us, and sometimes we won. The North Bronx where people are refined, we got here, and the boys in City College. That spirit you hold up will keep me going and maybe there'll be a maybe." Judith saw and felt that Shirley's mouth was pursed in a way that might have been cheerful or ironic. Her eyes in Judith's mixed affection and pity for a person who was there and not there.

He don't want any more of my money, he says. It stings like a hornet. I got bitten once as a kid in Hoboken by a dark, buzzing one who tiptoed angry into our kitchen. His sticking me felt like pulling out. But he should realize that since he stopped making any *gelt*, every penny he has is money I worked for, selling that cheap dreck to those PRs. But the fabric wasn't so bad, once. Para el hogar. Trying and waiting for them to make up what passes for their minds moving in two directions at once. At least not penny pinchers like the Jews used to be.

I'm his support, but I'm getting a hernia. In God we truss. And the expenses of his psychology are sky high! I'm supposed to ignore the fact that he's bleeding me dry, like a maniac parasite draining my bloodstream. Keeps me up all night repeating what I really should say to him: "If you torture me to death you won't be able to torture me anymore. So what'll you do for entertainment? But I don't say that. Never. I'm extremely

"I cook the food the way he likes. Well, used to like, so maybe he will again. He has to admit, though he doesn't say, that my breaded veal cutlets are a treat, golden brown on the outside, pale pink on the inside, substantial, juicy. I wash his clothes and wring and iron them so they'll be clean and neat, just in case. Sometimes I sing. You remember my favorite, the old song calling to the lover taken away, remembering his lips, looking forward to dreams lit by the light in his eyes. Knowing that 'in my dreams' is the only way to hold him again.

"I tell Ira he'll feel better if he eats, looks better since he slept. He doesn't quite, but maybe a little sometimes. I read to him bits from the book we read together, *Sons and Lovers*:

> She loved him so much! More than that she hoped in him so much. Almost she lived by him. She liked to do things for him; she liked to put a cup for his tea and iron his collars of which he was so proud. It was a joy to have him so proud of his collars.

restrained, and does he appreciate it? If I was more honest, I might get through to him, but she's always watching, ready to start bitching. Always ready to see his insanity as high-quality cleverness.

They're in cahoots with those bloodsuckers. His team. He pitches and they catch. But they're both on the same side, the moneytaking side. That *gonif* Mendelson. I said to him, "What are you doing to my son?" He said, "You're not thinking rationally." That means not stealing people's money. I shouldn't say any more to Ira about it. He denies it. "Can't you stop hammering at me?" I was doing nothing of the sort. Then I get excited and he clams up, but he's really going bananas, eyes darting around. And they say it's not his fault, *takeh*. He can't help talking nonsense that picks at me. I should tell him we're tickled to death to support him, but he doesn't believe it. He wants to support himself on nothing, like a ball suspended in mid-air. What's the good of talking to him about reality when he

"Ira says that's about Will, the son who went away, not the one she settled on. I say it's good he remembers. I know it bothers him to hear about hope, but he has to hear about it anyway. It's like his analyst. He says Mendelson upsets him by digging up terrible thoughts, but I tell him that's the way to get stronger, to face the music. Mendelson is concerned, not like that Gestapo in Long Island. We have to try. But Joel is only too ready to think the doctors are harmful, since they cost.

The hardest part for me is testing him on the post office schemes because I have to make him feel he's getting better, or at least he's as good as he ever was except time has gone by. I have to pretend his practice will lead somewhere, though I have my doubts. This deception takes something out of me, but better from me it should be taken than him.

"Hot milk with chocolate syrup I make because he says it helps him take his pills. Those pills keep his mind hanging on, give him another chance to realize that we want to make won't be reached? From reality I chased him away by trying to make him face it. That's not logical, a boomerang. You try to make sense and it's over the fence—a foul ball that can't be found.

It's a sucker's game to blame myself when the birthday present was from her. From Judith's side with her *kranke* brother Ben, a case and a half, always staring at the table, didn't know who he was. My brothers were right-minded, though they double-crossed me. Willie is a sap with his mail bag and box of little booklets, five cents each. Marcus Aurelius *takeh*. That's what those books are always telling those bookworms, "Mark us or else." You try to be sure what it means, but what it means is you've been sold a bill of goods and strained your eyes and mind. Marc's infected with the *mishegas*, and it didn't do Ira tremendous good.

Then there's Bernie, so cheerful it hurts, with his *shayne maydlach* and his *gezunt gelt*. What good does it do me that he's so happy when I can't play that game. He wishes he

him comfortable, his condition will improve as medical science advances. I said to him, 'You can live here. You don't have to let us bother you. We'll stay out of your way. Even your father, in his lunatic way, wishes he could be better and sometimes makes it.' Ira says, 'This place is gorged with the two of you, your bitterness, your fabulous plans for me, your making me take the medicine that eats away at my heart and brain.'

"I tell him the medicine is life, a concentrated form of life. He says life may be overrated, which I suppose is clever. Yoyel would say that's what you get from reading piles of books. I tell Ira life is what you make it. He says that's the trouble. I tell him you're young, you can get over the trouble. He says, 'With fried brains? With heaps of everybody's pity?' I say we know your brilliance is only hidden, but when I say that I'm a little afraid it may be insulting. He says, 'That would be swell, lavish, deluxe. But I wonder about your objectivity. You old people used to eat cow's brains. The butcher had a son, but that would be a battle royal. He always looked askance at me. Nice to me like charity. Me they didn't want any part of. The only one who ever stopped looking down on me was Abe, who was nice enough to drop dead. That party we had every day near the railroad station in Hoboken. All against me because I was too smart.

Newark was better with its park full of trees that Ira liked to climb in, to rest in their branches, until he ran away at the seashore. We had to call the cops, searching the sand and the waves till we found him a few blocks up the beach, looking in a circle for Jersey City.

For a while she cared for me. Even let me lick her and I think she really felt it, really came, but it's hard to be sure. So good-looking, both of us so happy dressed up on the boardwalk. Till she went back to her old craziness, and her nose just kept growing. Raised by criminals, swindlers, in false estate. My own life with behind the glass counter would take it from a tray and wrap it in brownish pink paper. You said it made you smart. My mind is not hidden. It's on a platter.'

"So Shirley, maybe he won't realize. Maybe he realizes too much. Maybe the effort I make, staying up late with him, listening to his *mishegas*, trying to get him to eat, to sleep—it's all for him like an overseer, pushing him into deeper misery, like a kapo working for the Nazis. The more I try, the more it hurts him. So how could this give me my reward, the hidden treasure that shines through my existence?

His resentment, his suspicion, tearing my *kischkes* out, it tells me loud and clear that I'm really with him, tells me with the strongest certainty that I'm giving him more than can be imagined, riches untold. My pain is his relief. It must be a measure of my love for him that he must be aware of on some level because it's there. There between us. The satisfaction I have to have is knowing I put it there and he's as good as gold.

my own wife, if she wasn't so bitter, *verklempt*, with no sexual feelings, no enjoyment but misery.

I took him to ball games, got him a hot dog he loved, with bright mustard squiggled from side to side. Looking down on the tan diamond of dirt in the sun. Showed him the greatest affection—didn't do any good. He just hid behind his *mishegas*. Like he was standing on a cliff holding us all at a distance.

How can I be blamed when I did more than I could? Enough misery and money to fill the Grand Canyon. She's just waiting to blame me to cover up the fact she spoiled him. Clothes she got like Little Lord Fauntleroy: fancy shorts with little belts. What she really got for him are the belts on the straitjacket. That's some stylish outfit. You have to laugh to make up a *lebedike velt*. Must be some fun somewhere in this mishmash of bad jokes playing reality.

Somewhere in this world, maybe above the world with God, there's a logic. Logic is Never mind what Yoyel did to him, that filthy maniac. Inside, Ira is as fine as watered silk. And he has a knowledge of it that keeps him alive—as long as I'm here. That's why I never stop singing to myself, 'I'll hold you in my dreams.' I can turn his grief around, bounce it off my hope. His sarcasm is not just heartless. He doesn't mean to be cruel at all. Marc says he's looking for a different way of seeing things. He's misguided in this world for sure, but he's out to find another world, to show us what's wrong, and when Marc gets back, we can try to make the value of what he's looking for clear, something *epes* new, A crazy person can be a genius, and Ira could fill the bill.

"I know what you'll say to me Shirley. It's my idea of him that I take satisfaction from. By imagining he can somehow be reached, I'm reclaiming him. So it's really myself I'm taking such first-class care of. And no matter how I jeer at Yoyel, I want Ira to live in the world Yoyel runs as the father of the family, with all his *krankheit*.

what holds the world together. You have to believe or you can't go on. So with all the medicine and devotion, he should come back, *takeh*. He must have it in him. He'll realize how I feel for him, part of myself. We'll be able to talk and I'll cut out my aggravation. As he gets older, he'll mature, a mensch. The other day I told him he was making progress and he laughed, sort of. Let's hope the devotion doesn't backfire. You have to have a positive attitude, not like the two of them with their misery sweepstakes: I can be more *verblunget* than you can. His nonsense she encourages him in—telling him to hate his father. She'll find out what good it does. Without a father to believe in you're lost. He's like God on earth. If you don't give your father credit, you're just what they call a bastard, stealing your life.

Still he could get better if he would listen to reason. I was always a top-notch father, gave him quizzes on the pillow when he was just a little child, building his mind. Vitamins are proven by science. There's But this is how things are, so if I can't reach Ira, if there's no connection between love and what it aims at, if there's no God, then there's no reason to do anything except mock and grieve.

"If there is a God, He will finally, in some final finally, bring Ira to remember, to understand, to cry. There were times when he said he was sorry—points of light—but he usually choked up before he could say more. And if God isn't, the thought is there, the notion made by the Creator who gave Ira life. Shirley, you'll say I'm not being realistic, but you remember I was tough when I had to be, for myself. When I left Dave and resisted Yoyel. What's most realistic is what I feel, more real than the garbage of sorrow. The light of hope shines for me now. It has to. It's here now and if things go wrong, it'll still be here. If happiness only lasts a minute, it lasts forever, Ira taught me this.

"To do good makes a person happy even if there's no reward. Doing good is the reward. To do it for a reward is not as right as to do it for goodness itself. Sure a real world that's not nonsense. *Reader's Digest* explains it clearly. A life of truth if we could only get there. We need to leave all this recrimination behind and look to the future. Cut out all this negative crap. The future looks bright ahead. We can count on that with one finger in the place it belongs. In the sky. May as well sing along with the disaster. It couldn't get worse.

this is selfish. Who can escape selfishness and breathe? But it's justified selfishness, Shirley, and that's why there's nothing better. *Shoin*.

"Once I said to him, 'There's knowledge in suffering. There has to be. And knowledge is happiness. What else?' He said, 'This knowledge is scrambled.' I said, 'So maybe you can unscramble it in time.'"

(Although it is within her, Judith stares ahead and cannot see Shirley's mournful smile of death, or hear her sardonic voice: "If you say you'll always have love for Ira, then you're affirming that you can't lose him, that he has no right to be lost, so you're stealing Ira from the God you need to believe in no matter how He torments you. The One you have to believe in to steal from. And why are you stealing him? Because of the dark, infinite universe of your desire to feel sympathy, your rabid need for someone to need you, a yearning that goes on forever because it can never be fulfilled. You are so terribly cursed with the incubus of happiness that you must be forever blessed with sorrow worse than sorrow, with myself, the smiling succubus of tribulation.")

Judith said, "I see his eyes looking through me with the blue tenderness of his dearest soul because we are both certain that we cannot live without each other. To doubt this cannot begin to make sense. This is the softness of our faces on which our consciousness rests. Without it, we don't exist. With it we rejoice. Our minds are locked together in a kiss that lasts forever, seizing more of the yielding flesh of ecstasy."

Shirley laughed and said, "*Azoy!*"

16

FISHING IN THE AIR

1967   1969

One afternoon in April of 1967, late in the second year that Marc was far off, Ira was hammering away at his post office diagrams, and the hammer was getting too heavy to lift. He was trying to memorize a scheme of address categories in the hope that he could get himself tested to resume his job, but he suspected that the scheme he was using was outdated. It had been years since the possibility of his being retested had been considered by anyone but himself, but the elaborate maze of the civil service preserved the illusion that there were still avenues that had not been exhausted, if one did not check carefully. It was a Kafka situation, but in the old days he saw Kafka as making fun of such fools. Now Kafka was too upsetting to read: Ira was required to be a fool.

He needed an activity, and Marc had indicated that painting might not be for him. Postal practice, while it represented a low level of possibility, had a comforting constancy. He had done it once; if only he could do it again. But now he couldn't: the categories floated away.

His finger tapped the paper.

"It's hard to be sure," he thought, "whether you really can't do this stuff or whether your concentration is just being sapped by discouragement after all this time, whether you're gone or just hidden. One thing you know for certain is that the pills are responsible. You wouldn't have all these empty spaces in your thinking if they weren't draining your brain. Your brain on the drain by the sink, being koshered with salt.

"Hmmm. I bet if you were to lay off the pills for just a few hours, you could get all this material together, like a feather. Then you can go back to the pills, and no one will be the wiser but you. Indeedimo. With a ho ho ho." He looked at the wandering, pullulating categories on the top of the sewing machine with a pained smirk. "Let's save money on medicine. Let's get lost. What could be more realistic than saving money? Why should someone like you believe this less than anything else?"

Judith watched him taking his thorazine, but he put his thumb and index finger in his mouth, while the pill was folded under his pinky, then washed down nothing with hot chocolate milk. Only an hour later, too soon for the missing pill to be unprocessed by his body, he developed a sense of gleeful exultation that made him believe that he could do better work. After an effort, however, he realized that it still wasn't coming together. "I should wait," he thought, "until it really takes effect." But now new ideas began to occur to him, ideas about freedom.

Marc felt so awake that waking had the sharp and shifting focus of a dream.

"It's only a half-hour from here, and just beautiful country." Jerry's head, shoulders and chest spoke, bringing up more of that California wine.

Miriam's honey voice purred, "It's a really neat place." The glow from the basement doorway in which Jerry rose caressed her right side, molding limpid silver sweeps of skin. Her eye was a circle of milky smoke. "There are scads of eucalyptus trees on the way."

Marc heard her sigh for the grey-green, odorous trees on the hills by the road. He felt himself held in her cunning sensuousness,

Stealing: A Novel in Dreams

in the thoughts of the couple she triangulated around him, in the lightness of her breath. Eight years later, he would look into Miriam's cloudy grey eyes on a bench in Central Park in New York, as Carol and Jerry sat watching the trees. Then Jerry was gone, and three years after that Marc realized what he had always known about Miriam: that he was too timid to have her, would always regret it. Now, in Berkeley, outside his sorrow, he felt as if he were starting on a journey, as if he didn't know what the road he was walking on led to. So he said to himself, "Relax, brother. The discovery of beauty justifies itself, and there is nothing wrong with wanting to live. Or if these propositions are not true, they are worth trying for, brother."

Jerry reached the table and hoisted two big maroon and green bottles with a sound of splashing squeezed in glass. "Imagine really good wine for a dollar-sixty-nine a half gallon. At that rate," bank bank (the bottles landed), "you don't have to stop drinking in 1969. After all, this is a year in which there's a moral purpose served by drugs and sex." (Why does another story stand next to yours, run next to it? Maybe this story holds yours until you can learn to ride on your own. But each story has to believe it is moving forward. If it sinks into the other, it will be lost. The runner has to keep running, the bicycle has to keep rolling, neck and neck, or they will realize they have fallen.)

"There are other connections that the pills are keeping you from," Ira thought. "They sure can't be reached through this postal crap. The reason that you have all these vacant areas in what you think is that you're being forced to fit your mind into someone else's patterns (guess whose?)—while the pills keep you from seeing the connections in your own mind."

Another voice said, "But this is dangerous. I could have a bad incident."

"It's dangerous because you're being held away from yourself. Can't you see how little alive you are in your safe state. As a drone without pay who can never catch up, who keeps falling further behind, what do you have that you should fear to lose?"

Ira's thoughts were exciting him so that he felt constricted by his not his room and had to go out. He feared leisure, especially in public, and tried to synthesize a purpose whenever possible. In this case, he walked to Zimmerman's candy store, four blocks away, to get a pack of cigarettes, though he already had quite a few. On his way, outside the Beth Abraham Home, he was struck by the sight of an approaching woman, who seemed to be Tammy, the girl he couldn't kiss.

He hadn't seen Tammy since high school; she had gone away to an Ivy League college. And it had even been years since he had imagined, with a pang, that he saw her in some tall, vital girl he passed. He soon realized with great relief that this was not her. Probably a nurse or volunteer from the Home. She seemed surpassingly lovely, as women sometimes do when they are first glimpsed. His head hung forward and he stood still and stared at her, thinking, "If such creatures exist, things can't be so bad." Even thinking, "Well, if I've seen her today, then today must be worthwhile. Yes, it's helpful to reach the stage where you don't have to worry about what to say to girls because you know it doesn't make a difference."

Marc filled a tumbler, hearing it percolate and fizz. "You know, folks," he said, "I've never had a chance to see how much I could drink in one swell foop." He gulped the turbid liquid in, feeling his chest and shoulders glow with a streaming, iridescent corrosiveness.

"I had to get far from my parents before I could find the space to relax. I felt pressure to work hard from the time I was six or seven, when my elder brother won a prize for selling the most copies of the *Newark Star Ledger*."

"Wha'd they give him, a watch?" asked Jerry.

Stealing: A Novel in Dreams

"He picked this fishing reel from a catalog. He didn't get a rod until about ten years later, but he kept this reel in a cardboard box in a drawer of goodies. It was shiny black plastic and metal and had this smooth like whirring, clicking mechanism."

"My childhood was such that I can't bear to be happy," he thought. "If Mom were to find a thousand dollar bill, her main reaction would be to worry. We're all that way." He spoke on, "Carol's done some amazing work with my case, but mostly I just try to excuse all this physical ecstasy by classifying it as a subdivision of grief, which is reality. Am I talking out loud or thinking? I have a constant foreboding of being doomed to progress—loving longer, writing better, moving with more strength. Gregor Samsa's dread that he might turn into a butterfly. What compels this happiness is horrendous."

When the woman saw Ira standing there staring, she was frightened. She thought of turning away, but didn't want to show fear. As she got closer, she felt she could see by his attitude that he was bemused and probably harmless. At first she thought he might know her and have something to say to her. When she reached him, passed him, and realized that he wasn't going to do anything but hang there, she couldn't help laughing.

Her first impulse was to make this a jolly laugh to express a flattered amusement. She was a compassionate woman who worked at Beth Abraham, a hospital for incurables. But as soon as she began to laugh, she realized that she couldn't make it sound too agreeable: it would be too much like a come-on to this stranger with something wrong with him. Women get killed. Her laugh ended up sounding defensive, sharp and derisive. She felt it necessary to teach him basic things he didn't seem to know about the rules that operate between the sexes—obliged to belie her own feelings by emphasizing that he had asked for it. He should benefit from this if he could benefit at all.

When Ira heard the beginning of her laugh, it occurred to him for a moment that she had seen how enchanted he was and was responding to his feeling. But then her laugh turned hard and his body, which had begun to relax, jerked back in pain. She was soon gone, after looking back for a cursory moment, and he said to himself, "Well, what did you expect? What else could she do to a stranger, a loony staring at her on the street?" He tried to hold to the cheerful first note of her response and take the whole thing lightly, but he felt something big turning inside him and he knew that this was a shadow of every relationship he ever had and that it would bring him down. Then he heard a voice say, "Hey, here it comes baby. Won't be long now. I can feel that old energy building." This voice sounded familiar, but he was puzzled by it. Some occasion, some ceremony, was approaching, instigating.

(The other knowledge should have been later, if a time could ever come for it. It couldn't be heard until a later that would never appear. It hints itself continually, too faintly to be heard. Time is the sound of its being unheard, the silence of dreams that speak not to us, but to each other, and go on speaking when we are not there, pleading for us in a voice we cannot hear except through each other, except in a dream. And when we hear it, when we hear how we have lost ourselves in each other, what we hear is terrifying and joyful, a knowledge that will never arrive.)

Ira went home to find his mother had returned from a shopping trip. He explained to her where he had gone and withdrew to his room, feeling something fermenting in him. "Maybe I should take that pill, as much as I don't want to— but I can't seem to raise the

"There is no known cure for normality," Marc affirmed. "One can only escape it by getting high. Once when I was very stoned, about half a year ago, I played with the idea of being someone else, my brother."

Marc wondered, "Can he be dead? Is it given to me to say

gumption to submerge myself in that trash. How could I decide? Aha. The voice of youth."

He immediately walked over to the chest of drawers and picked up from the top a letter he had received from Marc the day before; he began to go over the pages in consultation. It was a long letter, and though couched in ironic and self-deprecating terms, it was clear that Marc was doing well and liked California. It also criticized President Johnson and the war in Vietnam.

At first Ira wasn't sure what to take from the letter, but it led him to ponder on what he had heard from Marc and the media about Berkeley. "Well," he said, "well, well, well. Maybe I should get with it. Here it is 1967. High time old Ira-nee went on a trip. Yass, a visionary voyage. The external world being not too hot, maybe what I need is to make contact with the interior. Why should I be the only one left out of the party? Like 'Turn on, tune in, drop out!' Crazy man. Why it's easier than pie for us loonies to go tripping, Marco, my man. All we have

it? Have I assumed it, taken it? Or is he alive in my mind?" He went on speaking: "I realized then how exquisitely attractive insanity is to those who cross over into it. I stared at this wall and invoked what was on the other side of it, the demon of the unknown. But I was impotent, unable to pass through. All I could see was a wall. Never been much at hallucination. It was just obvious to me that it wasn't worth the trouble to keep even my own faith."

Jerry said, "Pynchon, talking about the Bay Area scene, refers to us as an army of failed suicides."

"Oh, wow. That's heavy," Marc said. And to himself, "I've always tended to think that Ira was doing what I would do if I had the courage. But suicide is absolutely wrong, a sheer waste, a dreadful crime against everyone else." And he heard a voice say, "Is it? Well, I guess that's pretty hard on me."

The others had gone to the kitchen and he decided to look through the house. He shot wildly up two flights of stairs, stopping for a long pee, from all to do is stop taking drugs." He laughed more than he had for a long time. "Well, all reet! Your hipster is the most pretentious form of loony, possible exception of your politician. These hippies have a point: a person should never be deprived of his imagination. Yuss, now we're getting somewhere, we're saying something, or something is saying us."

He felt a rhythm building that would make him have to go out again, but this time there wouldn't be a purpose he could define or control. He headed down the foyer toward the exit, saying to Judith, who was working in the kitchen, "Well, Mom, I blew it."

She was stung by the line. She'd been shaken by the weird statements from him and was reluctant to berate him for talking nonsense. She said, "You were just out." And before she could think of something more adequate, he was gone. She thought, "No matter what *mishegas* he comes up with, I owe it to him to count on the good part of him still being there. All the times I calmed the wine. The high pointed attic had redwood beams, a place he had wanted to be as a child. Country Joe and the Fish poster with big purple barbells. He lingered over a harpsichord Jerry had made from a kit, elegant and intricate. Then he careened down the stairs and reeled along the corridor between the kids' rooms, the neatest in the house, and the main bedroom. An immense green and yellow eye was painted on the ceiling over the wide, low bed he would never lie in.

"To make love is to turn inward," he thought. "I drift from Miriam, with her long, creamy legs, her wild memories of LA. I want to keep swinging across seconds of space. I waltzed through the empty rooms of Wiener's place the first time I got high. The green flowered curtain, clearer and closer. What I recollected of how a child felt."

The Knights' living room was still empty and Marc glugged down another tumbler of wine. He had had three pints. A picture window showed smooth streets placidly decanting him, helped him, must mean something."

As he walked out of the building, Ira looked up, and above the park he saw the light bleeding out of a discolored sky with a touch of yellow that reminded him of an old bruise, "like a patient etherized upon a table." He thought of himself strapped to the table learning the lesson of his life, the lesson of oblivion. Then he heard another voice behind him say, "Dawn's promising skies."

He crossed the wide street, which was occasionally streaked by the shadows of twilit trees, and sat on a bench outside the park. The top floors of the building he could not escape shone yellow in the setting sun. "The gospel of Blake, according to Saint Marc, says, 'I must create my own system or be enslaved by another man's.'" He chuckled. "This is going to be some system. Well, an excretory system designed by Rube Goldberg is part of the body of man. It can be passed through, or not.

"But enough of this frippery. We's got some serious business along moonlit hills varied with eccentric foliage that did not resemble the plants of the East Coast. He had been driven over by Carol while he was high, and did not know this neighborhood at all: wide, tastefully designed spaces washed with silver light, a continent away from the Jewish neighborhoods he grew up in, which he had heard referred to as ghettos.

"It reminds me of that steep, straight hill Ira used to coast down with his bike. Watching him soar down that hill is one of my earliest good memories. I think it was in Newark, but it was so far away that it was strange: I got there perhaps twice. Maybe it was in Orange. From the top of that hill we could see an enormous expanse of sky, and we fancied we could see the ocean on the vague horizon. No wonder it blows my mind when I go to Frisco and see the streets and buildings lifting away from each other."

Centrifugal force catapulted him out the door, stumbling down neat wooden steps into a radiant suspension of stillness. Now after eleven-thirty, no one here, bwah." He sat up straight and folded his hands together on his lap. "It's time to survey the estate." He put his finger on his chin. "What have we here?" He paused. "Well, lots of things, to be sure, and many of them quite charming..." (And a voice said, "You do drag it out, don't you?") "... but predominantly a young man who, as my *lantzman* Williams put it, is a pure product of America. And how does he feel about his craft, his vocation, his calling? Why, he's a mangy malcontent. Just listen to the scurvy wretch!"

"Feh! Calling? Don't call us, we'll call you. Who wants it? This is what I'm supposed to be? A demented creep? A searing threat to anyone who tries to love me? Lemme oudahere! Quick! Quick!"

(He was thinking of a Pogo strip in which Albert the alligator set his fake moustache on fire with his cigar. As he cried out, "Get some water! Quick! Quick!" he was surveyed by a father bug and his son. The father said, "Observe, Hermes, a duck with a red moustache.")

was out in the hills of Berkeley. "I want to see how things look in the moonlight, in Alphaville, among the shadows of forgotten ancestors, where images are negative, outside the wall."

He walked over to a tall hedge and peered into it. The white streaming that penetrated the hedge seemed to show more inside than daylight could. Sun gave only outline and green, but moon revealed a swirling inner chamber of self-possessed surface and edge. His gaze sank into rich shadow space secluded without coordinates in the heart of the deep night bush, and he whispered with its airy rustle:

> I thought love lived in the hot sunshine,
> But oh, he lives in the moony light.

"I stood on a sunlit hill in a vacation from my childhood. I sat next to a girl at the edge of a pool and reached into the water to find a world of shining, dancing blue light. When it was over, the swing Ira jumped off was rocking. Enough."

Stealing: A Novel in Dreams

The son said, "That's no duck." Father said, "Of course it's a duck. Don't you hear it say, 'Quick, Quick?'" Marc would catch this.)

"That's enough of that, young man. You better cut it out or we'll send you to a psychiatrist. You remember those guys. Your present good cheer is enhanced by the fact that you're scheduled to see one soon.

"Now then, in cases like these, and apparently (as the parents would have it) in all cases, what is necessary is to to accept one's position. They call it adjusting. Thus, he will find happiness and wisdom (make like Cicero). We must emphasize the positive aspects of the situation, and the supreme positive aspect of this one is its consistency." He rubbed his hands together and smirked. "It's well organized 'cause the old man's so coordinated. You can't contradict yourself when you have only one dimension. No loose ends here, old chap!

"Your venerable parents, your brilliant brother (uh huh), your august uncle, your touchy

He sprang down the street, his arches pushing his shoulders up in a shambling, effortless skip. The hollow brightness and the incline gave him a feeling that he was bounding on air, floating in light.

"When I was a kid I wanted to be a pilot, used to dream I could fly. My pillow was reshaped to the instrument panel, the machine gun handles. The possibility that I could lift my feet off the street if I concentrate on feeling light is still in the back of my mind, of my body. Only a few months ago, rushing through the rain and coming to a puddle too wide to jump, I caught myself thinking, 'Maybe if I lift myself carefully, I can hold myself up a little more, ease into it.' I can still see the yellow night lit pavement yards below."

Marc swooped down to a high curbstone. Along the surface from sidewalk to street, a clean cliff of curb sparkled with tiny bright points. Then he felt something pulling him down, so he looked up, stood up. The night extended to winking teachers, your so-called friends, your unfellow students, they all tell you the same thing over and over. Books argue it with you. The civil service certifies it. Gorgeous girls whisper it in your ear. Stones on the street hit you with it. Isn't it about time you learned it? They're telling you that you have only one fate." He slumped on the bench.

"This is my identity, a crowd of people going in the same direction. This is my heroism that was destined for me. This is my beloved, my only love that has always spoken to me, even when I was alone. Who can say nay? Hidey Hey."

A little bird suddenly appeared in front of Ira in the last light of evening. He had never seen one like it. It was all a uniform, soft gray except for the top of its head, which was black, like a thick skull cap. It had a long, narrow curved bill and precise little feet. It would hop from one spot to another and then be still so quickly that it was impossible to see any movement between the time it landed and the time it stood still.

stars over South Berkeley and Oakland.

"With my torso sloping downward on the curving rock, I had no place to lock my legs. I couldn't reach my hand, or could I? Couldn't pull without losing my purchase, what I own."

He swung his head from side to side, watching stars and moonlit trees sweep across his field of vision, grabbed a lamppost and swung around it like a discombobulated Gene Kelly, staggered a few feet, then came to a diamond-shaped field of grass. He was dizzy, and falling on his knees on the soft ground, he somersaulted twice and rolled around. Attempting to get up, he buckled and collapsed on his back. He lay straight, as he seldom did in bed, his joints relaxed, breathing against the earth and watching the stars continue to wheel. He felt expanded, as if there were a mountain range between his eyes and his toes.

"Ira looked unnaturally long in his coffin at twenty-eight. Why am I thinking of him so much? Because I'm free to." He closed his eyes to blot out

"Hmmh," he snorted, as if to say, "Well, whadda ya know? Reminds me a little of the jerky walk I sometimes fall into when I'm excited." The bird was hopping with so much superfluous energy, so much unpredictability, that he wondered, "Why make anything so excessively alive unless it were meant to be beautiful?" And soon he felt the bottoms of his eyes bulging with the onset of tears.

His heart felt lifted and he hoped he could cry. Then he heard a voice say, "He hoped he could cry." "Who said that?" he thought. "Who said he? And who is saying this? And saying it to whom? Ahah, trying to lose yourself in the crowd, eh? Don't kid yourself. I can't cry, any more than I can lose myself. Haven't been able to cry since being improved at Amityville. You can't cry by hoping for it. After all, crying is in fact a form of ejaculaton. What a crock, to want to cry so much that it cheers you up to come close. But I'm a sucker. I can't stop degrading myself by trying."

He leaned back and looked at the dense blue sky of early the night sky. "He seemed to be looking thoughtfully at the insides of his eyelids. Here I am. Here he is. Here we is. Wanna whine a little? Beg forgiveness? That's a good one. Indulge, mayhap, in some sensuous self-pity? Nummy nums. Precisely the kind of stuff that exactly got me where I am, buried alive inside you."

His eyes opened and he raised his head to scan the perimeter of the plot in which he lay. Feeling like a grounded flounder, he tried to recollect from which point he had entered the field. He concluded that the likeliest was a curving corner with a signpost: it seemed to be the highest. He hauled himself up and staggered over, expecting to find the way to Miriam and Jerry's from there. The sign said, "Tamarac." Had he heard that name?

He walked up Tamarac for two blocks, then another. No sign of house, car, or anything familiar—but the places he did see were pretty, with trellises, round windows, terraces. He didn't turn back to the lot because it hadn't shown him night with his eyes drawn open in what he considered a good position for crying. He said, "Mama," and saw his mother's face, saw her mouth draw taut and her wistful eyes film with grief he could never pay for. And he whispered, "Mom, I've lost you. I miss you. Come back to me. Let me cry. Give me tears. Marc, some of your emotions. Any name I can call. Daddy, daddy, daddy. Joel, Jahve, let me weep. I realize how you suffer for being such a bastard. Let me sob." But he could not forgive and there were no tears.

Ira reclined, chin on chest. "Birds are quick for protection, jerk, so they won't be spotted by predators. Yonder birdie wasn't made to be beautiful. It was made to survive by eating other critters. And if you assume it was made by God—an unsettling notion that kind of creeps up on you—then so were the others, whose purpose was not to survive. In the long run, the purpose of everyone is shonuff not to survive.

"Our feathered friends are looking out for themselves.

anything definite. He believed he must be above the Knights', so he turned down a street that seemed useful. Gravity impelled him to jog and swing his arms freely, cool air brushing his skin. Then, as the road flattened, Marc heard a murmur and noticed two men standing behind a station wagon with an open back fifty feet to his left. Were they whispering about him? He lowered his arms and attempted, with short breath and mixed success, to walk a straight line and look respectable.

"I'm not really loony, folks. At being straight I'm nothing compared to Ira with his miraculously bulging strait jacket, announcing his findings like an amazed scientist: 'I'm nothing. I don't exist.' What was he ever? Something to be misunderstood, to be constricted. I understood him better than anyone, and I managed to have no idea that he'd kill himself. And what did he do that kept him from having a chance? He tried too hard. Horatio Alger. Whatever anyone could do to

Who am I looking out for? I'm like that faggot Quentin, calling the bird his little brother. Come to think of it, little brother is quite capable of shitting in my eye. As for Mom, she's right there in the house, but I couldn't talk to her. You could never face an actual woman. Need some confidence to look for miracles. Anyway, her goodness works for his set-up. Only her nastiness resists him. Oh yes, and remember, you mustn't call Jivey's name. Mr. J. is busy right now, busy accusing folks.

"I can't escape my debt to the old man for one minute. No way I can have my own life. The world I've been waiting for to begin, can I take it from anyone else but him? Or his deputy junior?"

And a voice said, "Drop this world if you want to find out who you are. That's what they've been telling you all along when they tell you that you're nothing. Put your faith in your own transformation and step off this treadmill. Plant yourself in his bosom as a thorn. He'll feel what you take help him, he was always two steps ahead of them."

Having left the guys by the station wagon behind without asking for help, Marc looked across immaculate lawns into large empty rooms. In a few cases, they were lit, with fireplaces and solid, handsome furniture. "Ira would dig this. Yass, this is where he's to be found. On the outside looking in.

"Maybe I could knock and ask for shelter. Someone might know Miriam and Jerry, a girl in a nightgown, amused and sympathetic." He could sleep in any corner and might beguile her with his haunted lostness. He considered the possibilities, which were nothing to those he'd left behind. Later when he travelled, he tended to get lost, his real destination.

Climbing onto a short stone fence, he looked around, wavered, and thought he saw promise in the line of a wall. But after going a few blocks that way, he found the landscape obstinately turning from his expectation, writhing in disdain, trees holding themselves aloof, from him as a raging loss. He can deny it all he wants for the rest of his life. You'll be with him the way he's with you."

"And her?" he said.

"Looksee," a voice said, "You've finally found a way to get at her, to have her, to be inside her. You'll own her life completely and be all of the truth for her, all of her man. She'll cast him off complete when she sees his effect on you. It's the cat's pajamas, the land of heart's desire. And as for Marc, you'll be his father. He'll realize how he misunderstood you, what he did to you. Go to the head of the class. Man, you're giving yourself to all of them, not exactly in kindness, but not all in hatred either. Artificial insemination. Ain't reason wonderful? Bars of light whisper in streams of milk."

Then Ira saw his father turn the corner across the street, coming home from work. That meant it was after nine-thirty. Ira thought, "The world keeps defending itself by coming up with these surprises. But what is this?" He was startled by how old, small, and weak Joel the road leading to an incomprehensible declivity.

"This is an impossible situation. It doesn't seem to apply to me. I noticed at Miriam's that I enjoy pretending that I'm acting in a movie or written in the third person. But who's telling this story? Maybe my story's told by Ira. I started out depending on him and here I am in his situation, and he keeps feeding me material."

He turned toward a stack of timber he noticed in a nearby street and leaned on it, watching the bars of wood recede in smooth lines. "The unconscious lies in the past and the future, in imagination, outside existence, lost. The more alone I am, the better I talk to myself." He climbed on top of the planks, but didn't see much. He had no idea what to look for except the house itself. He got down and leaned against the wood, which felt rougher than it looked. "There must be a way out of this to be found by logic. I looked through the park for that cliff Ira was stuck on, thinking there must be another way to turn to find that magic place.

looked under the streetlight. Joel waved and he made a small hand gesture back. "Jesus," he thought, "he's over sixty. I'm wearing him out. I must be struggling against something he doesn't even have anymore, but I can't stop fighting. Where else can a fella go for satisfaction?"

Joel stopped on the steps leading to the entrance of the building and looked down. He said to himself, "More trouble." Then he turned and crossed Bronx Park East, which had hardly any traffic at this hour, and cautiously approached Ira slumped on the bench. Trying to sound deferential, Joel said, "It's late. Shouldn't you come in?" Ira said, "I want to think some here." Joel started to respond, then stopped (afraid to scold) and turned back toward the house. As Joel started to walk away, Ira surprised himself by saying, "This might be a spiffy time to see my buddy Mendelson."

Joel said, "A psychiatrist, *takeh*. At this hour to drag us out. You always want to see the doctor until you see him. We spent twice the national debt

Ira searched for a way to turn on the rocks—but that was me dreaming."

Marc stumbled on and came to a large, round brick wall. "Must be quite a mansion in there. Hey, what's that sticking out around the curve? A hand? An arm? Izzat Ira hung there? Naw, only a vine. Leave us not be pretentious, my boy. Real insanity is beyond your range. You can only gnaw feebly at the edges of it. Us loonies mos' decidedly do resent amateurs."

Around the corner of the curve, the wall was broken by an archway with stairs reaching out of it like a tongue toward the corner of the street. Inside the arch, the stairs led up to other stairs and the elaborate entrance of a glassed-in porch on a big house. The landscape outside the wall was uniformly unreal. No one seemed to be up, and he sank down on the three steps that extended beyond the wall, which were as close to public seating as anything he had seen all night.

"I need to rest and think, feel heavy. There's no direction to go that won't probably take me on doctors and it didn't exactly do you so much good. What you need, of course, is to make up your mind to help yourself. If you won't be reasonable, the best doctor in the world won't do any good, except to his wallet. Come and rest and you'll feel better in the morning. Then we'll see about a doctor—maybe he won't be necessary."

Ira held his breath for ten seconds and said, "You're a fountain of wisdom." Joel said, "I'd rather be a fountain of cream soda," and was glad to see Ira smirk wearily. Joel thought, "But he's too cute. So let him be cute. I'm not so peppy myself as to go for a round of psychiatricks." He foundered indoors.

Ira was struck by Joel's exhaustion: "He's *verblunget* from working to support my frolics. It's unfair to challenge him, no great fun to defeat the old man. It's not so much him, but the principle that's so stupendous. I may as well spare him, spare all of them. The fight's over and both guys lost."

Then a voice said, "You should confront a more worthy opponent. Joel is just a front, a further from anything I know." He leaned back. "I have no idea when light will come. It could be one a.m. or three. The ivy around this arch is like the diaphragm around a silver silent movie set. After a while, I'll think of something, see dawn, or build energy for a drive toward some vantage. Maybe the people in the house will notice me and call me in. I won't be lost here forever. The idea I'll never go back to who I was is self-indulgent. My real problem is I can never lose myself.

"The trip intensified when I looked into Miriam's eyes half an hour after eating the cookies. She looked back and said, 'You're getting high,' crystallizing my puzzlement into transcendence. I gazed into her awareness of me, feeling expansion breathe through my limbs, and said, 'Wow. I sure am.' The soft gray modulation of her eyes purring into mine. I followed her and gave her my devotion for a minute. Why did I lose touch?

"I kept trying to look into Ira's threatening eyes as he lay in the ambulance on his way to the feeble organ of the power that really put you in this position. If you take your argument upstairs to the real culprit, these folks will have a rest, and so will you."

"But am I really controlling this decision?" Ira wondered. "I want to save my mind, after all, whatever may be left of it. What else could I want?"

"Who do you think I am?" the voice said. "Harpo Marx? How 'bout a little responsibility around here? You think you're an innocent young hopeful like Marc. But it's crooked of you to deny that you've been through the meatgrinder, the broken looking glass. You're as full of it as Junior. You want to save your psychic *tuchas* for more years of wearing yourself and everyone else down, losing your last shreds of dignity and coherence. You can never be free of me and think 'cause I'm your reason. You'd best believe it, honey bunny. I'm the fundament you're sitting on. It's perfectly rational to be certain that whoever gave you a life like this doesn't deserve credit; and whatever can get you out

expensive sanatorium in Long Island where they mangled his mind. I meant to say, 'I know you think I'm doing this to destroy you. I'll always regret that I haven't got the courage to keep facing you without calling in the brain police. But can't you see in my yearning eyes I mean you no harm?'

"'You smug bastard. What right do you have to think for a second that you didn't mean him—me—harm?

"Well, I was uneasy about it even then, and I said to Ira, you in myself, 'Perhaps I'm killing you now by denying your will, I'm fated to destroy you. But how would it help if I cast off the only sense I can make at this point of what seems best? At least you see that I'm with you for these few minutes, if only as your enemy. I'm holding on to what I can grasp of my responsibility for your existence.'

"Ira probably thought I looked at him to taunt him while tormenting him. He once said there were woman who could kill you with a look of their eyes. No wonder he avoided my gaze. If he even knew I was there.

of it is your only boon. It's a banana split with pistachios, whipped cream, and raspberries. It's your golden wedding to Marilyn Monroe and her joyful mysteries.

"Well hey, I'm speaking to myself. Two voices that are both me. I have no way to know which voice comes from the deeper level of myself. Deeper level of what? Could you say that again? Nope. But it must be (mustn't it?) that the connection between the two of them is deeper than any one, and that one can't do anything without the other (whichever that is), never had and never will.

"Well, all reet. Now I know which side my butt is breaded on. Both sides. I've had enough of denying myself. Maybe I'm the one who hears them both, the deep *mishegas*. That's me. Buzuka, buzuka, buzuka, that's all, folks!"

He heard the rollicking *Looney Tunes* theme as he got up, crossed the street, and went up two steps to the front courtyard and two more to the main entrance, a door with heavy black metal grillwork over

Looking is as superficial and one-sided as words. The person I looked at most steadily was Carol, yet the time I enjoyed looking at her most, she was asleep.

"Her face was turned aside against the pillow on our honeymoon. I leaned over the fissure between the beds, which we put together all three evenings to be parted every morning by the maids at the Plaza. Her skin was clear and soft as untouched pudding, her eyelids as pure and happy as petals. The center of her mouth opened on the silent coolness of a bird's song. Her brow, which could sometimes crease with worry, was as placidly smooth as if the consciousness in it were only a limpid, drifting embrace of air. Why shouldn't I think that the clarity her soul kissed was myself? With every day, forgiving my craven soul, charmed by my obsessions, she helps me to deserve it. But it was not her that I saw, only my dream of her. She was asleep.

"What was Ira looking at when he fell? He may have been ecstatically happy, feeling the glass. Inside the lights were uneven—bright in places and dim in others—and the walls were dark mauve. Since the first floor was a passageway to their apartment in the back, it reminded him of what it was like to try to communicate with his father. He thought, "If you get smarmy with that aging maniac now, then what would be the meaning of the decisions you made when you were really there? For the first time in my life, I'm not on my way to the Glogover residence."

Ira pressed the elevator button and a metallic snap was heard, followed by sizzling and humming as the elevator descended. When it arrived with a crunch, he opened the outer door, which had a porthole, and stepped into the car. The elevator had been improved in the decade since he had gone up in it with Marc. It now opened and closed by itself instead of having a folding metal gate. He pressed six. There was another click, and the elevator whined softly upward.

wind rush on him. Did he see my eyes?

"I'm only too ready to feel guilt, but I can't blame myself. I did what I could and had no way of knowing what would happen. Eight years of roller coastering his craziness taught me that the greatest care could be disastrous, while any impulsive nastiness might help."

"Very clever. So you mought's well be nasty, huh? I especially like your earnest tone, like a professional, a person who appears to do someone a favor while he's manipulating him. This is known as psychology."

Marc said to no one, "I might have sacrificed my life for you without doing any good. The parents sacrificed too much—then held it against us. The way to be responsible for one's unconscious is to be healthy. What I can save will be saved by love, not fear."

"So you tell yourself in the groves of academe. And what have you saved?"

"I've, uh, saved my memories of you. You only exist in my dreams. Now that you're gone, it's the only life I can give you, when you come to me. Sometimes you come angry, like now, threatening. Sometimes you come softly, seeking love. We embrace and I tell you how glad I am to see you better and we weep for joy. Do you remember? This love, this hope, must come from you. You must have had it in you when you were alive if it remains to speak after you."

"Hoo hoo, thanks extra-large. I sure appreciate. First you conclude it's honky dory if you turn me over to the Gestapo because you're chicken; now you decide I'm alive because you can have delicious fantasies about me. It does me all kinds of good to be trapped in the mind you took from me, to be fabricated by your egotism. All you ever saved were your dreams. The worst insult to the choice I made."

"But you're here, Ira, aren't you? Here. Who's speaking if not you? The best version of you in existence. Here you are in action."

He felt a hand on his shoulder from above. Not caressing but definite, pushing his shoulder back to wake him. "Ira? Ira?" He was back!

"Okay, buddy, get up""

"What happened?" he thought. "I'm here on someone's steps. Uniforms. Two cops. Somebody must have called."

"We'll have to take you to the station. Let's not have trouble."

"They seem more amused than hostile—an act of theirs to keep it light, but I can't see much use in fighting. I'm one of the first to pull back at demonstrations. The other guys are up there confronting those billy clubs and I'm in back cheering them on. Still talking to Ira."

He asked, "What am I charged with?"

"Being drunk in public."

"But I'm no drunk. I'm a graduate student at the university" (well pronounced). "I got lost after some wine with friends." This couldn't be the real crime.

"You know enough to realize you'll have to come with us."

Marc got up lightheaded and navigated to the cop car by a series of small, careful lurches. As the car swooped down the

Stealing: A Novel in Dreams

hill, he stared at his feet, tried to think of arguments, and finally decided why he was so happy: "Busted for boozing, but I'm not holding and they don't know I've had grass. Just play it right. 'Be drunk'—Baudelaire. The charge is like quaint, like the fussy side of Berkeley.

"Exultation. Ira soaring cheerily. 'Wow, lookit all that space below me.' Breezing by the sixth-floor window of the redhead I was too shy with. 'Hey watch me, Brenda, I can fly!' Turn my body to adjust the wind on me like a shower nozzle."

They woke Marc and he remembered that Brenda had already moved out when Ira jumped. A cop behind a wooden banister recorded facts and fingerprints and took his wallet. Marc said he hoped the news of his arrest would not get back to the university. He had to spend the night in the drunk tank and was allowed one call. Miriam's warm voice.

"I see. Well, we were wondering what happened to you. It's three o'clock. Carol went home half an hour ago. I don't think she was really all that worried. We knew you drank. Are the pigs listening? She had to take care of Sybil. Well. You poor, foolish boy." She hung on the o's languidly. "Just sit tight in your snug little stir and don't worry and everything will be all right. I'll be real sure to call Carol and she'll rest serene. You take it easy now." Click

The call helped. Soothing to talk to Miriam, though Carol must be frantic. And wait a minute... something unpleasant, rancid, was rising around his diaphragm. Before he could diagnose or explain, Uroop, bluh! He threw up in a bright purple burst on the floor.

From (he apologized) a (metal door creaked) nearby closet came a cop with a mop, and he gave it to Marco to clean up that slop.

> But Marc had no idea how to clean up barf,
> and found himself disarmed by a tendency to larf.
> He was rather too lighthearted to learn,
>
> Which it took not long for the fuzz to discern,
> For tho he swung his mop back and forth,
> He was only spreading the glistening froth.

He apologized again—apology being to him like Merry Christmas to Santa—left the cop with the mop to clean up, and headed for his cell. The fuzz couldn't figure out how to force him to clean up, so being *non compos mentis* was to his advantage.

The drunk tank was long and narrow, with a heavy door at one end and a broken toilet jutting out from the wall of the other. The door, plated with metal, had a lockable, barred square opening above for talking and a slot with a flap and platform below for food. There were two cots attached to the walls on either side of the cell closer to the door than the back. Marc sat down on the one on his left, while on the right one sat a tall, thin young black man.

The door crunched shut, and the youth asked in a hoarse whisper, "What they got you for?" In the new silence, Marc whispered back that he was drunk in public, and the other said, "Same here. This is the place for us. What were you chugging?"

Marc said "Wine," and the guy said, "With you again. That's the stuff that'll get you going." Marc got a charge out of being in the same situation as this black man, but then he realized that he wasn't.

"My problems are not serious," he thought. "I don't have medicine for my asthma, but it isn't bothering me so far. Let's hope the English Department doesn't hear about this. I want to say something to this guy, but I'm not sure how. His dark face in this half-light, as if its surfaces preceded themselves, is a mask."

Marc asked, "Been in Berkeley long?"

"Year and a half. My name's Rick. Man, that Telegraph Avenue is really something else."

"I agree with you." Marc strove for enthusiasm. "It's fantastic. On a bus the other day I heard two guys in back of me getting up to Telegraph for the first time. Saying they were really going to spread it around. Pointing to houses and chicks. One of them was waving this wire coathanger. Said it was all the luggage he had."

"Yeah. Like there's all kinds of heavy people coming through." Rick's eyes were smiling. "I mostly hang around the Cafe Mediterranean. You know that place?'"

"I was only there once or twice." Marc couldn't afford it.

"They get to talking there," Rick said, "and I mean they really work things out: what people are living through and looking for instead of that off-the-wall jive in the university. And some of these chicks, they're really beautiful, body and spirit. They're not looking to put you down." His brows drew together with distress. "Does drinking make you like dizzy and foggy, even when you stop it?"

"Uh, I smoke grass more than I drink. I think the grass is slowing down my rhythm for good."

"I mean, I gotta stop all this drinking and chasing girls. It's hurting my brain. I get so turned around I can't remember things. If you can't remember what's supposed to be happening, you know, then you get to wondering if you're really there. And I have this trouble speaking, like words get lost, drowned out. I think it's going to kill me if I don't get off. I mean it's eating up my head." He looked ahead into space.

"I had a brother who took too much medicine. Made him sleepy. We had an unhappy home where I grew up. Parents always hassling. I think that's why he did it ... he stopped, though." Marc tried to make it sound positive.

"Do you listen to music?" Rick asked. "What kind of music do you dig? Do you like Hendrix?"

"Hendrix is a great guitarist. My favorite group is The Incredible String Band."

"I don't think I heard of them."

"Do you know Albert Ayler?"

Marc wanted to say that he believed in what the Scottish visionary string band and the black visionary Ayler had in common, but what they had in common here is that Rick had not heard of either. The prisoners agreed on Dylan, who had just put out an album with Johnny Cash.

"Is this guy Ayler like Cash? When I watch Cash on TV, he gives me icy chills, what he wants to do to me, when he looks in my eyes, like a knife in the brain."

"I doubt if Cash is a racist. He's part Indian—but his singing is flat. I never went for country music." He thought, "But I sang country to myself when I was brave, slopping the mopping."

"When I hear that music," Rick said, "I think about those hillbillies. Cold fire. They're unbelievable."

Marc wanted to tell him not to imagine dangers that weren't there, but he hesitated out of fear that may have been needless.

"And the cops. Wow," Rick said."Know why people become cops? Cause they groove on hitting people upside their head. Just want to get alone with you and bounce a few off you. Breathe down your neck and wait for a false move."

"Berkeley cops aren't as bad as Oakland ones."

"Those Oakland pigs. Big bullnecked black leather motherfuckers with their snarling dogs."

Rick noticed Marc watching him picking with his thumbnail below the second joint of his left index finger. "Did you ever have one of these sores that wouldn't heal? I mean I've had it for weeks, think it comes from the booze. Like I try to wash it, but it won't go way."

The oval concave gap in his skin, about three-eighths of an inch long, had the pink moistness of exposed epithelium, but it was clean and not bleeding—it looked like an open wound rather than an infection.

"You should stop picking it." The lightness of the exposed skin struck Marc with the idea that Rick was attacking his skin.

"Doesn't seem to help. Besides, you know, I have to keep it clean, and it itches like a mother." He put the gaping side of his finger in his mouth.

"Well, I think you should put on a Band-Aid to protect it."

"Yeah? Well I tried that. When it can't dry, it won't heal. Like, you know, it sticks to the bandage. And when you take it off, it hurts like hell and you're back where you started."

For an hour or two, Marc lay and thought of what he could say to Rick: "Quit hurting yourself... find a woman you can stay with ... use your intelligence to cut down on drinking." Sometimes he thought his rhetoric was lined up to begin, but all he did was clear his throat.

In the slow hours before dawn, he dreamed he was walking on Bleecker Street and saw a sign in a window announcing an appearance by Charlie Parker. He said "Come back" and he looked up to see Doris Roth, whom he had known before Carol but had never made it with. They smiled brightly to see each other again, and realized without speaking that despite their other lives, they had never stopped longing for one another.

She took his hand and led him to her loft. They climbed staircase after staircase, their hips and shoulders brushing lightly as they climbed side by side in the stairwells' limits. They felt the lives of their bodies singing to each other as their hands fluttered. They spoke in a conversation of

Ira ascended enclosed: "As I defeat gravity I'll draw my dispersed voices into me to sing in chorus. Not like Bach. Like that Ornette Marc digs."

The elevator's buzz created a field. of vibrations in which submerged voices whispered across the edge of audibility, the machinery talking to itself: "Brzzzt. Should we snag him?: What's ringing him? Megascholiosis."

When the elevator stopped, inhaling a click, he stepped into an empty hall: "Keep those noises down in the loony bin. Need clear voices to make sense.

"Got to walk quietly. Brenda lives right in there. Stairs steep, wall rough. My shoulder anticipates the heavy door. Better not make noise."

"Stop this, you fool. No one will understand the way you think they will—and besides, prayer, saying, "We can be free. We can be free." Her door had a dark eye in the middle of it, Doris's gleaming eye, and when she opened it outward and he walked into the eyedoor, he found himself suspended in a dark sky, and he heard an ancient Jewish voice:

"My mother would never tell me how many holes she had or where they were. Her eyes closed sideways. All of her skin is white and blue, woven of holes kissing each other. I plunge toward her vast inhalation. The hook of my fulfillment will sail on its line through the whispers of her memory, float in the clarity of her vision, the pure filament of her devotion, the space of her forgetfulness. The lost Shekinah.

"I cry out to my so-called brother as I sail through the sea of ink outside the wall. Want to find the God of your fathers? Touch me and I'll make you strong. Drink my blood and eat my meat. I can imagine I'm looking into my lover's eyes until the ground goes past me. Then I won't have anyone to love me but a foot stepping you won't be around. You should wait to find out what will happen. They might invent a new medicine. You could somehow get better. Mom might still divorce him."

"Can't you feel yourself coming alive, Clive? Going all the way into your being. Don't you hear these voices speaking together, all you? You've never been so rich, so busy. Your glorification approaches. I am your true will. This is show business.

"I'm humming the show tune, the one about petals and eyes, drifting in the pool, '... and this is my beloved....' Who am I to you? Do you see me the way I see you? How could you?

"I'll show you, you bastards. You think you can shit on me forever? I'll wring your hearts, curse your lives, nail myself to you as a man, not a kid. I'll show you I'm braver than you are."

"Terror is streaming like Freon in my veins, radiating through my skin.

"What, me worry? Dig the cat who says he's my true will. It is to laugh. Lots of yocks. Frozen band aids. Zany crickets on parade."

on the grass—and you, darling. Take my soul and make me your father." Marc looked into the clear spring night to see the blackness of interstellar space, the empty void that goes on forever. Movement, sound, and feeling disintegrated. Light was a tiny star point and he was looking into the dark clarity of Doris' eyes, and he realized he was attracted to her for the same reason he couldn't have her: she was insane. And the strength of his feeling for her was fear that he had killed her by not being able to give her his love.

There was a clank in the darkness, a rectangle of light opened, and something greasy thrust through it toward him. A slab of breakfast about three-quarters of an inch thick, gray flecked with yellow. Grinding its heavy lumps, Marc remembered from biology that albumin is the main ingredient of both egg white and semen. The breakfast cop told him it was seven o'clock and he'd go on trial sometime during the day.

Ira leaned on the door, pushed it open, and plunged out over the threshold onto the roof. He felt relief as the door reverberated shut without a slam behind him.

"The night encloses me. Only a few stars. The lights of the streets are far below." Now he could hear a faint drone from the ground. "The darkness holds me gently. My skin can see, my eyes can hear.

"Everyone has these voices, but they won't admit them. To be practical, reasonable, they have to pretend that they're speaking as single beings. (Don't you wish you could speak singly without feeling the best part was lost?) But I didn't make up these voices and they aren't new. I discovered them already speaking in my nerves. I know more than other folks, a big reason I frighten them."

"A *kranke meshuggah*. You think *I'm* going to blame myself for *your* choice? I worked like a dog for you. A son is his father's life. I put up with burning hell from you. A son to treat his

Marc was astonished at the density and sliminess of time in the stir—he who was used to reading all the time. Each half minute squirmed to a scream. Thinking of lockup makes one need an explosion that makes it worse.

He knew from reading Richard Wright that black people were born under arrest. His rich uncle Dave had declared he was entitled to a hundred times what the poor had because he worked harder. But Marc suspected what he now saw, that the poor had harder work.

father that way. You can blame me for everything, but I didn't shit in your pants. You're doing it to yourself because you're crazy and that's why it means nothing. I speak with the voice of God's mercy, His holy tears, when I tell you that you shouldn't do it because it makes no sense."

"When did that mercy appear? Maybe I can speak for it better than you. My feet shuffle forward slowly. Don't want to wake the lady to call the cops. Nothing to steal up here. I brush some pebbles on the roof that scrabble aside. With the graves vibrating against my soles in the dark, moist night, I feel as if I'm under the sea, in the realm of secrets."

"Don't do it, my son. Come back to the real world. Save my hope, save my life. We can talk. We can help. Sweet moments, happy times we had, we can have again. I'll take care of you. My beautiful son. You know I'll have nothing without you. Nothing. Why should you want to be so cruel to both of us, you and me? You have a life, all these years, made of the tenderness I gave you. I didn't advertise it, but I gave it. How can you fling it in my face like this?"

"Once you had me and I felt like I could cling to you forever. I felt that if I waited, you would show me a way to reach a place where my flesh could take light, where I would be blessed by the laughter of girls. But then I realized that you were never going to give me my real life. You're stuck yourself, transfixed, impaled, and you only want to take me back to that pig. So the laughter remains as a curse. What have I been waiting for? All the waiting didn't bring me closer. It brought me further away. My real mother must be in the sky, in the purity of the air, beyond corruption. You and I are brother and sister and I guess somewhere we'll always be waiting for each other, but not in life. You could never tell me in person what you tell me in my dreams. Maybe we're in a picture, in an empty room somewhere with a light shining into the night. Twenty-eight years is enough time to wait outside a window. I'm going in."

"You talk like a Hollywood poet, a devotee of the sky goddess Nut with her stars. But what are you actually doing, if you think for a minute. The hook you cast into the sky can only catch abstraction and escape, casting off the connections that make you human. Don't wipe yourself out for something your intelligence can't respect."

"Always a treat to hear some high-grade bullshit from you, Marc. What I'm doing is beyond your casuistry because I feel it in my bones. Been studying it all my life. All that pain and shame was flaying me, whittling me to my true shape, dream bones of suffering. Mom used to threaten us with the strap: 'You'll see stars.' Those are the stars I see, more real than anything you could know. And now that I move closer to my release, I feel more compact and impregnable.

"Now the night sky is clearer. I can see levels, ridges of cloud, extensions of space. The network of stars vibrates and trembles. If you concentrate on one, others grow dim. The stars burning my eyes are like voices in my mind beyond what I have heard. Lots of them come from long ago. I'm still saying the words I wanted to say to Marcy, to Marc, to Red, to Barbara, to the friends I made enemies."

"Now I understand what you meant."

"You could have helped me if you'd waited for me." (Is that kind or cruel?)

"Excuse me. I didn't realize that's the way it was."

"I knew all along you were lying."

"The music was crying at the moment."

"The can opener is too sharp."

"*bamotswol heslewt.*"

"Go fuck yourself with a file."

"Keep with me." (Didn't I say that before?)

"Now I have the power to go into all those voices. I can finish all those dumb conversations I had and didn't have with Marc. And what's that? I'm walking into the house I share with Barbara. My only claim on her is that I didn't know her. She's made roast beef for me and poured pineapple juice. She's here. She's touching me deeply. I have it now. Only now and it hurts too much. It kills me."

"My hands are on the tiles at the edges of the roof. Always been impulsive, not to say reckless." He swung his legs over the edge and sat down on the low wall with a wicked grin, looking at his lower eyelids.

"Ahmjes a-settin' hare on the river bank watchin' fer whut maght come aloang in the way of a oppurtunity." He settled back on his haunches and swung his feet vigorously back and forth like a version of Huck Finn.

"Ow." A grunt came out as a laugh. "Let's not overdo this thing. Don't want to bruise those heels. Maybe this is the time for caution. (Good a time as any, to be sure.) Lil thoughtfulness. Maybe this holiday spirit should be resisted, if only cause it's so enjoyable. What'll you accomplish here, bro? Mess up some pavement. Fill a box. But we know that puritan bullshit and where it came from: the father of lies. Stopped me from having a good time all my life." A fierce spasm of anger pulled his muscles burning tight, and he felt so close to jumping that icy fear surged over him, and he had to pull back.

"Whoa. I'm no athlete, and I'm pretty shaky. I'd better get back on the roof before the next event." He lifted his legs gingerly and, with his feet on the roof again, stooped forward with his hands on the tiles to catch his breath.

"Can't get much closer than that—without coming. So what'd you pull back for?'"

"Don't worry. The closer I get, the more I feel it drawing me, like the root of a tidal wave, lifting me over."

"Aaah. You're puttin' on airs, enjoying your little voices."

(The life that ends and the life that begins both pull us toward unfolding, toward telling our story, toward becoming one another. And as we cross each other, the hope of surviving, the movement away from death, becomes unbearable, shameful.)

Ira walked around the top of the courtyard. Everyone's lights seemed to be out above the fourth floor except for a TV on the fifth and a dim light in Brenda's place. Maybe she was making love to a boyfriend, but it was Monday. From the other side of the yard, he looked at the first floor. "Doesn't seem to be a light in our living room. Must be after 11:30. The news is over."

On the fourth floor, windows were lit and he saw someone's feet walk in slippers. His throat contracted and his mouth grimaced. "I don't want to see your home. I've had it with your love and conversation." He walked energetically back to the spot over his parents' living room where he had sat on the tiles. "What is it that you do to each other that makes you believe

At eleven, the prisoners were led out to join a double column of twelve men. A stocky guard spoke in a steady, rational administrative coo as he unloaded hardware along the lines: "Now this is a difficult point, fellas, and you'll have to be patient. The standard procedure for transporting a group of men is to link them in a manacle. With all that science has invented, this is still the only way to be sure people don't run off in all directions. Now I know that none of you guys are going to be foolish enough ..." And so on as he snapped the bracelet on each wrist, with two feet of chain between men.

He seemed to Marc to inculcate into them that whatever castrates you unctuously must be reason. "Our lives are forced into continuous lines, but if that you're not cutting each other up? Bright question, Ira. Everyone does it, but you cut yourself up. And when I judge myself, who's judging? My crave to be myself, which convicts me of either serving a master or thrashing into incoherence. Now you put your finger on it, my lad, and it put its finger on you. Someone inside myself I hate like murder, the stake I'm burning at. Every breath I let out struggles to be free."

Ira stood back and lifted his hands. with the intention of a grand flourish toward the sky, but as he spoke, his arms relaxed into a shrug. His low, husky voice was just above a whisper: "Yo, baby. Whaddaya saydere, Jahve, baby? Have I got an offering for you. Man, this is good stuff, first born." He closed his eyes, pushing the middle of his lower lip up, turned his head to the side, put his chin on his throat, and opened his hands upward, to express his benevolence and his extremely high quality.

"What I wanna say's 'You got it' I mean here's your fucking life!"

there are enough prisoners, another line is chained beside ours, confusing movement."

After fifteen minutes, they were rasped and clanked down a staircase and across a yard into a courthouse. Marc found himself in a room full of prisoners. A few were specifically political, and talked about how certain judges would punish people for protest actions. But the radicals left early, and the rest mostly talked about how innocent they were. Marc settled near Rick and listened to him rapping with a guy he'd latched onto. Isaac was extremely dark and squarely built, his hair sticking out in nubby points. He and Rick talked about auras or vibrations as Isaac's staring eyes, electric hair, and slow, droning voice projected buzzing in the air.

"This cat Samson got powerful vibes. He looks at people and they stop short."

"I've seen him on Telegraph," Rick said. "He has a deep walk."

A tall man who said he'd been framed as a thief said, "Is that the dude walks like this?" He

He stopped and considered. "Well, Maybe *fucking* is the wrong term for someone who got fucked in the head. Not trying to be pretentious, just accurate. Kayo, well here's your fuckable life, old man, old god. You know what you can do with it. I hope it gives you piles." His arms fell and he let out a sobbing laugh from his chest and slumped over, deeply satisfied.

His breath slowed down and he thought, "Now you went and did it. God or Satan or whoever is going to give you extra shock treatments for that. Well, I don't care. I've got my own world now. I've always been afraid. Might as well be afraid for something real for myself—for my own feelings, not some old man's. But of course it won't mean much unless I follow it up."

The tiles were raised in the middle like a turtle's back. Ira took a deep breath and put his right knee on the inside of the rise and grabbed the ledge with both hands, inside and outside, on his right. Then he put his left knee up and then raised that knee so that his left foot was on the tiles. "Good thing I pulled one hip after the other in movements that started fast and ended increasingly slow.

"That's him," said Isaac. "He practiced that walk for hours in front of a mirror before he got it right."

Ira had been concerned for years with walking the way a man really should. He charged at Marc with a massive stride to reach his apotheosis of commitment. He once let Marc know that he sometimes rubbed his prick before he went into locker rooms so it would look big. And after a vacation, he put lipstick on his undershirt to make it look like he'd made out, but they saw through it and laughed at him.

Prison was exotic for Marc, a chance to talk to people from whom he was usually separated, a source of pride, even a treat. Once he realized that he was not in danger, protected by the police, he had a ball, in his surreptitious fashion. It was a reservoir of material for storytelling, one of the high points of his life. "As if nothing can fail to benefit me, just as nothing can fail to hurt Ira. I attained this rehearsed," he said, though it wasn't true. Then he raised his right foot, pushed himself up strongly with his hands and stood on the tiles. His arms went out in front and behind to hold him steady at first. But then despite a low-degree tremble, he set his hands on his hips and his knees apart and stood up straight.

"Bravo. Give that man the clap. Quite a performance, though it was only to please an audience of local loonies. Very local—all in one body. I can't stay like this too long—won't find another ledge to step onto. And I couldn't get up this way again." He sighed deeply as he inhaled, thinking it was a sigh both of anxiety and of relief.

Then he saw his father's face and his mother's face in pain. Joel's pain was before an outburst. There was a terrified gleam in his eye and he seemed to glimpse a truth he could not bear. And then he was driven to rave, to attack, to excoriate. Judith's pain came to her as an afterthought: she looked down and pursed her lips as she condition when I got together with Carol, or maybe I blame her for a tendency I've always had."

For the others around Marc, however, prison was a grinding debasement. They were stuck with it, though they may have had as many dreams as he. And his efforts to show awareness of their plights were insulting to them, as if he could not help being destructive. Two weeks later he met Rick lit up on Telegraph and they shook hands. Marc regretted not having spoken earnestly to Rick that night, and when Marc put stress on how he really should take care of himself, Rick's face turned hard. "You take care of *your* self," he said, and walked away. The connection they'd had in jail had evaporated. So all Marc could do was tell himself to remember, remember, remember that every moment of happiness he had was stolen from someone else. The Jew Jesus was right to insist that every success was a crime. But he wouldn't remember. The truth was only a crutch he used to support his selfish life.

realized that something was dreadfully wrong. Her eyes glazed in smears of anguish.

"How I'm hurting them," Ira thought. "I'm slicing open their eyes, tearing out their hearts. Should I try to explain to them? What could I explain? That I love them? But I don't love them. That's what's wrong. I don't love them because they don't love each other, don't love themselves. Love is a disguise for destruction, and to recognize it puts me outside of life. To pretend there's love here would be a farce, a bad lie to die on, or to live on. Hey, if this is what love is, then what I'm doing is it. Devouring and being devoured.

"You've already taken responsibility, Ire. May as well be true to your miserable self. Yes, this clears things up marvelously. Should do it more often. But there's the old question. This sparkling wit, this scintillating humor, who's it for? Well, whoever it's for, one thing is clear. I'm fed up with him. What has he given me for my brilliance? By the time I was twelve, I could see how much better it was not to be smart. Of course I solved that problem by losing my mind. The handling of life's little dilemmas has always been a forte of mine.

If I moved my feet forward so that my heels were on the hump of the tiles, I'd have trouble holding myself back from plunging forward, but I already find it hard holding myself back. Eager to go. The closer I get, the better I feel. Enough procrasturbation. I need someone to count one-two-three, like diving into a pool."

Then he heard his mother say, "There, there, it's all right." And Joel said, "Attaboy, that's showing 'em." And Marc said, "I'll write the truth about you." And Marcy said, "I love you." And Red said, "You're a helluva guy." And Professor Magalaner said, "You're a brilliant young man." And Dr. Mendelson said,

The courtroom was empty. "Mr. Glogover," the judge said, "You are charged with being drunk in public. How do you plead?"

Marc thought, "Obsequiously." He said, "I did it, your honor, but I don't drink. It was just a fluke."

"We're clearing up your complex." And God said, "I forgive you, my child." And Ira said, "I'm saved." And Ira said, "Don't do it, you fool!" And he crouched a little, and then he jumped out.

"This great sense of flying and lifting. Is Brenda there? She'd be impressed. Can't see. Another social opportunity gone. I jumped up and forward off a swing, flying and landing perfectly on my feet (like a bird) to spring ahead. To run and save my brother. Then I was a hero. Maybe I'm a hero now, saving them all. The air is cool. I'm free. No responsibility. I can move any way I want. Can't make a mistake. No gravity. There was a decision I was supposed to make. To forgive them or not. Must have done both. Glad to be rid of that decision. Hot dog. This is the life."

There was a massive slam like his father hitting him in the head and his senses went out. "Uh, oh. Didn't sound too good, did it, Marc old boy? Yes, we're with each other whenever we're playing. Now I can forgive everyone and stop holding down the scalding terror. But

Ten days suspended sentence and a brief warning. He was essentially innocent. When he claimed his things, they said his wife had brought a book that hadn't reached him. He stepped into the sunshine with Northrop Frye to find that he was next door to Berkeley's innocuous City Hall. Five blocks from home in a city named after a man who maintained that the world was a dream.

Tired, but light-headed and expansive, he strode the clean serenity of Grove Street. "This feeling of springing from the ground to the swelling of my heart that I had after I met Carol, when I ran up the ramp on the last stop of the subway singing, 'Free at last.' That was the first time I walked home through the park from the West Bronx at night. It was a miracle I wasn't robbed on those late walks, but I had inserted myself into an ongoing miracle. Those were some of my happiest times, coming home late from Carol's. I'm on my way to her now. Bounding along through the empty air, the glowing silver levels, slopes and foliage of the where is my life? When will it come to me? *Payshi gulu solog.*" silent, moonlit park, shooting off hand gestures, shadow flickers, and crazy free ideas, like Ira when he was excited. Realizing that now I knew who I was.

17

THE RELAY

1967-68

Marc and his family flew in from Berkeley for the funeral and he found his mother swirling in hysteria. She hardly stopped howling and gasping during the entire four days they were in New York. "Why couldn't He take me? It should never have happened, my life. Let them bury me now. I only want to die." Marc was disturbed by her certainty that God took her son, and wondered if her "he" was really capitalized.

One afternoon when she was shrieking frantically, Marc tried to calm her down by saying, "Please try to take it easy, Mom. Remember, you've got to carry on." He knew as he said it that it wasn't especially true.

"Carry on," she said, lifting her eyebrows, "*Oy* am I going to carry on, my son!" In the midst of her turmoil she was chiding him, including his English major's diction, because he was out of touch with reality. Carol had already begun to criticize him in a similar way. Like the Laputans in *Gulliver's Travels*, Marc needed someone to follow him around and rap him over the head to remind him that reality was out there. He wanted women to control him for selfish reasons: he made his contact with life through them.

Judith blamed herself for staying with Joel: "I should have left him right away rather than staying with a lunatic. Other women get divorced and manage. Yoyel and Ira had no more chance than a falling body. It's falling, so it falls. It falls until the earth stops it." Her voice melted, then hardened. "But I was too selfish. Attached to old-fashioned ways."

Joel cried too, but he was more stalwart. "This could have been avoided. If he had listened to me and taken the vitamins in the first place, this never would have happened. I wanted to move to Long Island, where he could have had a decent home, valuable real estate. But she had to move to this hell-hole of a Bronx with her darling brother the swindler. Well she poisoned him but good with her rotten lies, and now look at the results."

Joel had long shifted from blaming Ira to blaming others for Ira. Once, when Joel was insisting more stridently than usual that Ira should have listened to him, Marc was moved by loyalty to Ira to say, "He had enough of you."

Marc felt uneasy, but Joel took it in stride: "So you're talking like your hero. You want to be another Ira, reading those crazy books. You're impressed by his accomplishments. Get in on the ground floor and you can work your way up to the roof."

The funeral parlor, not far from Yankee Stadium, was crowded with members of two families that were large without being close. The parents had asked a number of relatives to put Ira up over the years, hoping that some other environment would help him. Because they had been understandably turned down, there were few whose sympathy they wanted to accept.

Ira, though he was always tall, looked unnaturally long in his final home. The coffin looked like the hull of a ship, an ocean liner, and the cadaver seemed to be its smooth, stately superstructure. They had processed the body carefully, and there was no sign of injury from the fall. The flesh seemed hard and dense as stone—the skin was pale, clear, and waxy. The face was surprisingly undisturbed. The nose seemed large, straight, and dignified, like a tent. The mouth and brow were only slightly troubled. They seemed to be trying to concentrate. His eyebrows met in a few dark hairs between his eyes that added to the impression of focus. Marc looked at him looking thoughtfully at the insides of his eyelids.

Ira seemed to be trying to figure out what he should do to straighten things out. Marc thought, "Maybe the insides of his lids are mirrors in which he peers backward into himself, back into the past. I'm driven into the future while he's stuck in reverse time."

The cemetery was far off in New Jersey, and after a long drive, Marc was dazed during the burial. He kissed his rich uncle Dave and his beautiful cousin Linda in ways that were too erotic, on the lips. But his alienation was soon submerged in a massive convulsion of sobbing that swept over the group. Marc wondered if Ira would be proud. The three survivors were brought together in the deepest of that outcry, much as all four of them had been brought together earlier. But the sobs, wrenched to a climax as the coffin groaned into its hole, were fiercer now—in tune with the unheard wail that emanated from the invisible lost member of their lament, whose crying was outside any register.

After the grave was finished, Marc went with his parents to look at it. No stone was ready, and since Marc was married, a stone for three, Judith, Joel, and Ira, had been ordered. As they were starting back to the car with Uncle Bernie, who had cheerfully driven them out, Marc kicked something with his foot and picked it up. He didn't realize until he was a few yards away that it was a metal marker with Ira's name on it and a point on the bottom. When he tried to find the place in the earth where it had been planted, he couldn't. He decided it would be too disturbing to tell anyone, so he put it back on what seemed to be the right end of the right mound.

Later it occurred to Marc that he had moved the marker, and that the stone might go in the wrong place. How could he be sure it was an accident? When he was three, he hit Ira in the head with a hammer. If he had taken Ira's life, why shouldn't he see that even his grave was lost? While driving home Bernie said, as if to explain Ira, that among his three brothers, Joel was always known as the disturbed, angry one.

The next day, Marc, Carol, and Sybil flew back to Berkeley, where Marc returned to work on his Ph.D. studies. For a long time after this, he would insist that he had no way of knowing that suicide was a possibility for Ira. He repeated the arguments he had used to justify his trip west: that he had lost contact with Ira and had seen himself as unable to help because of Ira's hostility.

"I could blame myself. It's only natural to blame yourself when a relative dies and I have a huge responsibility: most likely, Ira would have survived if I had stayed in New York, but as I told the parents, it's irrational to blame oneself for things one couldn't know about in advance. A spiffy argument to excuse just about anything.

"Of course, I could ask why suicide never occurred to me—it sure suggests a lack of concern for Ira. I can rummage through the past and find clues that he was self-destructive. That scene on the cliff that I probably dreamed shows that I knew it deep in my mind. He was caught on the rocks of my mind. But that's seeing time backward, making the future cause the past. As if it ever didn't.

"Yet time has to move forward. It's under orders to. The forward stride of time is the way to life, the healthy way to live; while the backwardness drags one back to death, like grabbing one's own butt. I could let it haunt me and spoil my life and work, but what good would that do Ira?

"What I said to Mom is really true of me (what I say of everyone is): I have to carry on for Ira's sake, not to mention my family. He's in me more than he's in anyone else, even if the parents last. They were never on his side as I was, I think. I turn into him when I'm ironic or angry, or even jolly or strong. If I dream of him, that dream is more based on him than any other version of him going. I have to have children for Ira, and write for him. I'll return to him and understand him as well as anyone can. He'll live, grow, and change with me. I'll realize potentials in him that he never got to realize. It's an illusion, but it's all he's got."

He heard a voice: "You've got it all figured out, don't you, sonofabitch. You're going to make a corporation out of me, like a butcher who knows the use of each cut of meat. Whatever is good for you is good for me. Ain't that convenient? But let me tell you about *me*. You wanna keep moving forward, but I begin when you get dragged back. You wanna flush me, but I'll come flying out of that toilet. As you get older, you're gonna get further into reverse time. This is where I reside, as a bad dream. Until you die, I'll be your death coming after you. So you'll be begging forgiveness for the rest of your life like a broken record or a pious person. Every time you say something stupid or selfish to hurt someone, to hurt yourself, you'll be talking to me."

Marc was bent over his desk, his head on his hand. His eyes were clenched shut in grief, but his mouth had a little smirk. What he heard and what he answered made him feel like he was spinning in space: "Right on, brother, but you're still using my mind to speak. And you're going to work for me with no strike, providing me with hot and cold running inspiration. Sound like you, don't I? Why, I can find a new use for you every day, like a dessert topping that's also a rug cleaner. For example, you'll keep me from suicide. If things get rough for me, I'll think of what I owe you, and that'll keep me from giving up. No use to bluster, buster, cause we're going to be together for a long haul, and I won't be able to help degrading you, defiling you: it's my only way of bringing you to life."

The voice said, "I can see you won't give me any breaks even though I'm two yards under the weather. But looky here, I'm more dangerous now 'cause I've got your knowledge. I know what you're going to do better than you do, and what you love will take you back my way, back into reverse. So I can tell the story you emerge from. I can turn the movie backwards. Show me what you believe in and I'll show you your crime.

"You've given your life to love and freedom, but you suspect that your happiness hurts those who don't have it. You want to open everyone's minds with drugs, but can't you guess what those drugs will do to those who aren't ready for them? Whenever you find out what you want, you'll find yourself in trouble, confronting me." (That spring, Marc met Miriam Knight, who attracted him with her wild freedom. It would take seven more years, and Miriam was more effect than cause, but it was inevitable that Marc would commit adultery, bringing death into his love.)

"You take nourishment from the hope that people can be equal and together, but you should know that no matter how you hide it, the social position you are working your way into depends on and even consists of your distinguishing yourself from those mizzabobble wretches who haven't been to college, not to mention graduate school." (A month later, Marc got busted and met Rick, whom he could help no more than he could help his brother.) "Your striving to give everyone the power to express themselves freely is a by-product of your need to prove that you're smarter than others.

"This is in the future, but it appears only through the voices of childhood, such as your bosom buddy Ira's. So the future is already in the past, and you'll be finding me to turn you back at the crisis of every dream. You'll make it, because you've got scads of happiness, oodles of love with Carol. Not to mention you're as ruthless as a hyena.

"You've got books to take you beyond the world. But what do you think you'll find beyond the world? You'll have to keep squirming around me to be happy, living off me and pretending you don't. You'll have a wonderful life over my dead body.

"You tell yourself that you accept it, but you can't know it without getting rid of yourself. And you're infatuated with yourself, the self you never stop unsuccessfully trying to differentiate from me. You can never realize how much you gain from the casting of my rod into the sky. Because insofar as you confront how you benefitted from my death, you have to come to grips with your responsibility for it, your own hand on the rod. That'll keep you scrambling, so my services are indispensable to your dynamic success. Baby, I'm the best father you've got, better than that punk Joel, simply divine."

18

STEALING BACK

1976

"As much death as my father has taken is not enough," Marc thought. "The thumb jammed back flat against the wrist, the racking of his leg with two metal pins through the bones, the smashed left half of his pelvis, swathed in bandages like oversized diapers, the tubes in his arms and penis, the seventy-two years and the heart condition, could only pay for one night, it seems. Here it is only my second visit since the accident, and already I'm restless about spending the night at my parents'."

As careless as the nineteenth century, the parents had little awareness of how traffic worked. Crossing at a corner without understanding how cars could turn, Joel became the second Glogover to fly without a plane. Though he'd had a severe heart attack not long after Ira's death, and though he had been knocked for ten feet, he was still going to survive for a long time. He would end in comedy because if Ira's death hadn't demolished him, nothing would. After all his years of turning off lights and chilling the tropical fish to avoid the poorhouse, the settlement of the accident was going to leave him with more money than he knew what to do with, and he would end up leaving it to Marc in a form that Marc could never access.

The parents (name for a rock group?) had gotten a new apartment because they could not stay in the old one, and they were settling into a life of having money. She liked to buy fancy clothes and furniture, and he enjoyed playing obsessively with investments. They watched a great deal of TV and fought a lot. They had more moral impetus to fight than ever, for they had to blame each other for Ira's death to avoid blaming themselves—continuing the process of blaming each other for his life. But without the possibility of Ira, there was less urgency to the battle and it became more of a game. Perhaps it had always been more of a game than the kids could see, although it had seemed deadly. There are deadly games. The highest pitch of the battles was to save Ira, and this was what destroyed him. So their fighting was less fierce now, although she never forgave him, even insisting at her own death on not forgiving. And he was to continue to devote his life to attacking her, even twelve years after she died. Nothing else involved him so.

Judith, sitting sideways on the bus seat next to Marc, held tightly to the armrest and looked forebodingly at the air before Marc's face as she complained about her daughter-in-law. Carol's crime had been to make a reasonable suggestion about Joel's dubious investments.

"She's concerned about my money? She's not going to get my money so soon so she can keep up that estate over there, that mansion." Carol did not care for housework and cultivated entropy. "The only one she takes care of is the cat. I'm telling you, if a thief looked in the window to rob the place, he would think it was already ransacked and go away. Joel is lying in the hospital more dead than alive and she's worried about my money. Oh, is she taking care of you, my son."

Marc blamed her because he couldn't watch the pretty woman on the other side of the bus while she went on so loudly about his wife. In fact, he couldn't have been able to look at the woman as much if he were alone. He blamed his mom that his best friends were out of town and that he had forgotten to bring a joint for his heartaches. He remembered the twisted figure of his father tilted to the side, unable to straighten his back against the pillows. The grey face speckled with discolorations, elbow and shoulder crested with dark maroon shredded abrasions. The pale, bloated prefiguration of a death less noble than the marble statue of his brother encoffined. Until now he had expected to enjoy this one.

Standing over the feeble, grizzled crustacean that was left of his life's arch-villain, he felt more sympathy than he had in decades for that sweat-misted, high-arched forehead. He realized for the first time that Joel's whole life was unconscious, that the penetration of his dark, gleaming stare and his piercing accusations was always focused on a nightmare. Marc wondered if the old man had let himself get hit to finally atone for the suicide of his son. He had never admitted the slightest bit of his overwhelming responsibility, assiduously blaming his wife, the doctors, and everyone else.

Marc understood for the first time how Joel loved Judith when he saw the old man complain so spitefully. It made Marc feel the old familiar tug of temptation to burst out telling him that he was disgusting.

"Ooh, I'm sick as a dog! You don't know how it hurts. It hurts like nothing ever hurt before. She had to go and put me in this hellhole, this slaughterhouse. She found a hospital where they would treat me like she treats me. *Schwartze* dogs! Oh, oooh, oooh! It hurts me so much. She's got me where she wants me now and she's enjoying it plenty. Happy days are here again."

Marc was not able to fully condemn Joel's *schrying gevalt* any more than he could espouse Judith's disapproval; Joel was more than a demon and she was less than a saint. So Marc's perplexity, together with the worn-out nature of what they said, led him then as now to withdraw and meditate: "For thirty-five years, as if praying to the god of rancor, Joel blamed more than everything on her, inspired by her to the sublime. It was the bread and wine she served him by stroking him into paroxysms of vituperation with her coolness. And on her side, she desperately needed his accusations to make her feel pure and superior.

"So I ached through the long, reeling spasms of my childhood, suffering from the undeviating hatred of my parents for each other and from the charges that I was spoiled. Yet now I find they spoiled each other outrageously with spite and adored each other with incisions. The frozen fury of their devotion transcended realities they could never deal with: the Yankee world of techno-logic, the life of their firstborn and his death, the lacerated flesh, the antiseptic repression of a hospital. Whatever hurt them did not exist except as a manifestation of each other. Every stroke of bad luck spoke for the hostility of the mate. They could not lose because they had together made a world founded on loss, a world that lost everything.

"All these years I've wondered what was wrong with me, what kept me from understanding, only to find out that I understood all along. Their love was not some absent mystery, but this present frenzied savagery. Is this why I'm in love and could my love for Carol turn to such poison, with selfishness enough on my part to spoil it? Can one person remain present to another except as a misunderstood complaint?"

They reeled off the bus onto the ragged turf of Co-op City, an immense project built on a foundation of garbage. Judith, who was evidently in a good mood, alternated between imprecise, exaggerated accounts of how long it would take Joel to walk again and malignant visions of Marc's in-laws. Marc, despondent at the dull evening before him, mulled over lost loves, lost fractions of love, lost fantasies, lost photos of fantasy.

The only useful action he could conceive was to swig some gin as soon as they reached the parents' prophylactic apartment, in which alchol was one of the useless decorations. The velvet, antiqued, and brocaded finishes of the furniture tended to be coated with fitted plastic covers, making the place a sort of con-dominimum. The furniture was unprotected when Ira and Marc were messing it up, but now it was protected from nothing. On the main wall of the living room hung the two pictures Ira had painted by numbers.

"You know," Marc said, "this place is something you've both agreed on since you moved here. This swanky furniture, these lamps and drapes, you both think they're fine." There was a lamp hanging from the ceiling by a thick golden chain that had panels of amber colored glass molded in bas-relief. He didn't mention their battles over detailed choices, this *ungepatchked tchatchke* versus that one.

"As fine as silk," she affirmed, "and good deals we got on this stuff too. But we could never get along, and since Ira died, it's worse. We blame each other for Ira all the time."

Marc caught a glimpse of his brother's spirit flickering between them. "But what could he blame you for? The only thing you ever did wrong was to defend Joel."

"What I did wrong? I turned Ira against Joel. I went to work and left him alone. That man doesn't need facts; he has imagination."

"It's called paranoia," Marc said quietly.

"*Nu*, so paranoia if it makes you happy. But what's the use? We both want to have a home, but we'll never have it."

"You know," he said, "I think that you do love each other, but your love takes the form of conflict. You need to fight all the time. It's your main source of satisfaction."

"Satisfaction? From this satisfaction, I feel like I can't go on. Like I'm already in *drehut* and death will be a relief."

Marc was disappointed that she wasn't impressed by his theory. He fell back on repeating some familiar formulas about how she should learn to ignore Joel because he always said the same things and she knew they weren't true. He added that Joel had his own afflictions. But he felt himself sinking into the old family morass of frustration blooming with images of gentleness brutalized.

After he had engorged three gins and three pounds of hefty food, his perception expanded to manifest the next step of his path. He had heard through a friend that one of his favorite former students, Ronnie De, was living on West 85th. He got the number from information, and he glowed like St. Theresa contracting on a well-hung arrow when he heard those dulcet South Philly tones: "Great meyun. Come owun deown."

His mom threw back her head with widened eyes: "It's necessary to go to bums in the middle of the night, so go ahead. But don't you come back here. Oh, no. You can sleep on Riverside Drive. The door will be locked." He pitied her poignantly as he eased out the door to her faint echo of threats that were terrible to his childhood.

The soul for whom there is no rest moves from bus stop to bus stop, jubilantly running, with books lightly rebounding in his briefcase, floating on short wind through the night air. "Got to keep movin', gotta keep movin'. Hellhound on my trail." He sometimes missed buses in his eagerness to get ahead, as they passed while he was between stops. Now, as he was trotting beside the road, an out-of-service bus came by with its front door open. The driver asked where he was going and said he was going in the same direction.

Small talking in the darkened bus with a driver who wanted to escape from the city he wanted to escape into, he noticed the lofty, pale bulk of Einstein Hospital approaching. He hopped off, and though visiting hours were over, he Fantomas'd himself through the silent burnished lobby and up to the eleventh floor. He hadn't expected to visit Joel until the bus appeared. The old man was annoyed to be visited at 11:30, but realized that Marc wanted him to be impressed. He seemed to think of turning off the TV suspended above him, though he didn't actually do so. He was inspired in his ordinary way, and not bothered by the man trying to sleep in the bed next to him:

"She won't give me one drop of sympathy. You'd have to see how nasty she is to believe it. She knows how I'm suffering, but all she does is stand over me and gloat. She keeps hounding me to eat the food here, which tastes exactly like dried, salted rock. If you take a rock and dry it in the oven for a few weeks so it won't be too juicy. Filet of charcoal. The only thing she enjoys in life is whatever gives her a chance to be mean."

Marc chuckled, thinking he understood: "I never realized how much you two love each other."

Joel was stopped by this for half a second: "I love her alright, but she just gives me bitter gall. She hasn't got the slightest idea." The old man was crying with a feeble whimper. "Look what she did to Ira. Was that the love a mother should give her son? She destroyed him with her insidious lies."

Marc thought, "He's crying because they can't face the possibility that they may actually love each other. It would be terrible to them to break down their defenses. And he brings Ira in because he holds an article of faith that Ira's story illustrates her evil in the most drastic way, sure any reference to Ira is a point-blank attack on her."

The old man tried to calm himself by watching the TV, but it was showing an Elizabeth Taylor movie. Marc saw that his fear of women made him withdraw from the screen in an effort to see where reality was.

"I could have helped him. I wanted to do everything for him. How he suffered. No one will ever know how he suffered, how he was tortured. What did I do wrong? I meant to do what was best, but you couldn't tell what to do. It all seems like a dream. All gone wrong and disappeared like a dream into the air. You can't call back a dream because it never existed.

"You know his feet were no good. He had to walk on those stairs in the ballpark. Did you ever see those big concrete steps? He should never have done that. That's what made him worse."

Marc thought, "He's gone back to telling me what I don't know, back to his theories. Of course, he does know more about Ira than I do. Was with him for five years before I was born, and stayed with him when I went away. My claim to know more is egotistical, pretentious. When he hasn't got Ira or Mom to push around and he's helpless, I sympathize with him. He let slip enough to show that he has inklings of his responsibility, maybe even a tenth of it, which is a lot. I couldn't handle one percent of his responsibility. His injuries have allowed him to talk, to feel."

Marc said, "You know, scientists now claim that schizophrenia is caused by genes. Ira was born with it, and maybe whatever anyone else did couldn't have stopped it. So you shouldn't worry about what you did. It's no use now anyway. You were caught in an impossible situation." Marc didn't believe this at all. Joel was the cause of Ira's derangement, but he might as well put the mangled Joel at peace.

Joel, his circuits broken by the treasonous and incomprehensible suggestion that he could be to blame for Ira, gave no sign of understanding: he was hardly inclined to see that he carried the insanity. "I wanted to go places with him, do things like other people. A social life can help a person's mind."

Marc's lips curled at the thought of Joel hosting a party in a Napoleon outfit in an asylum. "He's back to attacking Judith, but then I guess that's his way of expressing love. And his attacks on Ira must have expressed love, too. I guess I can manage to see this as a kind of love, but that may be my problem, finding love in destruction. Right now, I think I've had enough. To be fair, they know how much I was responsible, but they don't mention it. Since my childhood they haven't referred to the incident with the hammer."

Having paid his dues, Marc roared down to the West side in a bright, clean, almost empty subway car, imagining the forthcoming dope, pulchritude, and culture, anticipating vision. He even saw subways as visionary, and one reason he didn't drive was that public transportation allowed him to think, to be transported.

On the IRT, he decided that the idea that Ira's problem was genetic was no solution at all, only another version of God the accuser, blaming Ira. "What if the parents, the women, and the brother whom Ira saw as destroying him were only enacting the outlines of his own hereditary disaster? Then everyone would be not guilty and the actual world would be heaven, like the magic world of normality that Kafka's figures hopelessly strive for. Why should it be wrong to be crazy? We're all crazy on the inside. The most extreme form of insanity is to be sure you're right. That's why it's so powerful.

"This happy ordinary reality is a beautiful dream, and rationality is a fantastic religion. It's nothing like the truth of life, and people who live in such a world of innocence are selfish and self-deluding, denying that their happiness depends on lowering others by being superior. Normality can't be separated from imperialism. It's worth it to make myself miserable rather than to fall prey to such horrible nonsense. So I thank Ira piously ten times a day, for continually showing me the truth, my thaumaturgical therapist."

"Hold on, bro. You say that rationality is for folks like Joel, but he didn't understand the explanation you just laid on him; and maybe no one is more attached to Joel than you. You cling to your happiness with Carol, and normality is a pretense you used to separate yourself from me. Put your feet where you like, you'll still be kicking yours jewly."

West 85th Street hadn't changed much in the fifteen years since Ira moved from one uneasy room to another around here. As Marc walked down it, an enormous orange woman leaned her globular hubs out of a first-floor window and looked him passing in the eye: "Hold the pickles. Hold the relish. We do it all for you at McDonald's." Was she talking to him? What could she do?

Marc bounded up the numerous stairs to Ronnie's apartment, gasping when he reached the top, not aware, but not unaware, of why he had come. Ronnie, as warm as ever after two years, still had good grass, but he was not thriving as they had hoped he might. His girlfriend Stephanie had moved out, and he had no immediate prospects for publication except for a novelization of a film.

In the past, Marc and Ronnie had shared their writing with each other, offering each other critiques. Marc regretted that he had brought no writing with him, but then remembered his attaché case. He had packed some stories to mail to Val, who had gone to San Francisco to visit her estranged husband. Marc was afraid that Roger might open the mail if there was a Philly postmark, so he took them with him to mail from New York.

Marc read stories about his brother and his wife to Ronnie and got the kindest comments ever. Then he listened to Ronnie's story about an orphanage and criticized it ungenerously.

At three Ronnie gave him the bed and settled on the couch. The bed was not long enough and Marc tossed diagonally, thinking of Valerie as a slim sunlit statue of Diana smiling with her whole body, a refulgent smile that couldn't be answered. He forgot Carol because he could never lose her. He didn't have to dream of her because she was within him. She was the container of his dream of Val.

He had never been in Annapolis before and was there for profit, for a victory, something he couldn't handle. Beyond a solidly planted terrace extended the sea. He saw the crest of a wave, the bright quavering surface purling back from a mounting ridge in expanding swirls of crystal. The bottle-green swell of the sea was framed by starshaped leaves of light green, evenly coated with a clear sunshine he seemed to have forgotten. The chirping of birds on all sides mixed in his head like a cold drink stirred by a glass rod. He wondered what he was frightened of and realized that he was afraid he would win.

He was awake and knew he had been dreaming of Valerie, forgetting that he had lost her. Ronnie was up too and he suggested a walk by the river. First, they drew in the glow of another joint and stumbled scrupulously down the shifting stairs. It was almost four and the cool night air streamed through their bodies, colloidal with mist. Nothing could be seen in the distance because it was foggy, and the dim, flat surface of the street seemed like a stage setting. They crossed a wide, ghostly highway only occasionally swept by the blurred lights of passing cars. It looked to Marc like the magnified bottom of a fish tank, its light diffused through water. He hoped they wouldn't come on the huge body of a dead guppy, floating with its silver stomach up.

Past the highway, they stepped downward together on a narrow path slanting through night-bleached grass. Marc followed Ronnie, who was talking about writing: "When you write something, you have to get into the words. I mean, like I pick up a paragraph I wrote two weeks ago and I can't do anything with it because it doesn't mean anything to me. But if I sit down and go over it a few times, the connections planted in the words grow up around them and I'm ready to build on it."

Wide, low trees writhing in thick fog framed the path, first on Ronnie's lower side, then on his. "I can dig it," said Marc. "When I write, it's always like there's an earlier version that I wrote and lost, and I'm trying to get back to it. But then, even when you're living, what you're doing and seeing is only one version of what's happening. It's going on in a lot of other versions at the same time, in the same place."

Ronnie said, "Now I have to find a new woman and I bet she'll be like Stephanie, striving to reiterate Stephanie, whose every belch now enchants itself. What splendid times we're having in the distance through the twisted telescope of the past. Every sad stumble that was has become the only possible dance step, with an audience of cheering laughter as if every bed of groans in the hospital was a triumphant appearance, the nurses in stitches, man."

As they passed the second tree, Marc realized that they had left the city, placeless in a cloud of cream soup, though they had been enclosed by it only a highway ago. Of course, this side had been invisible then, but the other side seemed more invisible because it had already existed. They shunted from disappearing path to appearing path on their way to the Hudson on its way to the ocean, pacing slowly as their steps flowed.

Curving, even pilasters on a balustrade reiterated to form an interlocking illusion of stone and vibrant green liquid, punctuated by wreathed urns too high to be looked into without strain and disillusion. The grass was firm and even, thousands of green teeth without a cavity. A tap of a foot on a flagstone brought him to Val's intention.

"Oh, hello, Marc." Her limpid skin held in a firm embrace the sunlight it reflected. Her upper lip was forthright, resting cleanly on the balanced, subtly curving vessel of her lower, serene with relinquishment. The centers of her eyes were a green stream running into the distance. More than that of any woman he knew, Valerie's face belonged to herself. This is why he wanted it so and could never have it.

They turned to another path, longer and more curving, descending athwart a damp stone slope penetrated by a tunnel. Ronnie lifted his head and protruded his chin to point before. And far ahead in the somnolent vapor, which seemed to be growing a little thinner, near the mouth of the tunnel, they saw an irregularly shaped tall white object standing by the path and slowly undulating.

Marc remembered when he was six years old and he had been in a field in Newark where he had seen a cloth-covered figure of human stature, shaped like a narrow, distorted upright trapezoid. When Marc asked what it was, his father had said it was a witch someone had wrapped in canvas. He wondered if witches could be men as well as women. That night he stood in a dream of the bathroom, looking over the little white octagonal tiles. When he saw these tiles, he heard the rapping clang of the marbles he and Ira had played with on them, and this sound made him feel how dense and hard the tiles were. In the back of his head he sensed that something was in the shadow in the corner behind the door and was watching him.

A canvas-swathed form appeared and began to inch toward him. It was not moving in itself, but it approached him almost imperceptibly over the tiles like a floating statue, or the way a shape of light, burned into your eyesight, will drift across your field of vision if you allow your eyes to relax. Was he going toward it?

It was not much taller than a fire hydrant, but then, neither was he. A fold of grey canvas fell asunder on the creature and something began to emerge from its interior and stick out toward him: a narrow pale bony hand whose fingers seemed to fuse together in a gesture of entreaty. His breath caught, surprising him with an audible, choking sound, as if he were giving himself away, as if the creature, which now seemed to be wrapped in a grey blanket, could hear what was inside him. The ridge of the outer edge of the bathtub extended smoothly to his left, shining softly white.

"We have only about an hour and a half," Valerie said, "till Roger gets here. We'd better not try ..." Valerie's wealthy musician husband would be back soon, but Marc would never see him. A dazzling white sail leaned against the wind on Chesapeake Bay. Marc thought, "Is it wrong to love two people? One can only feel love for one at a time, so one keeps switching. But isn't that a reactionary ordering of the mind?"

It was a couple. They had been embracing with hardly any movement in the mist, and he began to distinguish them as they slowly, gently disengaged from each other. They were both dressed in white shirts and pants, with long, light hair and slim, pliable bodies. One was looking down and the other was looking away. He couldn't see their features or tell if either one was male or female. As he and Ronnie got closer, the couple separated, after pausing to look at each other, and walked languidly away in different directions. Marc thought the one going up toward the city looked female, while the one going down toward the river looked male; but this perception might be only conventional, as might the notion that this couple would meet again not far away. He couldn't quite admit it, but there was a momentary doubt as to whether they were people.

"Did you see that?" Ronnie asked as they watched the figures deliquesce.

Marc said, "I was tempted to tell them that we didn't want to interrupt, but it would have interrupted. New York is more real than reality. Where else do you see something like that? But then, maybe I'd better confess something. I hate to say this, but I'm doing research. You see, I used to walk here with my brother Ira when he lived on the West Side. That was maybe fifteen years ago. We used to watch the river and talk. The beauty we felt is still here. I can't recall much of what we said. I would tell the parents to let him go and tell him to come home. Don't know which was worse. Both sides thought I was opposed to them, and I felt self-righteous." On saying this, he thought, "All I remember is myself."

"Go ahead and think," Ronnie said self-effacingly.

Marc thought, "He's too unselfish, as any friend of mine would be." He saw glimmers of light in the distance by the river. "This is the last place I really had contact with Ira," he thought. "The times I saw him after he lived on the West Side, he was too withdrawn into the poisoned well of his nightmare to be present. And the recovered Ira never really seemed to be there. No wonder I keep getting this feeling that he's still out there somewhere—pacing in the corridors of the city or on the slopes of this Park—still peripatetically trying to understand his problem, trying to find a way out."

Ronnie and Marc passed into the straight, round tunnel, massively arching down over them, their footsteps clacking back to clash upon themselves in echo. The ringing of stone and air superimposed on itself in the damp cathedral of night. Their eyes peered anxiously into the long darkness, trying to be sure that no one or nothing was there, that every shadow was lifeless.

Marc was writing about his dead brother as a demon falling through darkness outside the wall, when he heard a knock behind him. It was 2 a.m. in his attic study, and he wondered what the sound could be. He had already cut off a branch on a tree that had reached the roof. And it didn't sound like a raccoon. He paused with his hands suspended over the keyboard, heard another tap on the wall, and snapped his fingers. "I'm sane," he told himself. "I don't hear anything." He typed on hesitantly and soon heard two more taps in rapid succession.

"Marc," Val said, "Why is it so difficult? Why can't I adjust to it?"

"That's the way love is," he replied.

She tried to hold his meaning. She had wanted to learn from him what love was. Her eyes wandered vacantly as if she had withdrawn to look for something in her head. "God, I've known some good bad men. Love on a bed on a floor in a car in the woods. We did it in my granny's bed. It makes its own no place. Two people helping each other to masturbate, trying not to be alone."

He said, "I don't want to distress you." His hand was on her arm, claiming her. "I want to help you."

"You want to believe you're helping me." Her pupil, seen from the side, bulged brightly downward into an aura of sunlit sea.

"Well, the best way to believe that is to really help. Do you think I want to fool myself? If I'm wrong, tell me how to act. I know it's hard to help anyone. I've tried it, and I was amazed at the ingratitude I got. It finally occurred to me that merely by taking it upon myself to help anyone, I'm claiming my superiority. Yet people have to be able to help each other or we're all trapped. Maybe with time we could learn to get closer."

He took her other arm, thinking painfully, "Why does this sound like such bullshit? Why can't I express what hurts me so? Why do I feel so hollow? Religion is right about one thing. To love two women is to be in hell. The more you love them, the deeper the circle." After a still moment, he heard Valerie tap the flagstone with her foot. She knew what he was thinking, more than he was aware of.

Echoes of footsteps against footsteps mingled and faded as Marc and Ira emerged from the arching tunnel to see the expanse of the river before them, moving while still through the fog of pre-dawn.

"What should I do? What should I say?" Marc wondered. "Whenever I'm with him, I feel as if I'm in the wrong place, in a situation that can't exist." Marc looked anxiously at his brother's stolid face, trying to detect a sign of whether this was really happening.

Ira gazed at the wide, streaming field of milk toward which they walked, apparently trying not to let on that he was aware of anything unusual. He was thinking, "There he goes again, looking at me as if he can't believe I'm really here. No consideration for my affliction (he, he). Well, I can't afford to lose my temper, so I'd better pretend I didn't notice. After all, it's my craziness if I want that gangling lummox to think I'm for real. As if anything was real to him. My strict dependence on playing the role of a mysterious god forces me into a series of poses."

"Marc," Valerie hesitated, looking at his shoulder, "I don't know how to tell you this. You see you ...." She insisted to herself, "frighten me." She felt she was fighting for herself, to avoid being swallowed by him. But was there ever a chance of that?

He was moved to pull her toward him, pressing the sides of her back, feeling her spine with his fingertips, her breast on his. He was so suffused with warmth or anguish that it took him a minute to speak. Over her shoulder, a wave peak in the sea receded to a plain, and then to an invisible valley.

"It's terrible of me," he said, "but that impresses me as a compliment. That I should frighten anyone is incredible. You make me more than I am." He wrenched her in his hug. "I suspect that if you stopped fearing me, you'd have less love. I don't quite want you to believe me when I tell you the truth—that I can't hurt you." The swollen water receded in painful gradations as if it were embarrassed to realize that it was only water in a dream. If one drowned in it, would one wake up?

"Love," she said, "it's Carol you love. With me, you just make up theories to justify what you take. All we can find out about each other is deception, but maybe we can find something there, the truth."

One of those awkward pauses, parallel pairs of eyes speaking in gleams the dull light of the river. Perhaps they were both thinking, "Let's just sit and watch the water. People can sometimes communicate better without talking. We've argued this over a hundred times. Always it seems as if something has to be done, things can't go on this way, life can't get any slimier without smearing into chaos. But it goes on, or maybe we only hope it goes on. And we secretly suspect that if we acted for change, it would hurl us toward an abyss. That any movement forward between us will head for decline."

If this was what they were both thinking, it would have been a communion. But it was probably only Marc thinking it, not realizing he was playing ventriloquist with his perishing brother, giving him a voice by stealing his own away from him.

Marc didn't know what to say. He felt as empty as the lingering doorway of a house that has burned down. He heard the wind ripple in across the sea, as if the air were slapping itself, and felt a changing breeze on his arms. Val was thinking, "He's very sincere, until he gets me to bed. Then he uses me for what he wants." But she was caught in her beauty, and the syncopation of her breathing, close to him, contrasted and meshed with the undulating lights, swells, and plunges of the bay.

They talked on listlessly. His concentration waned. He realized with a twist of his ache that what he feared most was that he should be responsible for losing her. This was what kept him clinging to hopes of her for years after there was no basis for hope. And with another twist he realized that he only wanted her to do the act his wife couldn't do, to be lost.

Fearing the loss of contact, he spoke to assert the reality of the scene by taking an established role: "I guess there's no use nagging you, Ira, but you've gone through so many places now, and here you seem to be finding a problem again. I don't think this guy Stein has any such suspicions of you. You're building up a plot with very little basis in reality. That's fine if you can write it, but I mean, you worry too much."

"Lemme ask you something, Sherlock." Ira looked at Marc sharply, the hairs at the juncture of his eyebrows bending in concentration.

Marc looked in his eyes and fought his fear, thinking, "This is no dream that I can cast off. I have to see his reality if I'm going to help him."

"What do you know about it?'" Ira asked in a legal frame. "I mean, in order to investigate thoroughly, you have to be at the scene of the crime, *n'est pas*? But you, are you really here? Really listening to me? I think you're off in print somewhere, off with your books. Your books are just dreams kept at a distance, kept under control. And you see me as a footnote."

"That's not true," Marc asseverated. "If I wanted to read, I could do it in the library. I wouldn't have to drag my ass down here on the subway. I'm here to be with you."

"The two main reasons you come down here are first, you want to soak up summa that cosmopolitan atmosphere of Manhattan, and second, you've been ordered to report on the prodigal son to the parents. Well, be sure to tell them that I'm doing okay."

"Doing okay? Man, I wish you were. You haven't even bothered to unpack your stuff this time. You're living out of boxes. You haven't written anything in years that I know of. You aren't even looking for work. You have to make up your mind what you're doing. It wouldn't be so bad if you had a plan."

The corners of Ira's mouth curled in a saturnine grin. He started as if to speak, then stopped. His eyes shifted from point to point over the smoothly rippling surface of the Hudson, like water striders. "I've made my decision, my vocation, father. Something that matches my mind and involves a minimum of high-stepping. It's thought out, planned, solid—'massive and concrete,' as Wemmick would say. Indubitably more realistic than any other plan bar none.

"I'm going personally to be a professional tree. I can just whisper away in the breeze. What could be more serene? Yet hey, it's elevating and has growth potential." He pronounced carefully. "Taking a course on Orchard Street. Wanna have a lotta roots, so folks can step on me. Got a shovel on you, Guvnor? Dante would dig it. Tell the parents to send pay dirt. Plant a son in the Holy Land. Fertilizer by Marc. I can branch out. You can carve 'Marc loves Carol' on my trunk."

Convulsed in a seizure-like laughter through the nose, they quieted gasping. Light from a park lamp tinted pale green shone through the leaves of a tree behind Ira. Marc looked at the vague water. "Don't you have to forget about an awful lot to think that I don't love you? Think of all the stories of Looiyoo and the pillow fights and the bike rides and the Pogo letters. We both know you did everything for me. Why should I turn so callous so suddenly?"

"Because the world is run by parents. They've got the money and you work for them. But being a budding humanist or professional liberal artist, you don't want to feel guilty about siding with them against me, so you come off the wall at me with all that crap. To feel good by throwing a bone at me. You're supposed to know about motivation. What do you think it is that makes people keep saying to themselves, over and over, 'I did all I could'?"

Marc came back to find Val's hands trembling near her thighs as she spoke, "Look, this won't work, you know, it's my fault. I'm some kind of cold turkey." He thought how honest she was and he remembered, as she reached an eye and a hand toward him, that he had once said that the rich attack people by feeling sorry for them.

The tapping persisted, and he turned to make sure there was no face peering through the third-floor window in the corner behind him. Feeling his chin brush his shoulder, he was reminded by the diagonal angle across the attic of the old dream in which he looked at the corner of the bathroom. He saw nothing in the gap below the blinds but night air and the trees across the street. So that should be okay. He tried to type on, but as the knocking continued intermittently, he found tension building. Finally, he leaped up and rushed to the window, determined to confront it, no matter what. If it was malign, he'd just fight it. Better than passively letting it approach from the rear. He wrenched the blinds up with a clatter and looked out.

A deep breath. What he had to say was a set speech, but he put his heart into it: "I'll always be happy, Val, I'll always feel light when I think of you. You're so beautiful and kind and smart."

Turning toward the house, anxious to flee though she had no hope to flee to, Valerie steadied herself by feeling the regular movement of her thighs against one another, as if riding a horse. The cool shining doorknob hastened her withdrawal from the scene. She felt she had never been there. "But then," she thought, "where was I?"

The broad Hudson, filled with itself and softened with mist, seemed stationary. Marc tried to calm his mind by staring at it for respite from the barbed claws of his brother's thought. Sooner or later, Ira brought him up against a question that he could not answer. And he might worry about that question until it became the question of which his life consisted.

Suddenly, he saw one of the dark grey stones on the light grey edge of the embankment flinch. Two minutes of scrutiny revealed no further movement and he began to think of it as a trick of his head. Then another motion appeared a few yards on and he was able to follow it. Soon he perceived scurrying rats along the edge of the river.

Ira spoke: "That's not T. S. Eliot, my boy, that's life. Rats know more than intellectuals do about how the world operates. If you try to be nice, do something that's not based on selfish defensiveness, someone will grab you and jab his snout into you and gnaw your flesh. The way Joel treats Mom. So you chew at me with your first-class advice for a while and tell yourself that you're helping.

But you're really helping yourself, giving yourself a helping. Want some cranberry sauce?

"And while you're at it, you'll also take notes for some book you plan on. Don't miss a twitch. The more it hurts me, the more it's worth to you. But of course you're not actually doing it. You're just observing without having any influence. The food just happens to fly into your mouth. And you'll happen to survive if your old competition is eliminated and the albatross-turkey is gone."

Ira was driven to his feet by energy crackling through him. He paced tensely back and forth, his heels springing off the ground, hands gesticulating shakily at his sides, mouth and brows pursed as his eyes stared shining downward before him. Marc found it impossible to argue with his older brother because he felt that everything Ira said was true, so he consoled himself with the reflection that it was only part of the truth, an unlivable part.

His heart heaving, Marc looked out the attic window and saw below him on the lawn two men who had been throwing pebbles. The bigger one began to piss on his hedge. It was Bob, whom he had betrayed, his friend Bob, whom he had wanted to help and had ended up screwing deeper into purgatory. He had returned from Ireland. It was terrible to see him, but it saturated Marc with joy. He thought, "What have I done to deserve this boon?" and rollicked down the stairs to let in Bob and the other student with him. They got high and read the story he had been working on. For a time, he felt like a writer, but when he was done, Bob had to go away for good, still betrayed.

Ira halted his incantatory strut and stood fixed, staring at Marc. "Do you really want to help me?'

"Of course I do," Marc answered apprehensively.

"Then follow me," Ira said, and he began to walk firmly across grass to the southeast. Marc sprang after him and they strode over some fields and along a road between banks of stone. Then they climbed laboriously up a slope interspersed with scraggly bushes, outcroppings of granite, and rough, flaky stretches of mica schist.

Finally, they trod across some flat ground like pavement and up a stone staircase bending along the curve of a wall, shadowy and vacant with the approaching dawn. As they stepped up the stairs, Marc had trouble keeping up with his energetic brother, who seemed to be approaching something he longed for.

Marc looked toward the sea; his vision rushed towards him. He had won. When Val was gone, he told himself she was too honorable to look back. So he fell on his knees gasping. The horizon embraced his temples and he felt the pulsing of the sea in his blood. He crumpled, turning, and fell on the grass. The immense, radiant sky wheeled above him, through streaks of diffuse cloud. His innocence was a trick he played knowingly on himself.

The sweetness of the receding sunbeams flooded him, drenching his flesh, and he groaned and rocked with pleasure. It reminded him of certain times when he had awakened early in the morning filled with a glow of well-being and convinced that all of his problems were illusions. He wanted to explain to Val, even to her husband. He felt that if he could make anyone understand how happy he was, then they must be happy too. In his contracted vision, he saw the falling sunlight sweeping across the waves, giving the surface the clarity of vitreous humor. Only later would he realize that he had thrown her away and that they would miss each other for the rest of their lives.

At the top of the stone steps, we emerged onto a large terrace floored with dark stone and edged by a curving balustrade high above the park. There was a gap in the balustrade, a gate leading nowhere. At a distance from the edge were several white pillars about eleven feet tall. Probably originally there had been a bandstand with a top on it. The place seemed to be built for a ceremony or a memorial.

"Listen," I said, "I finally realized that we didn't understand the parents. They really loved each other tremendously, incandescently, and that's why they were always so nasty. It's their way of giving. I mean, it's difficult to take love. Blake thought that the purpose of all human life is to struggle to accept love:

> And we are put on earth a little space
> That we may learn to bear the beams of love

"And the parents spent so many years of hard times trying to forget childhood in order to survive that they couldn't possibly have any idea where we were at. Yet they were still toddlers inside or they wouldn't have had such tantrums. So if you only look beyond the external complications and realize the central truth, you'd see that it isn't really that serious after all. Just a misunderstanding. They did love each other, and they loved us. So you have reason to be glad. You can forget all that bitterness."

Ira grinned and nodded his head. "Boy, you really are a full bucket. You could look at a cat eating a mouse and say it was love. You might have a point, but it wouldn't say much for love. And while your theory may do you oodles of good, I've got a different point of view. Seems to me I've been waiting for love all my life, love anyhow, anywhere, from anyone with anything. For a while, I thought I'd get it from you, but all I ever got from you was a reflection that drained the mirror. And with girls, they only wanted to use me to please themselves—but the ones who didn't, I always mistreated. And that must go back to the parents, who each wanted to prove that the other was wrong. Look at *pater noster*: everything he says is trying to prove that he's completely right, so everyone else must be just as wrong. I must be the one he did the best job of convincing, his number one son. And with Mom, it was always something to wait for, to prepare for, something we were never quite ready for. I wanted love and I got theories."

"But this theory doesn't want to prove you're wrong," I protested. "I mean, you're not wrong. You can take life. Love is there. We all want to give it to you, to embrace you."

Ira's cheeks and forehead softened to a gentler sadness. "Looka here, my starry-eyed youth, that sounds sweet, sweet as a charlotte russe, but it helps you more than it helps me. After you've made love to the air, after that radiant embrace, it's hard to go back to mere people." And then I remembered that he'd jumped. He looked directly at me, his eyes serious, trying to make me understand. I looked away from him and cleared my throat heavily, choking on his death.

"Right now," he said, "I'm imprisoned in your dreams. I don't think I can ever get out. It's bondage, man: I can't do anything, can't have a point of existence that doesn't speak for something hidden in you, even my attack on you. And it's degrading too, 'cause you use me to give vent to everything you deny; all the waste matter of your mind, you evacuate through me. I don't want revenge, though. I don't want to be a demon. All I want is for you to recognize me as a human being who has, who ever had, a chance for his own life. Look at me, please, Marc."

I struggled to look up, but I couldn't. Was it because I still felt that he might be a demon? I tried to speak to his soul: "Every moment I never gave you, every word I never spoke, they've all multiplied within me. I was only a kid. I hear them moaning in my chest at night. How can I see you fully when I can't bear to see myself? When will the dead stop nibbling away at the living? Aren't your moments torn from my own?"

Suddenly a figure was flinging about with rapid, jerky motions behind the pillars. As it rounded the last pillar, I was shaken to see that it was a coat without a head. I looked more carefully and saw by the hands and feet that it was a small, thin, white figure, evidently a child, wearing a coarsely woven, badly worn, grey man's overcoat. For an instant it reminded me of a picture of a concentration camp victim, but it looked more ludicrous than grim or menacing, ambling along jauntily with its pale, tendrillar hands in parallel motion. It really wasn't so bad, apparently a jolly lad. Romping, bouncing and swaying pointlessly, like a weasel on its hind legs, twisting through its trunk.

The best thing to do would be to put my arms around it, to embrace it. That would give me a chance to look for the eye in the chest. I wouldn't have to open the coat much to see the eye if it had a red light beaming from it. But no, if I put my head on his chest, it would be like going into him and I could never get out. But this is really too much of a trick to throw at me when I'm tired, and the coat seems smotheringly heavy; though it's making lots of random movements, waving arms, bouncing feet, it's definitely moving closer, really coming right into me. Into my heart. Am I a man? Can't afford not to be.

Swiftly I step aside, plant my feet strongly, grab the loose arm of the coat, pull back toward the edge with my nearer foot, wheel around and fling it through the opening, over the edge of the terrace. As I turn, wrench, and heave, I say to myself, "Go down, you bastard. Go smash!"

Neatly done. I raise my heels off the stone in jubilation. For a moment, the creature hangs in space, as in a Roadrunner cartoon, receding from me. But the boy sinks a few inches before the coat, so I don't get to see if there's a head. When it drops, my head moves toward the edge to see where it went so silently. Perhaps I cast it off too soon. Perhaps it was an innocent child. I should have grabbed its hand rather than its sleeve, but I might have found a bony hand whose fingers were fused in a gesture of entreaty—and then where would I have been for the last twenty-six years? I didn't hear it fall. Perhaps I can still reach it or see it. The fall may have opened the coat.

The balustrade has vanished. The stone is smooth and moist. It begins to tilt downward like a forehead. With the energy of my spin and hurl, I'm slipping toward the edge. The heels I raised in my excitement—can't seem to settle them right. If I press down on my feet, it makes me slide. It seems to be a hundred feet down. I can hear birds singing below me. Maybe I'll see the boy if I fall. Did Ira see me when he jumped? My shoulder seems to be too far out in the air for me to regain my balance. If I try to move back, it'll set up a reaction and push me forward. But there's actually nothing to worry about because Ira is standing there, and with him, I'll be all right. The one I threw over was someone else.

My chest is over now and my waist may be. The parts of my body are yearning outward. Better not look down: it'll tip me forward, but I can look to the side, look up, even if I can't look back. The sky is aching and blazing with the blue and pink of dawn, so beautiful it fills me with sweet longing, as if I could possess it. My knees are at the edge and I can't seem to stop them. But I'm sure it's okay, 'cause I think I can see Ira at the edge of my vision. He is quite substantial (I hope he isn't me), and he's definitely close enough. He has only to apply a few pounds of pressure to tip my wavering form back. I say, "Kindness is life, and you always wanted to be kind." I know for sure without a doubt that what I say is true. And I reach my hand out behind to him, where he can't miss it if he has eyes, even one eye. And I say, very clearly, "Help me."

GLOSSARY

This glossary provides brief definitions for the Yiddish (or more broadly, German) words and phrases presented in *italics* within the text.

azoy—thus, so.
bumicas—female bums, tramps.
davening—chanting prayers while bowing repeatedly.
drehut—hell or underground.
epes—somewhat.
fapitzed—dressed up in a fancy way, decked out.
fleegles—wings or arms.
gelt—money.
gezunt gelt—flourishing money.
gonif—thief.
goy—non-Jew.
kinder—children.
kischkes—guts.
kranke—sick.
kranke meshuggah—sick, crazy person.
krankheit—illness.
kvetch—complain.
kvetching—nagging, complaining.
lantzman—countryman, one from the same land.

lebedike velt—things are not bad (literally, "livable world").
lebedike velt mit gelt—things are not bad with money; wealthy.
mamzer gonif—bastard thief.
meshuggah—crazy person.
mishegas—craziness.
nebbish—insipid, boring person.
nu—so what? so?
plotz—die.
schmatta—rag.
schmekel—small penis; diminutive of schmuck (penis).
schmendrick—fool.
schmutz—dirt.
schrying gevalt—crying out in alarm.
schul—synagogue.
schwartze—black.
shayne maydlach—pretty girls.
shoin—already.
shoin fertig—that's final.
shoin gut—alright.
takeh—indeed, really.
tsitskes—breasts.
tsuris—misery, suffering.
tuchas—buttocks.
ungepatchked tchatchke— idle decorative object, plastered with superfluous ornaments.
vans—cockroach.
vayizmir—woe is me.
verblunget—confused, lost.
verklempt—upset, tense.
vilde chaia—wild beast.
yenta—talkative, manipulative woman.

About the Author

Shelly Brivic is an internationally recognized James Joyce scholar and a retired university professor. He has written extensively on Joyce and other modernists from the perspective of Lacanian psychology. His most recent scholarly work is *Revolutionary Damnation: Badiou and Irish Fiction from Joyce to Enright*, published by Syracuse University Press in 2017. *Stealing: A Novel in Dreams* is his first novel.

CPSIA information can be obtained
at www.ICGtesting.com
Printed in the USA
BVHW041316201118
533634BV00013B/150/P